CALLING
on the
Matchmaker

Books by Jody Hedlund

A Shanahan Match

Calling on the Matchmaker

Colorado Cowboys

A Cowboy for Keeps
The Heart of a Cowboy
To Tame a Cowboy
Falling for the Cowgirl
The Last Chance Cowboy

Hearts of Faith Collection

The Preacher's Bride
The Doctor's Lady
Rebellious Heart

Michigan Brides Collection

Unending Devotion
A Noble Groom
Captured by Love

Beacons of Hope

Out of the Storm: A Beacons of Hope Novella
Love Unexpected
Hearts Made Whole
Undaunted Hope

Orphan Train

An Awakened Heart: An Orphan Train Novella
With You Always
Together Forever
Searching for You

The Bride Ships

A Reluctant Bride
The Runaway Bride
A Bride of Convenience

A SHANAHAN MATCH
Book 1

CALLING *on the* MATCHMAKER

Jody Hedlund

BETHANYHOUSE

a division of Baker Publishing Group
Minneapolis, Minnesota

© 2023 by Jody Hedlund

Published by Bethany House Publishers
Minneapolis, Minnesota
www.bethanyhouse.com

Bethany House Publishers is a division of
Baker Publishing Group, Grand Rapids, Michigan

Printed in the United States of America

Library of Congress Cataloging-in-Publication Data
Names: Hedlund, Jody, author.
Title: Calling on the matchmaker / Jody Hedlund.
Description: Minneapolis, Minnisota : Bethany House Publishers, a division of
    Baker Publishing Group, 2023. | Series: A Shanahan match
Identifiers: LCCN 2023026948 | ISBN 9780764241963 (paper) | ISBN 9780764242236
    (casebound) | ISBN 9781493443758 (ebook)
Subjects: LCGFT: Christian fiction. | Romance fiction. | Novels.
Classification: LCC PS3608.E333 C35 2023 | DDC 813/.6—dc23/eng/20230620
LC record available at https://lccn.loc.gov/2023026948

Scripture quotations are from the King James Version of the Bible.

This is a work of historical reconstruction; the appearances of certain historical figures are therefore inevitable. All other characters, however, are products of the author's imagination, and any resemblance to actual persons, living or dead, is coincidental.

Author is represented by Natasha Kern Literary Agency

Baker Publishing Group publications use paper produced from sustainable forestry practices and post-consumer waste whenever possible.

23 24 25 26 27 28 29   7 6 5 4 3 2 1

1

ST. LOUIS, MISSOURI
JANUARY 1849

"Nip along with you now, Finola." Madigan bounded onto Broadway, dodging an omnibus that was slogging through the thick mud. "The matchmaker is waiting."

"Have patience." Finola Shanahan followed her younger brother and tiptoed into the mire. She bunched up the black habit the Sisters of Charity had so graciously provided for her to wear whenever she accompanied them for charity work. "I'm going as fast as I can."

"Mam and Da are done putting up with your impertinence." Madigan shot her a warning look. The sixteen-year-old was already a handsome fellow with his big blue eyes and brown hair, turning the heads of the local lasses wherever he went.

Of the six Shanahan children, everyone claimed she and Madigan resembled each other the most. And aye, she had the same blue eyes and brown hair. But when God had been doling out the freckles, He'd forgotten to spread them out between her and Madigan. She'd ended up with them all.

The winter wind rustled against her hood and sent a chill down her back. "I'm a dutiful daughter."

Madigan released a snort. "And I'm the pope."

Guilt nudged at Finola. She *was* a dutiful daughter in almost every way except one. . . . She wasn't cooperating with her parents' efforts to find her a husband.

Madigan leapt over a half-frozen puddle. "They're just trying to make a good impression on the matchmaker, dontcha know."

"I'm well aware, to be sure." They might want to impress Oscar McKenna, the local Irish matchmaker. But she wanted to frustrate Oscar enough that he'd refuse to help her parents. And being late for the meeting was a good start to that effort.

As she took another tentative step into the busy thoroughfare, the mud sucked at her lace-up ankle boots.

A faded yellow hackney rumbled down the street toward her. The coachman sat slouched, his head down, the brim of his top hat pulled low. He didn't seem to be looking where he was going. Rather, he held the reins loosely, as if the team of horses knew the route well and didn't need his directing.

Finola forced her feet to move more swiftly after Madigan. In the late afternoon of the dreary January day, the St. Louis traffic was heavy, especially on Washington at Broadway so close to the riverfront where factories, warehouses, and stores crowded the mostly unpaved streets. Apparently now that the gray skies had finished spitting a mixture of rain and sleet, everyone had come out to finish the day's work.

As a beer delivery wagon filled with casks lumbered from the other direction, she paused. The driver wasn't paying attention to her any more than the hackney. A dray from the levee followed, piled high with boxes of merchandise and hogsheads of tobacco.

Madigan was already on the opposite side, and as he spun to check on her progress, his eyes widened. "Holy thundering mother, Finola! Get out of the street before you get run over."

He waved his arms, motioning her back, his gaze darting to the hackney coach that wasn't slowing—not even a fraction.

It was less than two dozen paces away from her, and the driver's head remained down, the reins still loose, the horses trotting forward with no intention of stopping for a lone woman standing in their path.

"Hurry, Finola!" Madigan's voice took on an urgency that prodded her pulse into a gallop. She tried to make her feet follow suit, but as she spun, one of her boots snagged in a rut. In the next instant, she felt herself going down.

She braced her fall with her hands and knees, the layer of mud cushioning the impact. But at the nearing rattle of harnesses and the creak of wheels, she scrambled to push herself up.

Horse hooves pounded closer.

She clawed at the mud, slipping and sliding and attempting to find footing.

Several shouts—including Madigan's—advised her with increasing fervor. But her heart was suddenly beating too hard to hear anything clearly . . . except the toll of the death bell.

She was going to die. And there was nothing she could do to stop it.

"Hail, Mary, full of grace, the Lord is with thee." The words clogged in her throat, the rest of the plea for mercy drowned in a frustrated cry as she tried to wrench herself free.

But with each move she made, the mud coated her more, seeming to lock her in place.

"Lie flat!" A deep voice penetrated her panic.

Even as she began to brace herself for the impact of the horses and carriage, a man slammed into her and rolled her to her back, throwing himself over her and covering her body with his just as the horses passed by her on either side. Their hooves slapped so close, she held herself stiffly.

The man shielding her also held himself rigidly, clearly intending to take the brunt of the harm from the horses. He

7

ducked his head next to hers, near enough that his cheek bumped against her bonnet and his heavy breathing echoed in her ear.

She cringed, waiting for a hoof to hit him, but only mud splattered against them.

A moment later the horses were gone, and the green hackney wheels were rolling past. The low underbelly of the vehicle box slipped over them, brushing close to her rescuer's back so that he flattened himself against her even further.

Thankfully she had a slender frame and was on the smaller size of the average woman. Even so, she did her part to mold against the street, attempting to keep the man from getting hurt.

As the shadows of the hackney gave way to the cloudy day above them, the man lifted his head and scanned the street as though gauging whether he needed to protect her from any other oncoming traffic.

Apparently seeing no immediate threat, his body relaxed against hers, and he returned his attention to her. "How do you fare?"

Finola found herself peering up into blue eyes so dark they were almost black. Deep set, they crinkled at the corners with concern, and his fair brows bunched together above a fine, narrow nose. His hat had been knocked off, and his toasted blond hair fell across his forehead in disarray.

His gaze held hers intently, as though he wouldn't be satisfied until she reassured him she was fine. She did a quick mental assessment of her limbs, wiggling her fingers and toes simultaneously. Nothing seemed to be missing or broken. "I think I'm alright."

He glanced again over his shoulder and then down the street in the opposite direction. The wagons all around them had come to a standstill.

Too little, too late.

As if thinking the same, her rescuer homed in on the hackney, the only vehicle still in motion, slogging away at the same careless pace, as if it made an everyday occurrence of running over pedestrians.

He frowned, his square jaw hardening. The angular edges were covered in a light brown layer of stubble. Though his expression was serious, she was suddenly aware of just how handsome he was.

"Saint Riley to the rescue again!" someone shouted.

Saint Riley? Riley Rafferty hailed as Saint Riley of the Kerry Patch?

She'd never personally met him. But the Irish community in St. Louis had always been small enough—at least until recent years—that she knew of almost everyone, saw almost everyone at one point or another at a parade or mass or a wedding or a funeral. So of course she'd seen Riley Rafferty from time to time over her twenty-three years.

But he was several years older and wasn't in any of her family's social groups. She'd never given him a second thought until last autumn when she'd witnessed him dive into the Mississippi and rescue a drowning steamboat deckhand.

Over the past four months since that rescue, she'd observed him on occasion from a distance and had marveled like everyone else over his daring deeds.

And now, here he was.

Her breath snagged in her chest, this time not out of fear of being crushed by an oncoming conveyance. No, this time, she was breathless because the heroic Riley Rafferty had saved her life.

Her body awoke to the realization that his full length was covering her—a broad chest, muscular torso, thick arms, and long legs. She knew from watching his dripping-wet body emerge from the river that he was a strong man with muscles in every conceivable place. He had the kind of body that could make a nun blush.

Even so, his presence wasn't heavy or suffocating. Instead, she felt safe, as though the world had stopped and nothing or no one could hurt her, not as long as Riley was with her. The feeling of security was odd, one she hadn't felt in many years.

"Finola Shanahan!" The next shout was Madigan's from above her. "What am I going to do with you?"

At the mention of her name, Riley's brows arched, and his eyes lightened a wee bit to a midnight blue. Did he recognize her?

More likely he recognized her family's name. Her da was one of the most prominent men of St. Louis. And one of the wealthiest.

Riley seemed to study her more carefully, his gaze slowing as he passed over the freckles on her nose and cheeks.

Of course, there were other Irish Shanahans in St. Louis, and he might not realize she was the oldest daughter of the iron magnate James Shanahan, sole owner of Shanahan Iron Works.

"You're sure you're not hurt, Sister?" Riley's eyes, full of questions, met hers.

Sister? Did he think she was a nun? She supposed the confusion was only natural since she was clothed in the habit. Should she correct him?

"Come on with you now, Finola." Madigan thrust a hand toward her.

A part of her wanted to clear up Riley's mistake in thinking she was a nun. But what was the point in doing so? She had every intention of joining the Sisters of Charity . . . just as soon as she could convince her parents to allow it.

First, she had to thwart their newest plan to use the matchmaker to arrange her marriage. Once she foiled their efforts, they'd surely agree that after so many failed matches, the only bride she was suited to become was a bride of Christ.

At the sight of Madigan's outstretched hand, Riley started to push away. She had the urge to grab him and prevent him from leaving her. The need was completely irrational. This man was a stranger. And she couldn't remain in the middle of busy Broadway any longer than she already had.

As Riley gingerly crawled off her and stood, the watching crowd cheered and clapped.

Madigan bent down and began to help her to her feet. All the while, she couldn't tear her sights from Riley.

A young lad hustled toward Riley and reverently handed him his hat. Riley squeezed the boy's shoulder in thanks before he situated the work-worn felt hat on his head. He waved and grinned at the onlookers as if he'd just finished putting on a theater production he'd been rehearsing for weeks.

Although Riley's breeches and woolen stockings were heavily splattered with mud, his coat and the linen shirt underneath were fairly mud free. Unlike her clothing . . .

She didn't need to glance down to know she resembled a sow who'd just had a grand time flopping around in a pigsty. Not only was her front caked in mud, but her backside was too. She could even feel splotches on her cheeks and forehead.

No doubt, Riley thought she looked a fright.

As if hearing her silent assessment, he swung his attention back to her. The seriousness was gone from his expression. Instead, mirth added faint stars to his eyes, and his lips quirked at the corners, as if they weren't comfortable anyplace other than in a smile.

Was he finding humor in how she looked?

She started to swipe at one of the splotches on her cheek but then stopped herself. It didn't matter what Riley Rafferty thought about her. It didn't matter what any man thought about her. Not now. Not any time.

She pulled herself up to all of her five-feet-three inches. "Thank you for saving my life, young lad."

Riley's brows rose. "My pleasure."

Absolutely no one in her right mind could mistake Riley as

being anything other than a full-grown man. But treating her suitors as though she were sixty years older than them always seemed to douse any growing sparks. Not that Riley was a suitor. And not that he had any growing sparks. But it was best if he knew she harbored no attraction toward him. None.

"You're quite the boy." She reached up and pinched one of his cheeks just like a grandmother would do. "Keep up the good work."

With that, she slipped her arm into Madigan's and tried to nudge him on his way.

When Madigan didn't budge and continued to stare at Riley with wide-eyed admiration, she jabbed her elbow into his ribs harder.

He released a low *oof* before stumbling forward and leading her the rest of the way across the street. Fortunately he'd been the one carrying her bag with her change of clothing and shoes, and it had survived the escapade intact.

As they made their way down Broadway, he didn't release his grasp of her arm, retelling every detail of the rescue from his perspective, as if the brush with death wasn't already clear enough in her mind.

On the next block, she dragged Madigan past a printing shop until she reached the alley behind it.

Her brother didn't resist but followed along warily, likely having had enough drama for one afternoon. "What are you doing now, Finola?"

She nodded to the back of the livery stable on the opposite side of the alley. "I'm needing to change before I go home."

Madigan's lips curled up into one of his irresistible grins. "I'll not be arguing with you there."

"Good." She crossed to the livery door and peeked inside to find it was as deserted as always at the late-afternoon hour. She'd have no trouble finding an empty horse stall and putting back on her garments like she had on previous occasions.

She always changed out of the robe lest she cast suspicion upon herself. Yes, her parents knew she was heavily involved in charity work with the Sisters of Charity. But they believed she'd given up her aspirations for becoming a nun, as they'd suggested, and didn't know she still held the desire very dear to her heart.

They also didn't know that she'd purposefully driven away all her previous suitors so she could enter into service. Of course, after she'd recently sent her last suitor running into the arms of another woman, she'd hoped her parents would finally resign themselves to her being single and might even suggest that she become a nun. She hadn't guessed they'd be desperate enough to enlist the help of the matchmaker.

"Get along with you now, Madigan." She shooed him away.

"I can't show up without you—"

"You know as well as I do, we'll both fare better if you nip ahead and let everyone know I'll be there in a wee minute." Maybe in addition to her tardiness, she could earn another demerit if she arrived looking like a swamp monster. Doing so would certainly give Oscar McKenna pause and make him think twice about arranging a marriage for her. More likely that strategy would backfire, and Oscar would decide she needed to marry a man who also looked like a swamp monster.

Whatever the case, she didn't want to mortify her mam and da. She might be full of shenanigans, but she wouldn't intentionally hurt or embarrass her parents.

Finola shook the habit but couldn't dislodge the mud.

Seeing her futile efforts, Madigan heaved a sigh and handed over her bag. "Fine. But mind you, no more dawdling, or you'll get me in trouble for sure."

"I'll hurry, so I will." She was already ducking inside the livery's back entrance and heading for the closest stall. Low voices wafted from the front of the establishment, but from what she could tell, the rest of the building was deserted. Only the scent of damp hay and horseflesh greeted her.

The shutters in a window above one of the stalls were open, providing enough light that she could see well enough. She slipped into the stall made of planks rather than split railing. The door, too, was solid, giving her the privacy she needed to change.

She dropped her bag and started to work her way out of the habit. The loose-fitting garment was easy to divest. Her boots and stockings took a little more effort to shed. When she reached her damp chemise and drawers, she crossed her arms and shivered.

She hadn't thought to bring a change of undergarments. Though she was daring, she wasn't daring enough to go without them. She'd have to make do.

With cold fingers, she fumbled with her bag, wrestling to remove her bodice and skirt.

The sudden crunch of hay and gravel under footsteps entering through the livery's backdoor brought her to a halt. As the steps drew nearer, she held herself motionless and ceased breathing lest she draw unwanted attention.

The crunching paused near her stall. Then a moment later, the latch began to lift.

Her heart jumped into her throat. She cast around for a place to hide. But with only a trough built into the wall and a smattering of grooming equipment hanging from pegs, she had no place to go.

The door inched open.

Ach. She'd done it again. She'd gotten herself into another predicament.

2

*R*iley wasn't sure why he'd followed Finola Shanahan into the livery. But here he was.

He pushed the door wider. Why had she pretended to be a nun? And why hadn't she corrected him when he'd addressed her as *Sister*?

Maybe he wanted answers. Or maybe he was intrigued by a woman who had the audacity to pinch his cheek and call him a young lad.

His grin kicked up just thinking about it, and his mind replayed the first moment he'd exited the bank to see her stepping off the boardwalk into the mud. An internal warning had gone off, one he seldom ignored. He'd watched her begin to struggle. And he'd witnessed the flash of panic cross her face when she realized she'd run out of time, that she was going to be hit by the hackney.

By that point he'd already bolted into action. He'd known he wouldn't have enough time to whisk her out of the way of danger. So he'd done the only thing he'd been able to think of—try to stay between the team of horses and the hackney wheels. He'd gotten knocked around by the horses and would have the bruises to show for it. But it hadn't been as bad as he expected, and he'd kept her safe, which was the important thing.

Of course, the whole time he'd been rescuing her, he assumed she was a nun. He hadn't stopped to question her identity until her brother crossed into the street and shouted her name.

After that, it had taken him only a second to place her. Even though she didn't have the same red hair as her father, she and her brother had distinct Shanahan features—especially the dimples in their chins.

The Shanahans had gained a reputation for their charity and kindness—especially to immigrants. James Shanahan owned large portions of Kerry Patch and had originally allowed immigrants to squat on the land for free.

Over recent years, Shanahan had built tenements and charged a low rent that even the poorest newcomer could afford. From what Riley could tell, the fellow was one of the better landlords who actually made repairs and improvements on his buildings whenever he could.

Riley rested his hand against the stall door. Maybe that's why he'd followed Finola. Because he was afraid that any other man who realized she was the daughter of one of St. Louis's millionaires might take advantage of her.

Or maybe he was just fascinated with her.

Women normally didn't dismiss him so easily. Especially pretty young women. Not that he cared about pretty young women. He'd lost his desire to be with a woman the day Helen left downriver on the *Monarch*. In the two years she'd been gone, he'd been perfectly content being single. And he had no plans to change that.

As the stall door widened, he paused. He ought to head right back to the wagon shop. He had heaps of work waiting for him. Rafferty Wagon Company had more orders for wagons than the Mississippi had gnats. In fact, they had double—even triple—the orders at the start of 1849 than they'd had for all the first half of last year.

In part, the demand was growing with the influx of immigrants into the city that had been dubbed the Gateway to the West. When he and his dad had moved to St. Louis back in '30, the city had still been relatively small with a population of only fourteen thousand. Almost twenty years later, it had swelled to sixty-three thousand.

It was still growing. Every day, steamboats arrived from New Orleans, weighed down with immigrants eager to claim land in the West. And every day, a portion of those people came to the Rafferty workshop, seeking wagons that could take them to their dreams.

The rumors that gold had been found out in Sacramento Valley in California were only adding to the need for wagons. Men were hardly talking of anything else these days, so much so that now more than just immigrants were itching to head west. Droves of fellows were waiting for the heavy ice on the upper Mississippi and the Missouri to break up, with every intention of traveling to California and trying to strike it rich.

The truth was, Rafferty Wagons couldn't keep up with the demand anymore, not even with the new apprentices and several journeymen they'd recently hired.

Riley took a step back. Duty called. He'd taken enough time out of his day to place orders for more lumber and iron and to run other errands. He had only a couple of hours left to finish trussing the underside of the axles on his current wagon project before he would have to head over to his campaign headquarters for the evening.

He started to turn away, but at a scampering from inside the stall he hesitated. He'd watched Finola send her brother away and then sneak in the back door. Was she in some kind of trouble again?

There was only one way to find out. He shoved the door open the rest of the way.

A horseshoe flew straight at him and hit him in the chest. Through the layer of his heavy wool coat, he could hardly feel the iron bounce against him before it fell to the ground cushioned by hay.

Something else flew his way—a farrier's nailing hammer. He dodged it before it could hit him. "What the devil!"

At the sound of his voice, Finola paused with her arm stretched back, ready to throw again, this time a hoof nipper. Her eyes were wide and wild, the blue as bright and captivating as it had been when he'd first looked into them after saving her. It was a shade he seldom saw, like the sky on the eastern horizon along the river after sunrise.

"Riley Rafferty?" The surprise in her voice was genuine—and was it tinged with relief? "What are you doing here?"

What *was* he doing there? He still didn't know.

"My father owns the place." He said the first thing that came to mind. In addition to the wagon shop on Front Street, his dad had invested in several liveries in the area, mostly to have teams of horses and mules that he could sell with the wagons.

Those going a longer distance, however, needed oxen, and William Rafferty, being the savvy businessman he was, had purchased land south of the city to breed and sell oxen.

She lowered her hand, clearly deciding Riley wasn't a threat and that she didn't need to attempt to impale him with farrier tools.

"What are *you* doing here?" He mimicked her question, but as soon as the words were out, his gaze dropped to find that she was standing in nothing but her undergarments. Silky undergarments that clung to her body and left little to the imagination.

Sweet saints above. She was half naked. Not only was she curvy, but her arms and lower legs were bare, showing miles

18

of pale skin covered with more of the same freckles that were sprinkled across her face.

He swallowed hard. He needed to tear his gaze away from her, but he was a starving man at a feast. He'd denied himself womanly pleasures for so long that this glimpse was awakening hunger in him. Hunger he didn't want to feel.

He let his sights drop to her slender feet and her delicate toes.

As if just realizing the indecency of her attire, she gasped. Her gaze darted around. She was searching for an escape, or a blanket, or perhaps a cloak to use in covering herself. But in finding nothing, she glanced at the tool still in her hand. And then she threw it at him.

He tried to tell himself to move, duck, or even lift a hand to at least block the thing. But he couldn't move, was too dazed to do anything but stand still like a daft old man. In the next instant, the hoof nipper hit his jaw with a thud before it fell to the floor next to the other items she'd thrown.

She stared at him, at his jaw, then released another gasp before cupping a hand over her mouth.

A sting in his flesh told him the tool had punctured his skin. He lifted his hand to the spot, and when he drew it away, blood coated his fingers.

"Oh holy mother, have mercy." She dropped her hands from her mouth. "I don't know what came over me."

He knew exactly what had come over her. Righteous indignation for his behaving like a bull in heat. He'd deserved to be hit with the nipping tool. In fact, he deserved to be whacked over the head with a four-by-four for gawking at her state of undress instead of immediately retreating from the stall.

Before he could let his attention wander to her chemise and drawers and all her bare skin again, he spun on his heel and closed the door behind him.

"I'm sorry, to be sure." Her voice was stretched thin with worry.

He leaned back against the door and took a deep breath, trying to make his lungs and heart start working again. Then he scrubbed at his eyes, as if that could wipe away the image of her in her undergarments.

But it didn't. The picture of her standing in the stall practically bare was at the forefront of his mind once more. Bother it. He had to think on something else. And fast.

The wagon for the government. The axle. The flat strap of iron he still needed to add to give the wagon the extra strength and structural support to make the long haul over the Santa Fe Trail without falling apart.

At the shuffling of garments, he guessed she was putting on her clothing. Thank the good Lord for His mercies.

She gave a tiny huff, and suddenly his mind was right back on her bare skin.

The wheels. They still had to be boiled in linseed oil. Then they'd need painting by one of the apprentices. Green. He'd have the wheels painted green this time.

"Riley?" She seemed to pause in her dressing.

He closed his eyes. "I'm here."

"Don't leave yet."

He really should. "I won't."

The rustling resumed.

Finola had the prettiest pale skin he'd ever seen. And her freckles only added to its appeal, as if they were meant to be kissed one by one. What would it be like to lie next to her in bed and spend the day kissing each and every freckle?

Heat shot through him like liquid metal.

He straightened and rubbed at his eyes again. What in the blazes was wrong with him? He had to get himself under control. "Maybe it would be best if I left." His voice caught, and he had to clear his throat.

"Wait a wee minute." She had the lilting hint of Irish brogue that some of the natural-born children of immigrants had even though they'd never lived in Ireland.

His muscles tightened with the need to flee. But another part of him wanted to linger.

Before he could make up his mind on whether to go or stay, the stall door opened. "I'm nearly done."

He stared ahead at light coming through the back of the livery. From the corner of his eye, he could see that she was dressed and stuffing the nun's robe into her sack.

The tension in his body eased, and he slowly pivoted to face her.

She released the bag, the robe only halfway tucked away, and straightened.

He gave her a once-over only to realize that half the buttons on her bodice weren't latched and her feet were still bare. Even her feet were pale and dotted with freckles. No doubt he'd find a trail among the freckles and trace it, starting at her toes and working his way up her leg.

Blast him again. He had to get out of the livery and away from this woman before he said—or did—something really stupid.

"Since it looks like you're okay, I'll be on my way." He spun and began stalking toward the front of the livery, betting that she wouldn't follow him.

"Don't go." Her footsteps padded behind him only a few paces, then halted. "I want to doctor your wound."

"It's a small cut." At least he hoped it was. "Nothing to worry about."

"I have some medicinal supplies given to me by the Sisters of Charity—"

"I'm fine." Without slowing his stride, he pushed past the stalls and entered into the haymow. Tom Dooley, who managed the livery with his dad, paused midsentence in his transaction with a fellow standing just outside the wide double doorway with a pair of bay Morgans. Gangly with his tattered clothing hanging on his sticklike frame, Tom had yet to regain all the weight he'd lost during his final year living in Ireland.

When Tom and his dad had shown up at the wagon shop last summer begging to work with the horses, Riley hired them even though he hadn't needed more help at the time. He figured it was the least he could do to ease the suffering of those who were escaping the terrible starvation in Ireland after recent years of failed potato crops.

"Don't mind me, Tom." Riley didn't dare look over his shoulder at Finola. He didn't want to draw attention her way, not when she was yet in a state of undress. Although Tom was a good man, one look at Finola and he'd be following her around like a pup wanting his chin scratched.

"Didn't rightly expect to see you." Tom tipped up the brim of his flat cloth cap. Something in the young man's eyes slowed Riley's steps.

"I'm just passing through."

"Oh, aye. Big Jim's looking for you, so he is."

Riley halted, a sudden hitch in his chest. "Big Jim?"

"Aye."

The fellow never left the wagons. He had every right to do so, was a free man and a master craftsman. But he preferred a quiet, simple life and kept to himself.

"Spit it out, Tom." Whatever had happened must have been serious if Big Jim needed him.

Tom hesitated. "'Tis your old man. He's in a bit of a bother."

Riley's body tensed. "What kind of bother?"

"He's had a heart attack."

Heart attack? Was his dad—?

"He hasn't fallen off the perch yet." Clearly Tom saw the

unasked question in Riley's expression. "But from the sounds of it, he won't be able to hang on for much longer."

Without waiting to hear more, Riley bolted through the hay-mow and barreled out of the livery, already on a run toward home.

3

*F*inola rolled excuses for her tardiness around in her head as she approached the rear entrance of her family's spacious home on Third Street.

With a glance both ways to make sure no one was watching, she darted across the gravel road that wound to the rear of the house where the coach house, summer kitchen, and privy were located.

"Finola." Madigan's call came from the upper balcony that ran the width of the second-floor exterior.

She paused and peered up at him leaning against one of the large white pillars. The many windows were all closed now. But in the heat of summer, the French-style galerie and the windows facing the river breezes kept the home from turning into a furnace.

Madigan leaned over the iron railing. "I told Mam and Da you were helping a new family get settled in and lost track of time."

It was mostly the truth. At least the version of truth Mam and Da would accept, namely that she'd gotten so involved in her charity work that she hadn't heard the church bells tolling the top of the four o'clock hour.

"Thank you, Madigan. I don't know what I'd do without you."

He tapped at his cheek and then nose. "You've still got mud."

Wiping at the spots on her face, she rushed up the several steps that led to the back entryway. After her second encounter with Riley Rafferty at the livery, she'd been so rattled she was surprised she managed to exit clothed, much less free of mud.

She felt horrible for injuring him. She hadn't meant to, had overreacted. After all, it wasn't as if he'd known she was changing in the stall. He'd assumed she was a nun and had no reason to suspect she was unclad behind the closed door.

Aye, perhaps he shouldn't have stared quite as long as he had. But that didn't excuse her throwing things at him. As if that wasn't enough, he'd received terrible news about his father.

She paused at the door, hand on the knob, and offered another silent petition for his father's health. After how Riley had saved her life today, the least she could do was pray for him and his family.

With a final entreaty heavenward, she forced herself to open the door and enter. The clatter of pans and the carefree chatter of the cook and scullery maid came from the lower-level kitchen along with scents of roasted chicken and potatoes with hints of rosemary and thyme.

Even though she wanted to dally in the hallway and relish the familiar sounds and scents, she'd already delayed long enough. It was past time for her to join the meeting.

She climbed the short staircase that led to the central hallway. The long carpet runner on the tile floor muted her steps, allowing her to approach the parlor at the front of the house undetected.

Only Winston, their longtime butler, nodded at her from where he stood near the parlor door. In his usual impeccable black suit, the tall, silver-haired man regarded her with a censuring frown.

She offered him a bright smile in return and an innocent shrug, as though she wasn't aware of how late she was. But she'd never been able to fool the older man—none of the Shanahan children had ever been able to.

From the parlor, the animated voice of Oscar McKenna rose above all the others as he shared one of his many tales of matchmaking.

"When she went into that old farmhouse for the first time," Oscar said, "ach, it stunk something terrible, so it did. That bride lasted a day inside before rushing out and telling her new husband that the barn smelled better than the house and he'd better do something about it. The very next day the farmer set about patching the walls of the barn with cow dung and whitewash, the same way he had the house. When he finished, he told her that now she couldn't complain that the barn smelled better."

Da's laughter mingled with that of Mam's.

A smile tugged at Finola's lips, but she quickly wiped it away, trying to muster the inner strength she would need to withstand the matchmaking.

She pushed forward through the wide entryway into the parlor, the fanciest room in the Shanahan home, tastefully furnished in rococo style. With light spring green-and-gold wallpaper and matching green draperies in the front bay window, the room was bright and cheerful on the wintry afternoon. Large gilt mirrors and cornices seemed to rival the sun in their brilliance.

A fire was burning upon the hearth, the white marble mantel a French import and one of the finest in all of St. Louis. Not that she cared about such things. But it certainly showed just how hard her da had worked over the years to establish himself and prosper in America.

Her da sat in one of the wingback chairs upholstered in a green floral silk damask. At the sight of her, he stood and offered her a welcoming smile, one that, as always, brought out the dimple on his clean-shaven chin. "Here she is." His eyes regarded her warmly. "Our Finola. Out saving the world, that she is."

Attired in a sharp navy suit with a frock coat, he dressed the part of a successful businessman, his starched turned-up collar embellished with a dark silk cravat tied into a flat bow. To others he was an imposing man, with brawny muscles that strained against his clothing and a fiery temper that matched his fiery red hair.

But to Finola, he'd always been a loving and giving father. "I'm sorry to keep you waiting." She meant it. She hated to disappoint him. And she hated to disappoint Mam too. If only she knew how to convince them her plans for her future were for the best. But her efforts at actually *telling* them had never gotten her anywhere. And she'd been left with no choice but to *show* them.

"If you're sorry, lass, you know what to do." He pointed at his cheek.

She crossed to him, lifted on her toes, and pressed a kiss against his cheek.

He in turn tweaked her nose, the sign that all was forgiven.

Mam, sitting on the settee of a matching green floral, patted the spot next to her. Her expression wasn't as warm as Da's. Frustration creased her pretty face. "We've been waiting for you. Poor Mr. McKenna has been here nigh an hour."

Everyone said she looked like Mam with her dainty features, porcelain skin, and brown hair with tints of auburn. Da claimed that Mam had been the prettiest Irish lass he'd ever laid eyes on when she walked off the steamship gangplank. It hadn't mattered that she'd only just arrived in St. Louis or that he'd been ten years older than her seventeen years. He went right up to her and told her he wanted to marry her.

Mam had smacked his cheek and walked away. But like most

people, she couldn't resist James Shanahan's efforts. And after a few months, Da won her heart and her hand in marriage. Finola had come along less than a year later.

Finola nodded at Oscar McKenna in the wing chair opposite her da and then at Bellamy, his youngest son, standing behind his father's chair. It was rumored that at twenty-two, Bellamy was in line to take over his father's matchmaking duties since there was speculation that Oscar was growing too old to know the needs of the younger generation.

Oscar certainly had the look of an older man with his thick gray hair and veinous nose—as though he'd had too many draughts of Guinness in his life, which was certainly a possibility since he owned and operated one of St. Louis's busiest pubs.

If Finola had to take a guess, she'd put him at sixty. She supposed in his younger years, he'd been a dashing, dark-haired heart-stopper the same as Bellamy. Even though Bellamy was a full-blooded Irishman who'd immigrated with his family ten years ago, he had the swarthy skin of an Italian and would certainly not need a matchmaker to find him a wife.

Mam slid a hand across the settee and poked Finola before cocking her head toward Oscar.

Her mam was right. She still needed to apologize to Oscar. "I regret I was delayed, Mr. McKenna."

And she did regret it. She shouldn't have made her elders wait. Such marriage-avoidance tactics were simply too rude. She had to stick with what she did best—estranging ardent suitors.

"Ach, don't be troubling your mind." Oscar waved a hand. "Bellamy and I have already worked out many of the details with your father for your dowry and the sort of young man he'll be expecting us to find for you."

"What sort did you decide upon?" She tried to keep her tone calm, but her stomach was already churning at the prospect of going through the matchmaking process. She'd watched Oscar at work with other young couples, and he was good at what he did.

That was precisely the problem. She didn't want him to be good. Maybe she ought to insist upon the untried Bellamy to take up her case. He'd turned his attention to the large painting hanging above the piano and was clearly bored with the matchmaking process.

Oscar exchanged a meaningful look with her da. "I always say that one of the main jobs of a matchmaker is to help you young people open your eyes and see the positives in other people that you might have missed."

"Is that so?" Finola tapped a finger against her lip, trying to appear contemplative of his statement. "I'm sure Bellamy would have some good suggestions for suitable men with qualities I might have missed. Right, Bellamy?"

He shifted around, crossed his arms, and leveled his magnetic dark gaze upon her. His eyes were keen, as though he'd already seen right through her ruse even before she had the chance to put any plans in motion.

She hesitated only a moment before pushing forward. "I'd like Bellamy to pick the potential candidates. I think he'd do a fine job."

Oscar's bushy brows rose.

"Not that you won't do a fine job too, Mr. McKenna. But I do think Bellamy needs to gain more experience. Why not allow him to handle my match? It would boost his reputation in the community and allow him to take over for you more swiftly."

Bellamy's gaze hadn't budged from her.

She dropped her attention to her lap, waiting with what she hoped was a demure and innocent air.

"What do you think, Oscar?" Her da's tone seemed to hold consideration for her idea. He always liked to encourage young men to pursue their aspirations and would probably see this as a way to help Bellamy.

"I don't know," Oscar started. "Bellamy's still so young."

Bellamy released a soft snort. "I've watched you and Grand-dad at your matchmaking for years."

"'Tis true enough." Oscar rubbed his big hands together, clearly warming to the idea. "Bellamy is no dozer. And he's as wily as a leprechaun."

At another poke from Mam, Finola sat up straighter.

"Will you cooperate with Bellamy?" Mam's question was pointed. No doubt she suspected Finola intended to obstruct the matchmaking efforts.

"Of course I'll cooperate with Bellamy."

"You won't cause him any problems?" she persisted.

"Not one wee bit."

"Finola Shanahan, you listen well to me now." Mam's tone was thick with the Irish brogue that hadn't diminished over the years. "If we allow Bellamy to make your match, then you need to promise you'll do just as he says."

Finola folded her hands in her lap. "I will." She wouldn't interfere with Bellamy's planning or manipulate his choices for her, but she would, as always, have plenty of tricks for making sure her matches would not find her suitable. But that was neither here nor there at the moment.

Around her, the parlor grew silent, accentuating the footsteps in the room above them as well as Enya's singing.

Finally, her da took a step toward Bellamy and stretched out a hand to shake on the deal. "She's in your care then, son. I have every confidence you'll be able to find Finola a perfect match."

4

*R*iley clutched his dad's work-roughened hand between his own. He hadn't moved from the chair beside his dad's bed since arriving yesterday, except for when the doctor had visited for a checkup.

The doctor's prognosis had been as grave as Tom Dooley indicated, and Riley hadn't wanted to miss any of the last moments of his dad's life, even if he was sleeping most of the time and groggy during the few occasions he'd awoken.

The door behind Riley opened, then closed, followed by the patter of feet—one of his sisters coming to see if he needed anything. With the draperies drawn, the room was dark, only a sliver of daylight filtering in to mark the passing of the night and the start of another day.

A gentle hand came to rest on his shoulder. As the slender fingers squeezed, he caught a whiff of jasmine perfume. Lorette.

The sixteen-year-old was the closest sibling in age to his twenty-six years and always seemed to understand him best. Though she was technically his half sister, he didn't see her that way. He adored her. He adored all four of his blond-haired, blue-eyed little sisters. And he'd grown to love his stepmom too, although their start had been rocky.

He'd been but a lad of eight when he'd woken one morning to

make breakfast for his dad, only to find a pretty young woman in their apartment, her long blond hair streaming around her. She paused, with one hand stirring eggs in the frying pan and the other flipping slices of ham on the griddle. She smiled at him. "Good morn, Riley. I'm Eleanor, your new ma."

He narrowed his eyes at her. "I don't need a ma." He and his dad had gotten along just fine without anyone, hadn't they?

Eleanor had turned back to *his* cast-iron stove and resumed *his* job of cooking.

He had half a mind to stride over to her and drag her out the door. She was a thin waif and didn't look old enough to be anyone's ma. "I can take care of my dad by myself."

At his declaration, she paused, and this time turned her full attention upon him, her beautiful eyes brimming with tears. "I can see that you've done an excellent job taking care of your dad. But I'd like to help, if you'll let me."

He started to shake his head, not understanding why she was near to tears. But before he could say anything else, his dad ambled out of his bedroom, yawning, shirtless, and his hair tousled. He hadn't seemed to see Riley standing by the table and had gone directly to Eleanor, settled his hands on her hips, and drew her sharply against his body before bending in and kissing her hungrily.

Riley had only been able to stare.

Eleanor allowed the kiss but a moment before pulling back and pressing a hand against his dad's bare chest. "I was just introducing myself to your son." She nodded and smiled again at Riley.

At the reminder that he had a son, his dad jerked away from Eleanor. He swiped up his shirt from the back of one of the kitchen chairs. As he stuffed it on, he didn't meet Riley's questioning gaze.

In that moment, Riley had known he'd fallen short of being

what his dad had needed. Somehow he'd failed so that his dad had gone out and gotten himself a bride without telling him.

Eventually, Riley had realized that Eleanor had grown teary-eyed because she'd been sad that at eight, he'd already been responsible for so many things. And of course over time, she'd made it nearly impossible not to love her. Not only had she been beautiful, but she'd been good and kind and tender to him. She still was.

Each of the four daughters she'd borne William Rafferty were every bit as beautiful and good and kind and tender—just like her.

Lorette squeezed his shoulder again. "Ma says I'm to sit with Dad so you can sleep."

Riley shook his head. "I'm staying right here."

"I told her you'd say that." Lorette stepped up to the bed and stroked their dad's cheek. Covered in a layer of scruff, Dad looked nearly as young now as he had the day he'd married Eleanor. He'd aged well, with only a few creases in his forehead and cheeks. His blond-brown hair was untouched with silver, wavy like Riley's. And his body was still as muscular and strong.

The fact was, William Rafferty was too healthy and young at fifty-two years of age to suffer from a heart attack and die.

Riley pressed his dad's hand and was surprised when his dad gripped back. A second later, his eyes flickered open. "Riley?"

Riley leaned forward into his dad's line of vision.

"I'm dying, son." The raspy words fell from his dry lips.

"No." Riley couldn't keep from protesting. "You can't give up yet."

His father's lids closed, and he sucked in a struggling breath.

Clutching a rosary, Lorette had started to back out of the room, obviously wanting to give him privacy with their dad, but Riley cast her a pleading look. He didn't want to be alone in Dad's final moments. He needed her to stay.

As usual, he didn't have to say anything for her to understand

33

him. She merely returned to his side and placed her hand on his shoulder again.

"Do one last thing for me," his dad whispered.

Riley grasped the man's hand tighter. "You know I'll do anything for you."

His eyes cracked open. "Do you promise?"

"Yes." The one word came out in a rush of passion.

"Then get married again."

Riley almost jumped up, but with Lorette holding his shoulder and his dad clasping his hand, he was trapped. "Ask me for anything but that."

His dad released a long, uneven breath. Was it a sigh of disappointment?

Frustration rippled through Riley, and he bent his head and closed his eyes to keep from overreacting. His dad had been pressuring him over the last year to take another wife, telling him he'd waited long enough, that he needed to put the past behind him and move on with his life.

Every time they had this conversation—which had been more frequent over recent months—his dad insisted that marrying Eleanor had been one of the greatest blessings of his life, that it had helped him work through his grief.

And each time, Riley didn't have enough courage to tell his dad the truth—that he wasn't grieving for Helen, that he never had. In fact, he was ashamed to admit that when he'd gotten the news the *Monarch* had hit a snag and sunk, he'd almost felt relief that he was free.

He'd been the one to convince Helen to get married, had wanted to make things work. After only a few months—after the miscarriage—she'd grown tired of being married to him. Finally, during one particularly bad argument, she'd packed a bag and said she intended to live with her sister in New Orleans. When he'd come home the next day from work, she'd been gone.

He blamed himself for her leaving. Maybe if he'd done more for her and loved her better, she would have been happier with him.

Whatever the case, he'd made a mess of one marriage, and he had no desire to get involved with another woman. As far as he was concerned, his desires were dead and buried.

The image of Finola Shanahan half naked in the livery stall flashed into his mind—her beautiful curves, pale skin, and those freckles . . . Heat flared to life low in his gut.

So maybe his desires were still alive and strong. He was only a man. But that didn't change the fact that he didn't want to get into another marriage anytime soon, maybe not ever.

"I want to go in peace," his dad whispered.

Riley lifted his head to find his dad watching him, his brows drawn above sad eyes.

"But I can't get married." Riley's return whisper held a note of desperation that surely his father could hear.

"I just want you to be happy, son."

"I am happy—"

"And I want you to have a family." Dad held out a hand toward Lorette. "A whole bunch of daughters as sweet as sugar-coated candy."

Lorette took his hand and kissed it, tears springing to her eyes as easily as they did to Eleanor's.

Dad then reached for Riley's face, brushing the injury on his cheek, the injury Finola had given him yesterday. The sting reminded him of how feisty and beautiful she'd looked when she'd thrown the tools at him. "I want you to have a son too. One as courageous and determined and loyal as you."

"Don't worry." Riley's chest ached with the realization that this was his dad's good-bye. "I'll take good care of Eleanor and the girls. They'll be my family."

"You'll attract more voters if you're married."

"It's possible." His campaign staff had already told him that. "But that seems like a shallow reason to take a wife."

With the death of the mayor last month, a special mayoral election was being held in April. With Riley's widespread fame, some of the local Irish leaders had convinced him to run for office.

After the past few weeks, the grassroots campaigning had taken off, and he was gaining ground, even among the rest of the St. Louis non-Irish population. But his campaign manager, Father O'Kirwin, insisted he needed to be doing more, including getting married.

Dad closed his eyes, the exchange clearly making him weary. But in the next moment, he opened them and spoke again, this time more forcefully. "If you want me to rest in peace, then you'll do this for me, son."

William Rafferty could be persuasive when he wanted to be. The man hadn't earned the reputation as the best wagonmaker in St. Louis based on skill alone. He was also smart and confident and tough.

As his dad held his gaze, Riley knew he had no choice but to go along with the wishes. How could he deny a dying man his last request?

He couldn't. That's what. "If you really want me to—"

"Lorette?" Dad pushed up to his elbows with a sudden burst of energy. "Send for Oscar McKenna."

"The matchmaker?" Riley straightened in surprise.

Lorette took a step toward the door but then paused. "Now?"

Dad nodded. "Immediately. Tell Oscar this is urgent."

"Hold on." Riley held up a warning hand. "Not so fast—"

"Now, Lorette." Dad's tone was strong and sure.

Riley wanted to continue to protest, but if the matchmaking mission would give Dad renewed motivation to fight for life, then he couldn't object.

As Lorette exited, Riley reclined in his chair. Yes, he'd do just about anything for his dad. It's partly why he'd run for mayor. He wanted to make his dad proud. And if taking a wife would please his dad and the constituents, then he had to set aside his objections and his fears and give the idea a chance.

Dad fell asleep again, and Riley couldn't keep from hoping the next time his dad roused that he would forget all about the matchmaking. When the room door opened an hour later with a breathless and flushed Lorette followed by Bellamy McKenna—and not Oscar—Riley let himself relax.

He didn't have anything to worry about. Even if his dad did persist with the marriage planning, without Oscar present, they wouldn't be able to make any solid arrangements.

Lorette made quick work of pulling the extra chair around the bed so it was positioned next to Riley. Shyly, she offered it to Bellamy, her cheeks still pink.

Riley narrowed his eyes at Bellamy, who was shrugging out of his coat and unwinding a scarf from his neck. The man had better not toy with Lorette. She was too young to court.

Bellamy didn't seem to be paying any attention to Lorette. Maybe she was the one with the fascination, and maybe Riley needed to make sure she wasn't getting any notions about marriage yet. After all, he would soon be the man of the house, and he'd have the responsibility of helping his sisters find advantageous matches.

"Thank you, Lorette. You may go." Riley offered her a smile to soften his dismissal.

She hesitated but a moment before she nodded and left the room.

Once he was alone with Bellamy, Riley shifted in his chair to face the fellow. Though the draperies were still pulled and the room dismal, they had enough natural light to see. "Look, Bellamy, this is my dad's idea—"

"Where's Oscar?" His dad's question was weak and breathless

again. But his eyes were wide open, and he was staring at Bellamy expectantly.

Bellamy gave his dad a nod of greeting. "Oscar has the philosophy that one can never drink too much Irish whiskey."

"And . . . ?"

"And as a result, he rarely works when the sun is shining so brightly." Bellamy spoke with the seriousness of a priest delivering a soliloquy at mass. But from the glint in his eyes, Riley guessed he had a sense of blarney that rivaled the best.

"Didn't Lorette explain that I'm dying?" Dad studied Bellamy's face like he was a riddle that needed solving.

"Your daughter made your wishes clear, so she did. But I'll be telling you the same thing I told her. That if you want a matchmaker's services in the morn, then you'll not be seeing Oscar Fingal McKenna. You'll have to make do with the matchmaker's son instead."

Dad's lashes fell, but not before he could hide his disappointment that he hadn't been able to enlist Oscar's services.

Bellamy didn't seem to notice—either that or he didn't care. He raised a brow at Riley. "So tell me, Riley Rafferty. What kind of woman would ever be able to meet the high standards of Saint Riley of the Kerry Patch?"

Was that sarcasm in Bellamy's tone? Was he making light of Riley's many heroic deeds? Riley scrubbed a hand across his mouth to hold back a defense of himself.

Bellamy's eyes darkened, and his lips quirked with the beginning of a grin. "Ach, I don't care about your grand reputation. But I can tell you this: any woman who cares even a wee bit about your fame won't be right for you."

Dad relaxed back into the bed. "Sounds like we might have the right man for the job after all."

Bellamy shrugged. "The list of candidates won't be long."

Dad gave a weak smile, but a smile, nonetheless. "If they're sensible young women, that's all that matters. And if her family is able to gain Riley more support in the election, then even better."

It was Riley's turn to study Bellamy intently. He'd thought Bellamy would be more like Oscar, who was a what-you-see-is-what-you-get kind of fellow. But the young man had more wit and depth of insight than Riley had expected. Under other circumstances, Riley might have even liked Bellamy. But this morning after a sleepless night, the fellow was getting under his skin like a pesky wood shaving.

"Since you're clearly the expert," Riley said, "and already have my future figured out, why don't you tell us which women you're contemplating?"

"There's only one at the moment."

"One?" Riley's question came out at the same time as Dad's.

Dad continued first. "Now, Bellamy, we need more than one option. We're not paupers with only pennies, and we have plenty to offer a woman."

"I guarantee you'll like the option and want none other."

Riley wanted to roll his eyes at the matchmaker's arrogance, but he held himself in check. "You can't guarantee—"

"I've a notion that I can."

"Not to add to the low opinion you have of me—"

"I don't have a low opinion of you. But you'll not be needing a woman patting your back when you have the rest of the city doing it already."

"Very well, but if I get married again, I prefer to have a wife I find at least a little attractive."

"Naturally. I wouldn't want to be the cause of you gouging your eyes out because you can't stand the sight of your wife."

Dad released a rumbling chuckle.

Since that first morning Eleanor had come to live with them, Riley had lost count of the times he'd caught his dad getting handsy with her, always touching and kissing and whispering and laughing. It had been clear as a cistern of fresh rainwater that his dad had been attracted to Eleanor and couldn't get enough of her or she of him.

A part of Riley had always longed for that kind of relationship. He'd hoped for it with Helen, but in looking back he could see that most of what they'd had was little more than lust.

"Then tell us." Riley rolled his shoulders, trying to loosen the tension that had taken up residence there. "Who is this sensible woman immune to my charm and fame?"

Bellamy pivoted in his chair to squarely face Riley, almost as if he was preparing himself for a show and didn't want to miss a single moment of the unfolding drama. Bellamy quirked a brow, seeming to ask if Riley was ready for the momentous revelation.

Riley lifted his brow back.

"The one and only woman on my list for you is . . ." Bellamy paused dramatically. "Finola Shanahan."

Finola Shanahan?

Riley couldn't hold back a snort. "Nice effort, Bellamy. But the Shanahans run in different circles than the Raffertys and will be seeking a more advantageous match than me."

His dad didn't say anything. For a second, Riley wondered if he'd gone back to sleep. The meeting with Bellamy was surely wearing him out. But his dad's eyes were wide open, and he was watching Bellamy with a keen new interest.

Of course Dad would be interested in a union with the Shanahans. Who wouldn't want to marry into one of the wealthiest families in the city? Being connected to them would go a long way in aiding Riley's election efforts, especially if James Shanahan was willing to use his influence to help Riley.

But Riley couldn't consider Finola Shanahan, could he? Not after their embarrassing interaction at the livery.

Bellamy narrowed his eyes upon Riley. "I heard what happened yesterday, so I did."

"You did?" How? Had Tom Dooley seen Finola and him after

40

all? Had the lad gone and told everyone about it over drinks at Oscar's Pub later?

"Why don't you tell me your side of the story." Bellamy crossed his arms, the seriousness of his expression saying that he wouldn't settle for anything less than the truth.

Maybe Finola had been the one to blab about their encounter. If she'd informed her parents about the way he'd ogled her, maybe they were demanding that he marry her out of respect for her reputation.

He might as well admit the truth. "Look, Bellamy. I don't know what Finola said and what you've heard. But I didn't realize she was half naked when I opened the stall door."

Bellamy didn't move, but his eyes took on a new sparkle.

"You saw Finola Shanahan naked?" Dad's voice rose with a note of surprise.

"No." He glanced toward the bedroom door, guessing that all four of his sisters were hovering in the hallway and had just heard Dad. "I didn't see her naked." He made sure his voice carried so that all the ears eavesdropping would know the real facts. "She had on her unmentionables."

Dad shook his head. "As if that's any better."

Guilt pricked Riley. He should have been more careful yesterday. At least he wouldn't have to worry about needing to gouge out his eyes with Finola, that was for certain. Even fully clothed, she was a beautiful woman with attractive features. Not only were her blue eyes unique, but her brown hair with hints of red reminded him of fine cherry hardwood.

For a moment both Dad and Bellamy watched him, waiting for him to give them further details regarding the encounter. Once again, his mind flashed back to the sight of her standing in the middle of the stall wearing nothing but a thin layer of silk. And once again desire shot through him.

"Aye, so, you're remembering how she looked." Bellamy nodded with a half grin.

Bother it. Riley jumped up from his chair so quickly it clattered to the ground behind him. How could Bellamy see inside his head so clearly? It was uncanny, that's what.

"I was asking you about what happened on Broadway when Finola pinched your cheek and called you a good lad." Bellamy stood, too, and reached for his coat. "But your story is much more entertaining."

Riley wanted to roll his eyes at his own stupidity. "The story needs to remain private." He hoped that not only would Bellamy keep quiet but his sisters too.

"Dontcha be worrying, Riley." Bellamy flung one end of his scarf one way around his neck and the other the opposite way. "I'll have you married to Finola Shanahan by Shrove Tuesday, so I will, and then you'll get to wake up every morning and see her n—"

Riley cut Bellamy off with a curt shake of his head and nod toward the door.

Bellamy followed his gaze, then dropped his voice to a whisper. "What?"

"Don't say it."

"Say what?"

"You know."

"No, I don't."

Riley bit back a sigh. "Let's stop talking about her being naked."

"I was going to say that you'll get to wake up every morning and see her nice smile." Bellamy's eyes held false innocence, but clearly he'd gotten from Riley the response he'd wanted. "But looks like your mind is thinking about only one thing."

Again, his dad chuckled.

Riley palmed the back of his neck, the heat rising there. Apparently, his encounter yesterday with Finola had awakened his desires more than he'd realized, and now his thoughts were a fire-powered engine on a narrow track driving toward a single destination.

Maybe his dad was right that he needed to seriously consider marriage again. And maybe by enlisting the aid of a matchmaker, he could avoid the mistakes he'd made the first time. In the process, he'd make his dad happy, and he'd benefit his campaign to become the next mayor of St. Louis.

He highly doubted Finola Shanahan would give him the time of day. But he couldn't deny that he was open to seeing if she would.

5

$\mathscr{A}$nother night had passed, and his dad was still alive. With a prayer of thanksgiving at the forefront of his mind, Riley trotted down the narrow stairway of the tenement, the sour waft of cabbage and fish a permanent scent embedded into the thin walls of the building.

At midday the tenement was fairly quiet, the crying of a babe coming from behind a closed door and the squeal of little tykes at play from another. Most children—including his sisters— were at school. Dad and Eleanor, like many others, took full advantage of the free education offered by the city. Jefferson School over on Wash Street wasn't fancy, and the classrooms were crowded, but it was a fair share better than no education at all.

Not only were most children absent from the tenement, but the majority of adult residents toiled long hours each day to provide for their families. Largely unskilled, they took whatever employment they could find. Many of the men labored as stevedores, loading and unloading cargo from the dozens of steamships that carried goods to and from St. Louis. Others worked in factories or in construction.

Some of the lucky Irish like his father had a trade and were able to establish a profitable business for themselves. But most struggled not only to provide the basics for their families, they also faced an increasing hostility among the non-Irish of the city. Just recently on one of his excursions into the wealthier shops and businesses, he'd noticed a Help Wanted sign in a window that said: *No Irish Need Apply.*

Such discrimination set Riley's stomach to churning worse than a summer storm blowing off the river. At times like that, he wished he could do more for people than just rescue them from danger and death. It was why he'd so easily agreed to running for mayor. Because he hoped the position would allow him to make a difference for not only the Irish, but for all those who were struggling in a city stretching at the seams.

Tucking his coat lapel closed and pulling down the brim of his hat, Riley pushed open the front door of the tenement and stepped out into another gray winter day with no sunshine in sight. Today, he wouldn't—couldn't—complain about a single thing. His dad was alive and that was all that mattered.

A bitter gust of wind greeted him as he paused at the top step of the building his family had lived in for ages. Even though his dad had grown prosperous and could afford to move into a better place, he'd chosen to stay in the Kerry Patch and live a humble life among the Irish community. Not only that, but the residence was close to the wagon shop.

Riley pulled in a deep breath, the chill in the air filling his lungs and clearing his head. After the past two days and nights spent by his father's bed in the dark room, he was not only tired, but he also needed a breath of fresh air. And though he'd been reluctant to leave his dad's bedside, Eleanor had finally all but pushed him out the door, telling him to go to his apartment or go to work or go do anything besides worry about his dad.

Riley glanced west past the rows upon rows of dingy tenements that lined the street, some of them with nicknames like Clabber Alley, Wild Cat Chute, and Castle Thunder. In the warmer months, the view would have been congested with the clothing hung out to get a blow from lines that stretched from the upper windows of residences on either side of the street. But during this time of year, most women didn't do laundry, or if they did—like Eleanor—they strung up lines inside so the garments wouldn't wear out from so much freezing.

He shifted his sights to the east and could see all the way to the river through the dark haze that came from the nonstop exhaust pumping from the city's many coal-powered factories and smoke billowing from dozens upon dozens of steamships that docked along the levee. The loud bellows of the smoke-stacks were so common, he almost didn't think about the noise.

But the stench? With the tallow factories, slaughterhouses, and tanneries nearby, the smell of hot fat, blood, and rotting flesh was constant. In addition, many places didn't have proper sewer systems, so people were dumping sewage into creeks, ponds, and the Mississippi River. If that wasn't bad enough, privies were being erected without any direction, and some were too close to wells and cisterns.

In one part of St. Louis, an engineer had developed limestone sinkholes to form a natural sewer, but Riley had heard that during heavy rains the sinkholes backed up, forming large ponds of human waste that only added to the stench.

When he became mayor, he'd find a better solution.

"Well, young Riley Rafferty," called a stoop-shouldered man shuffling up the steps. "Good day to you."

At the mention of his name, one of the nuns entering the tenement across the street halted, and her back stiffened.

"How's your father getting on?" the older man asked.

"Rightly, we think." Riley cast a cursory look at the neighbor before focusing his attention on the nun. "He seems stronger this morning."

"Good, good."

The nun paused, allowing the others to enter the building

46

ahead of her. Riley couldn't see much beneath the black robe and bonnet she was wearing, but the petite size fit the profile of Finola Shanahan.

Riley's heartbeat picked up speed. It couldn't be her. . . . He was only wishing it was so because he hadn't been able to stop thinking about her since Bellamy's visit yesterday. No, Riley hadn't been able to stop thinking about Finola Shanahan since the day he'd met her. And Bellamy's suggestion that she was the one Riley was going to marry had only made matters worse.

Riley willed the nun to turn around.

As if sensing his beckoning or his stare, she glanced over her shoulder in his direction. He barely had time to glimpse bright blue eyes and a freckled nose before she started through the door.

"Finola!" He hopped over the iron stair railing, then leapt to the ground, landing with the nimbleness of an alley cat.

She hesitated—had clearly heard him call her name—but continued inside, letting the door close behind her.

With a burst of renewed energy, he darted into the street, dodging the traffic coming from both directions. Heedless of more greetings being tossed his way, he made a direct line to the tenement Finola had entered. He took the front steps two at a time and tossed open the door to find her already nearing the landing of the second floor.

"Finola, wait."

With her back facing him, her steps faltered. It was clear she wasn't keen on seeing him again. Was she embarrassed from their interaction in the livery stall? Or perhaps Bellamy McKenna had already approached her father and begun the discussion regarding a possible match. What if Mr. Shanahan didn't want to give his daughter in marriage to someone of Riley's station?

Even so, with or without the matchmaking, he wanted to

see Finola again. In fact, now that she was within his sights, he wasn't sure he could walk away without talking to her.

"Hope you're not making plans to roll in the mud again today." He climbed to the bottom step, ready to bound after her if necessary. He wasn't used to having to chase after women. Usually it was the other way around.

She held on to the rail a few seconds more before she pivoted. Although the brim of her bonnet cast a shadow over her face in the dimly lit stairwell, he found himself finally getting a full view of her pretty features, her pert nose, well-rounded lips, the adorable dimple in her chin. And the freckles. They liberally sprinkled her nose and cheeks, putting her in a class of beauty all her own.

Against his will, his mind conjured the image of all the freckles hidden beneath the layers of her gown.

Bother it. He couldn't let his thoughts go there.

"Playing nun again, I see." He gave her a once-over, the baggy robe indeed hiding what shouldn't be hidden.

"Hello, Riley." She spoke quietly, calmly.

"Are you going to explain to me why you're dressed as a nun?"

"'Tis none of your business, Riley Rafferty. But if you must know, the good Sisters think I'll draw less attention covered like this."

He could see their point. With the Kerry Patch riddled with gangs and a growing population of riffraff, no one would dare touch or harm her if they thought she was a servant of the church. She was safe cloaked in nun's clothing.

Even as she gave him the excuse, she dropped her attention briefly to the landing, as though she didn't want him to see the entire truth. Perhaps there was more to the nun's clothing than she was disclosing.

He took another step up, wanting to span the distance between them, but he was afraid she'd rush off if he came too close.

How was it possible he'd never noticed her in the Kerry Patch before? Of course, he was rarely in these parts during daylight hours since most of the time he was at the wagon shop working and his apartment was above the shop. And he supposed even when out running errands, he wouldn't have paid a group of nuns any special attention.

She twisted at the simple belt cinching the habit. "A moment ago, I heard you say that your dad is doing better."

"He is. Thanks be."

She nodded solemnly. "I've been saying prayers for him morning and night. And I'm happy to know he's recovering, to be sure."

She'd been praying for his dad? "Thank you, Finola. That's kind of you."

"Does the doctor expect him to make a full recovery?"

"He says it's still too early to tell, but with plenty of rest, it's possible."

"That's wonderful. I'm happy for you." Her gaze was sincere, devoid of the spitfire that had been there during previous interactions.

From the genuineness of her tone, he believed she truly cared enough about people that she was glad his dad was alright.

"And you?" Her question dropped a decibel. "How is your injury? Better, I hope?"

"My injury?"

She looked pointedly at his cheek and then his jaw.

Oh, the cut. He lifted a hand and brushed the spot, still tender. "This little thing? I hardly know it's there."

She watched him as though searching for the truth.

He let his smile broaden.

"Then you've forgiven me?"

"As long as you've forgiven me for—well, you know."

She glanced up toward the second floor where the door to an apartment now stood open with two Sisters just inside. They were already distracted by the family within and didn't seem to be paying any attention to what Finola was doing.

"I propose we forgive each other," she said in a hushed tone, "and then we never have to think on either incident ever again."

He doubted he'd be able to forget what he saw, wasn't sure he wanted to. "Too late for that." He let his gaze drift over her. What was he doing? He gave himself a mental slap and forced himself to focus on her face.

Her eyes widened, showing her surprise at his admission. What exactly had he admitted? That he found her attractive? That he didn't want to stop thinking about her? Maybe both? There was nothing wrong with that.

"You have to wipe the moment from your memory," she insisted.

That would be impossible. "I'll do my best, but you must know you're unforgettable, Finola Shanahan."

Her cheeks turned pink. "You cannot say things like that."

"What? I can't tell the truth?" He grinned. "Would you rather I lie?"

"It's not lying if you restrain yourself."

"Once you get to know me, you'll learn I rarely restrain myself."

"I do not plan to get to know you." Her voice turned sassy.

"Is that so?" The more he talked to her, the more she intrigued him and the more he wanted to get to know her. "Well, you'll find I'm irresistible."

"I'm finding that you're rather arrogant."

"And you like me. I can tell."

"Certainly not, Mr. Rafferty." She bunched her robe into her fists, twisted around, and started up the next flight of stairs. "I guess I'll need to keep praying, this time for your wayward soul."

"Thank you. I need the prayers."

"Aye, you do." With a final glare, she ascended the last step and crossed into the apartment. A moment later, she shut the door behind her and closed him away from view.

As soon as she was gone, he wished she'd come back out and talk to him longer. Something about their exchange brought him to life.

He watched the door for a few more seconds before he retreated down the stairway. Striking up a whistle to an old Irish love ballad, he exited the building and started toward St. Charles Street.

He wasn't exactly sure what he would say to Bellamy McKenna when he arrived at Oscar's Pub. But he knew one thing. He no longer needed his dad to convince him to meet with the matchmaker. Riley was going there of his own free will. In fact, there was no other place he wanted to go and nothing he wanted to do more than to tell Bellamy to arrange a meeting with Mr. Shanahan.

Riley whistled all the way to the end of the street before reality hit him harder than a toppling wall of bricks. He stopped short, causing everyone around him to do the same and stare at him expectantly, waiting for him to jump in and rescue somebody.

But the truth was, the one who needed rescuing was him. Being Saint Riley of the Kerry Patch wouldn't be enough to win over James Shanahan. He had to be and do more to prove that he was worthy enough for the Shanahans and for Finola.

But what could he do that he hadn't already done? His list of accomplishments included rescuing people from burning buildings, saving passengers from drowning on sinking steamboats, halting deadly brawls, preventing robberies, catching runaway feral livestock, providing fuel during an ice-storm crisis, and more.

Even if he listed everything he'd ever accomplished, his heart told him it wouldn't be acceptable, not for a man like James Shanahan.

No, he needed better qualifications, something that would truly show he was a worthy man. Would his bid for mayor prove that he had aspirations? Could he somehow convince Shanahan he wasn't just running for mayor, but that he intended to win?

As he continued the rest of the way, his mind whirled with all his options. Upon entering Oscar's Pub, the scent of tobacco smoke and beer hung heavily in the air. The dark-paneled barroom contained a few lanterns attached to the wall, providing only dismal light. But oil paintings hung on every wall and were bright and cheerful landscapes of Ireland, many of County Wicklow. *"My home, the most beautiful country on God's green earth, so it is,"* Oscar McKenna always boasted. *"Right on dirty Dublin's doorstep."*

A polished mahogany bar counter ran the length of the room with the shelves behind it holding rows of spirits in all shapes and sizes. Bellamy was drying a glass and conversing with a patron seated on a stool at the counter.

Since it was still before noon, Oscar wasn't at his usual table at the back where he conducted business. But the leather ledger where he kept a record of all his matches was there, putting a claim on his spot, a place no one else ever sat. From what Riley had heard, the ledger had been passed down from father to son for several generations of matchmakers.

Would it soon go to Bellamy? Even if not, Riley was too impatient to wait for Oscar. And since Bellamy had been the one to meet with him in the first place and start the matchmaking process, it only seemed right for him to continue.

At the sight of Riley, Bellamy straightened and raised a brow.

Riley grinned as he crossed toward the long counter. "I'm ready for you to set up a meeting with the Shanahans."

"Are you now?" Bellamy was watching him again, as he had the day he'd come to Riley's dad's bedside, as if he was entertained by people and their reactions more than anything else.

Good thing Riley didn't mind putting on a performance. He spread his arms out wide and faced the few men who were seated around the pub, those who were too old to work or too drunk. "Hey, folks," he called to them, drawing their attention. "What do you think? Should the matchmaker set me up with Finola Shanahan?"

As the men whistled and cheered their support, he gave a mock bow before he turned back to Bellamy.

The young matchmaker was finally grinning. "I'll hand it to you, Riley Rafferty. You have guts, that you do."

"That you do." The older patron, Georgie McGuire, was grinning too—or at least was grinning with the few teeth that remained. Ginger-haired, he had a cowlick on top of his head that made him look like a rooster. With a pale face and purplish nose, he was a permanent fixture at the bar.

"Do you think James Shanahan will agree to meet with me?"

"I know he will, since I've already scheduled for you to meet with him."

"Sweet saints above." Riley groped for the counter. "You did?"

"Oh, aye." Bellamy's eyes sparkled now too.

"Oh, aye," Georgie echoed.

Riley sank onto the nearest stool, his mouth going suddenly dry. "When?"

"Tomorrow night at seven o'clock. And see that you're not a minute late."

"I'll trot over there right now to make sure I'm plenty early."

At that Bellamy chuckled, and Georgie made a humming sound at the back of his throat.

Riley was half serious. How had this happened to him? How had he gone from being opposed to taking a wife one day to acting as if he'd swallowed an ancient herbal love potion the next?

He guessed in part his awakening desires had to do with the

fact that when he'd vowed to his dad that he'd get married, he'd finally given himself permission to move on from Helen.

Yes, the thought of making mistakes again still terrified him, but he couldn't forget he was no longer the same inexperienced and immature man who'd married Helen. He'd grown up, and more importantly, he was taking his faith seriously and doing his best to live an upright life. Surely this time he'd prove himself to be a better husband.

Riley reached for the glass of stout Bellamy was sliding his way. He took a sip and wet his tongue, then wiped the foam from his upper lip. "Are you going to tell me why James Shanahan agreed to meet with me? Is he impressed with my bid to become mayor?"

Georgie was still grinning, his front gums showing. "His little gal is turning into an old biddy, that's why. And everyone knows that long-churning makes bad butter."

"Finola hasn't been churning for long." Bellamy poured another glass of stout. "No, James Shanahan likes a man with ambition, and he sees your potential."

"Not sure *ambitious* is how I'd describe myself."

"And he's taken a shine to the idea of working out a deal that Rafferty Wagon Company buys Shanahan iron for their wagon parts."

"Has he now?" Maybe he had more to offer the Shanahans than he'd realized.

"But neither of those are the real reason Shanahan is interested in you, Riley."

"What's the real reason then?"

Georgie's gaze was darting back and forth between them. "She's as stiff as a brass bedstead?"

Riley shook his head. Finola was anything but stiff.

Bellamy's eyes twinkled as though he'd heard Riley's thought. "Shanahan didn't tell me in exact words. But I guessed what it was, so I did."

"What is it?" Riley rubbed a thumb around the rim of his glass.

"Maybe someday if you haven't figured it out on your own, I'll tell you."

"Fair enough." Even if Shanahan was willing to meet with him, that was only the start. He had to make Finola like him. And that might prove the biggest challenge of his life.

6

"*F*inola Shanahan. Sit still with you now lest I burn you and leave a welt on your pretty neck." Mam held a piece of Finola's hair wrapped tightly around the wand of the hot iron hair curler.

A welt on her neck? Finola peered into the vanity table mirror at her reflection. Would a welt make a terrible first impression on tonight's caller?

The neckline of the light blue silk evening gown dropped off her shoulders and dipped in the center, allowing for plenty of room to show a blemish. The straight panel of lace bertha hanging from the neckline would only highlight the disfigurement. Aye, marring her skin with a flaming red welt might work.

But as Mam pulled the hair curler out and left behind a perfect ringlet, Finola could only cringe at the prospect of putting herself through such pain in order to alienate the matchmaker's first match.

"There, so it is." Mam stood back and examined Finola through narrowed eyes.

Finola hadn't wanted all the fuss over her appearance tonight. But Mam had insisted on Finola looking her best. "You never get a second chance to make a good first impression," Mam had said.

Now with but minutes until the suitor's arrival, Finola looked the picture of a perfect lady with her hair parted down the center and smoothed back into an elegant chignon with long ringlets hanging on either side of her face.

"This one is too loose." Enya stood on the other side of the cushioned bench. She, too, was studying Finola, her green eyes luminous and her red hair exquisitely styled as always. She wore a peach silk that brought out the warm tones of her skin, so different from Finola's. Having just turned twenty, Enya was most certainly old enough to get married.

"Maybe Da should make this match for Enya. She never has any trouble turning a man's head."

"You never have any trouble catching a man's attention either." Enya held out the bothersome strand while Mam wrapped it around the prongs that were now growing cold and would need to be reheated over a flame. "The trouble you have is in keeping his attention."

Finola only sniffed. She wouldn't be keeping tonight's man's attention either. At least not for long.

Da and Mam had refused to tell her the name of Bellamy McKenna's prospect. Did they think she'd undermine the meeting if she knew who it was? Or perhaps skip it?

They weren't entirely wrong. She'd always been able to come up with excuses in the past to avoid suitors—headaches, stomachaches, dizziness. She was quite adept at forcing sickness when she needed it. That way she didn't have to lie. Maybe she still had time to do so for tonight.

The problem was, such tactics only delayed the inevitable meeting. Aye, she'd learned that the only way to truly eliminate a suitor was to make the fellow so dissatisfied with her that he called things off.

What if Da and Mam weren't telling her because he was twice

her age and wouldn't be put off by anything she might do to make herself distasteful?

A shudder worked its way up her spine, but she cut it off just as quickly as it started. Bellamy McKenna would start with the young and rich and handsome among St. Louis's upper class. There were, after all, still a few men left that she hadn't scared off.

The gilded oval mirror in front of her reflected her as demure, beautiful, and elegant, the low-pointed waist and bell skirt highlighting her womanly figure. But that wasn't the real her.

Her gaze shifted to the reflection of the opposite wall of her bedroom to the faded rose-colored wallpaper and the three empty squares that were a brighter pink. Even though she'd taken down the framed doily artwork she'd painstakingly crocheted, she hadn't been able to erase their memory. And even though she'd boxed up the doilies from underneath the rose-patterned bedside lanterns, she could still picture the delicate white fluted edges she'd crocheted to look like rose petals.

Not only had she boxed all evidence of her crocheting away, but she hadn't allowed herself to crochet a single stitch since the day of the accident seven years ago. . . .

Enya pulled the strand of hair tightly. "You wouldn't be in this situation if you hadn't pushed away all the handsome men who have already shown interest in you."

"I didn't push them away."

Mam and Enya both pursed their lips and shook their heads in a similar curt fashion.

"I can't help it if they didn't like me once they got to know me." Finola tried for an innocent look, but after so many failed courtships, it was only natural for everyone to suspect she was at fault.

Enya released Finola's wayward curl and scrunched it next to the others. "I plan to pick my own husband, someone handsome and dashing."

Mam scoffed. "Mind you, smart and sensible make for a better husband than handsome and dashing."

"Maybe for you." Enya's eyes flashed with her easily ignited temper. "But not for me."

"Truth is truth, and how you feel isn't changing that, so it isn't."

Enya stepped back and fisted her hands on her slender hips made even more slender by the tightness of her corset that pushed her bust up so that it peeked out of her neckline. She already had the curvy figure of an ancient Celtic goddess, and the corset only made her all the more irresistible. "I like Bryan, and I wish you would accept him."

Mam placed the hair iron down on the marble top of the vanity, then started across the bedchamber to the door. "We'll not be accepting him for you, Enya."

"Whyever not?"

Mam didn't pause until she had her hand on the door handle. "We've been over this already, that we have, and there's nothing more to be saying."

"Even though you deny it, I know it's because he's Protestant."

Mam didn't respond and instead held herself rigidly.

Finola's gaze darted between her mam and sister. Though Enya had Da's red hair and fiery temper, she took after Mam in almost every other way, including the fact that both were strong-willed and stubborn. Because of that, they'd been clashing since the day Enya had kicked and screamed her way out of the womb—as Da liked to say.

"I'm old enough to decide for myself what I want." Enya's statement was low and filled with challenge. The words weren't new. Enya had spoken them during other arguments. And she'd likely speak them again. The trouble was that the arguments were growing more frequent and more intense, causing Mam's eyes to crinkle at the corners with exhaustion and Da's smile to show itself less frequently.

Mam took in a breath, squared her shoulders, then answered with a calmness that was clearly forced. "I'll not be arguing with you tonight, Enya. This eve is for Finola, and we'll not do anything to compromise her chances of finally getting a match." Before Enya could form a retort, Mam opened the door and stepped into the hallway. "Now come along with you, Finola."

Finola gripped the cushion of her chair, and she wished she could tell Mam she didn't want to get matched, that this would all be a waste of time.

But even as she opened her mouth to say something, the words got lost inside, just like they always did. What more could she say to change her parents' minds than she already had?

Maybe if she were like Enya, she would have been able to voice her wishes more forcefully. At the very least, she could have brought it up on another occasion and insisted that she needed to go into service to the church. The trouble was that every time she considered saying something more, the moment just didn't seem right.

Like now.

Enya glared after Mam, her eyes brimming with bitterness. But Mam's footsteps were already firmly leading away from the room.

Stifling her own frustration, Finola let go of the cushion and stood. With the tension her parents were experiencing with Enya, she didn't want to add to their problems. She would simply have to handle this new matchmaking effort her own way.

She took a step, only to have Enya grasp her hand. "You don't have to do this, you know."

Finola shifted so she was face-to-face with her sister. She lifted her other hand and cupped Enya's cheek. What should she say to this dear sister who had been the one to speak up for them both during their childhood? She loved her sister and her parents both and didn't want to disappoint either side.

"We aren't living in the Dark Ages, Finola." Enya was as serious and passionate as always. "We don't need our parents or a matchmaker to tell us whom we can or can't marry."

"Don't worry about me. I can take care of myself."

Enya wavered, seeming suddenly so young and uncertain.

Finola pressed a kiss to her sister's forehead. "I heard you composing a new song earlier on the piano. Will you play it for me later?"

"I don't have it quite finished."

"I still want to hear it." She squeezed Enya's hand before she released her and followed after Mam.

Her mam was waiting several paces away from the top of the spiraling marble stairway that led to the grand entrance hallway. Mam placed a finger to her lips and cocked her head down the steps.

The men were exchanging greetings, among them her da's voice and Kiernan's. She wasn't surprised her da had invited Kiernan to be a part of the matchmaking process. After all, as the oldest son and heir to the Shanahan fortune, Kiernan would have to form an advantageous marriage soon.

Perhaps her brother had even been the one to suggest sitting in so he could prepare for using the matchmaker himself. Only a year younger than her, Kiernan was reaching marriageable age too, but Da and Mam had made it clear they intended to see her wedded first.

Although Kiernan hadn't complained about her string of failed relationships, she could sense his growing frustration with her. As far as she knew, Kiernan didn't have his sights set on one particular woman, but lately he'd been dropping hints that Finola needed to hurry so he could have his turn.

"My father sends along his greetings," Bellamy said. "But he's busy making another match tonight, that he is."

"It's that time of year," her da said good-naturedly.

"Oh, aye." Bellamy's voice held a note of sarcasm. "Everybody is scrambling to find their special someone before Lent.

Rue the poor man or woman who has to celebrate Christ's resurrection as a bachelor or a spinster."

Laughter wafted up the stairway. And Kiernan's sounded strained.

Finola's chest pinched with guilt that only seemed to be getting stronger every day. Maybe her delays were making Kiernan more unhappy than she'd realized. She didn't see her brother often. Between her charity work and his many business endeavors, they were rarely at a family meal together. Or maybe she'd just been too preoccupied with her own future to take his into consideration.

"Let's hope the discussion tonight is fruitful," Kiernan said.

She'd been selfish and inconsiderate. From now on, she'd have to work more rapidly and stringently to bring about the dissolutions of all the relationships.

Her mam poked her with enough force that Finola knew it was time to make her grand entrance. She started forward, and when she reached the wide stairway with the carpeted runner, she stepped down, the high chandelier oil globes lit and shining upon her.

The men were still talking. And a familiar voice joined the conversation. "I admit I was surprised when Bellamy told me he'd arranged the meeting." The voice belonged to none other than Riley Rafferty.

She stumbled and had to grasp the rail to keep from falling.

At her clunky movement, all eyes shifted in her direction, including Riley's midnight blue eyes.

What was he doing here?

His face was cleanly shaven and his waves of blond hair were parted on the side and combed into submission. Instead of the simple attire he'd worn on previous occasions, he'd donned formal evening wear including a dark gray vest over a starched white shirt, matching gray trousers, and a black broadcloth tailcoat that fit snugly and showed off his muscular form. He held a black top hat and carried himself with the assurance of one who was as comfortable in an opulent mansion on Third Street as he was in a dingy tenement in the Kerry Patch.

Riley seemed to be taking in her appearance in the same measure, scanning her hair, gown, and the dainty slipper showing at the hem. Without the nun's attire and the mud, she probably looked different too. What did he think?

As his gaze traveled back up to her face, she found herself holding her breath. Not that it mattered what Riley thought about her appearance tonight. She wasn't making her grand entrance for him. She was making it for . . .

She glanced to the rest of the men, trying to locate the newest suitor, the one Bellamy had picked for her to meet first. But the only other men present were Bellamy, Kiernan, and her da. All three were dressed in evening suits in a similar fashion to Riley. And all of them were watching her.

Where was the mystery man who was coming tonight?

As though answering her unspoken question, Riley took several steps toward the stairs and looked up at her with a seriousness that sent strange flutters through her heart.

"How pleasant to see you again this eve, Miss Shanahan."

She pressed a trembling hand against her chest before she realized she was doing so. Riley Rafferty couldn't be the suitor. Could he?

Why else would he be visiting? Here? Now?

A strange sense of panic bubbled up, and her gaze darted to Bellamy. The young matchmaker must have made a mistake to arrange this meeting with Riley.

But Bellamy stood with his arms crossed, leaning against the doorframe to the parlor, the hint of a smile upon his lips, as though the evening was unfolding exactly the way he'd hoped. No doubt Bellamy had heard about Riley coming to her rescue and then her reaction afterward. Had he also learned about Riley seeing her changing clothes in the horse stall?

At Bellamy's imperceptible nod, she had the feeling he was answering a silent yes to both questions.

She gave him what she hoped was an imperceptible frown back, one that told him she wasn't pleased with his prying.

The clearing of her mam's throat from behind was equivalent to a poke, another signal to behave. And in this case her mam expected her to greet their guest politely.

Finola gripped the rail again and took another step down. "Mr. Rafferty. I was not expecting to see you."

She hadn't expected to see him yesterday in the Kerry Patch either. But after the encounter, she only had to ask one or two questions to find out everything she wanted to know about the Raffertys.

They had lived in the Kerry Patch neighborhood almost from its inception. And instead of building a big house with profits from his burgeoning wagon-making business, William Rafferty had invested his money into buying other businesses.

He owned several liveries and a large dry-goods store that specialized in items needed for the overland journey west. Not only that, but William gave a portion of his earnings back to the community, helping to build better roads and fund the school on Wash Street.

Even so, Riley wasn't the type of man Da would want for her. Surely Da preferred a wealthy, cultured man from among St. Louis's elite families.

Aye, she needn't worry. There was a misunderstanding. Her da would soon set everyone straight.

Drawing in a breath of resolve, she continued down the steps. "How is your father getting on today, Mr. Rafferty? I do hope well."

"A sight better." His gaze was riveted to her.

"Mr. Rafferty's father suffered a heart attack earlier in the week." She offered the explanation to her father, Kiernan, and Bellamy.

Kiernan had the same imposing build as Da and an intensity about him that could often be intimidating to those who didn't know him well. His hair wasn't as red as Da's—more auburn, making him a fine-looking man wherever he went.

"Bellamy informed us." Da offered Riley a sympathetic nod. "We're glad to know he's on the mend."

Riley smiled politely at Da. "He's as tough as buckboard if not tougher."

She was nearing the last of the stairs, and as she did so, Riley held out a hand as any gentleman would do to assist her descent. "You look lovely this eve, Miss Shanahan."

"Thank you, Mr. Rafferty."

As she paused two steps above him, their conversation from the tenement yesterday played through her head, especially the dark shade of blue his eyes had turned as he'd peered up at her and told her she was unforgettable.

When he'd scanned her as if he was remembering exactly how she'd looked in her chemise and underdrawers, she'd been mortified. But strangely, she'd liked his attention—although she would never in ten lifetimes admit it to him.

Tonight, his blue eyes were lighter, less playful, as though he was taking this meeting seriously. She knew she could do nothing less than use good manners in return.

She placed her hand in his. As his fingers closed about her white kid gloves, the warmth and solidity of his touch penetrated the silky layer. What would it be like to hold his hand without the glove between them?

Hold his hand? Really? What was coming over her to wonder about such a thing?

She kept her attention focused on the final steps. The moment both her feet were standing solidly on the hallway tile, she tugged her hand free.

Thankfully, he didn't let his hold linger. With nothing more than a last glance her way, he allowed Bellamy to usher him into the parlor with Da and Kiernan.

Bellamy paused in the doorway, cocking his head toward the settee and chairs near the hallway fireplace, which was crackling with flames. "I don't mind you waiting nearby, Finola. And I certainly won't mind you voicing your questions or concerns when we're finished."

Mam and Enya had already descended. Through a gap in the doorway down the hallway, Finola glimpsed the faces of her other younger siblings, including Madigan. Having the matchmaker there to begin negotiations was a momentous occasion, and she didn't blame her siblings for their curiosity.

"Thank you, Bellamy," her mam said as she began to guide Finola toward the settee. "We'll be just fine sitting out here, so we will."

Bellamy nodded but then paused and gave Finola a steady look—one filled with assurance and confidence. "It'll work out just the way it needs to. You'll see."

She wanted to blurt out that he was wasting his time with her, that she was a hopeless case, that instead of helping to solidify his standing as a successful matchmaker ready to take over for Oscar, she was about to ruin his reputation.

But before she could confess, Mam situated her on the settee and took the spot next to her.

7

*A*ll Riley could think about was the fact that Finola was sitting in the hallway just outside the parlor, and she was the most beautiful woman he'd ever laid eyes upon.

Why was it that every time he saw her, she was prettier? It wasn't just because her evening gown was off the shoulders, giving him a feast of her pale freckled skin. He'd tried not to stare so that her parents didn't think he was pursuing her to get her into his bed.

That wasn't why he was doing it, although he had to admit, the more he thought about her, the more he was looking forward to being fruitful and multiplying.

Bellamy had informed him on the ride over that the meeting was nothing more than a simple get-to-know-each-other. If the introductions went well, then they'd set up another night to pluck the gander, the process of negotiating what the prospective bride and groom would bring to the marriage. Once the details were worked out, they'd eat the gander, which was an old way of saying the bride's family would provide a meal to celebrate the match.

Tonight's meeting was the true test. If he didn't pass it, there would be no plucking, eating, or any other gandering.

But as far as he could tell, the meeting with James Shanahan and his son Kiernan was going well. They'd discussed the newly elected president, Zachary Taylor, a Whig, who would be taking office in March, and how President Polk had finished installing gas lights in the White House just in time for the new president to enjoy them.

They'd also conversed about the end of the war with Mexico now that the signing of the Treaty of Guadalupe Hidalgo was completed. As part of the negotiations with Mexico, large sections of land had been given to the United States in the West. Shanahan was interested in the new territories and what that meant for the growth of the country. More importantly, they discussed the implications for the growth of St. Louis as more people arrived, eager to head to the new territories.

They deliberated Riley's bid to become St. Louis's next mayor, and Shanahan inquired about the issues that Riley wanted to address, including more housing for immigrants, safer drinking water, additional paved streets, and more. Although Shanahan didn't specifically offer an endorsement, Riley sensed the man liked his plans, and hinted that his support and backing would be an advantage to marrying into the Shanahan family.

By the time they'd talked for the better part of an hour, according to the mantel clock, Riley had finally ceased perspiring and settled into the wing chair he sat in across from Shanahan.

"So, Riley Rafferty." Shanahan uncrossed his legs and sat forward, a Cuban cigar dangling from his fingers. "You think you can win over Finola?"

The question knocked into Riley, jolting him out of his comfortable lull and pushing him to the edge of his seat. The chit-chat was over, and now the real meeting was about to begin.

Shanahan's gaze was direct. "Bellamy believes you're up for the task."

Riley shot a look at the young matchmaker, who was reclining on the settee as relaxed as if he were on a Sunday picnic on a summer day.

Bellamy had indicated that he'd shared all the details of the Rafferty family so that Shanahan knew everything there was to know about the Rafferty businesses, wealth, and background. Bellamy had even told Shanahan about Riley's first marriage and that he'd been a widower for the past two years.

In addition, Bellamy was almost certain Shanahan had hired a private investigator of his own to do more digging into the Rafferty family. It appeared that Shanahan now knew more about the Rafferty family than even Riley did. Bellamy had reassured Riley that Shanahan wouldn't have agreed to the meeting if he'd found any concerns.

Even so, Riley pulled in a deep breath and tried to quiet his nerves. It was only natural that a loving father would want this match to be more than a business transaction. To be honest, Riley wanted it to be more than that too. "Even if the marriage starts off as an arrangement, I believe it's possible for love to eventually develop."

It was Shanahan's turn to exchange a look with Bellamy.

Hadn't they liked his answer? "I assure you I would work toward that end—"

"That's all well and good, Riley." Shanahan stood, took a drag on his cigar, and then began to pace. "But the issue here is . . ."

Riley's muscles tightened in preparation for the news, sensing it wouldn't be pleasant.

"The issue here is that Finola is . . ." Shanahan stopped in front of the fireplace and cast Bellamy another look.

Before Bellamy could come to the man's aid, Kiernan spoke. "What my da is trying to say is that Finola is a bit of a pickle."

"Pickle?" Finola's indignant voice burst from the sitting area in the hallway.

If Riley'd had his way, he would have included Finola and her mother in the parlor with the men. But Bellamy had warned him that the Shanahans were traditional when it came to the roles of men and women, and that the meeting would include only the men.

"Aye, a pickle she is." Kiernan raised his voice to make sure Finola had no trouble hearing him.

Riley waited for another comment from Finola, hoped she'd say something in response. But at a murmur of women's voices, he suspected her mother was curbing any more participation in the men's-only discussion.

"Finola is a good girl, that she is." Shanahan started pacing again. "But none of her previous suitors have lasted."

Riley hadn't bothered to consider Finola's previous courtship history. But it was strange that as one of St. Louis's most eligible and beautiful women, single men weren't fighting over her. "Why don't the suitors last?"

Kiernan rolled his eyes. "Because, I'm telling you, Finola is prickly and sour—"

"That's not true!" Finola's call was quickly cut off, probably by her mother.

Shanahan gave a curt shake of his head to Kiernan, clearly reproaching him for speaking ill of Finola. Or perhaps for disclosing something he shouldn't have. "As I said, Finola is a good girl. It's just that the fellows are too particular."

Too particular? With her sizable dowry and her beauty? Surely even the faintest of hearts could overlook a few minor imperfections in light of what they stood to gain in a woman like Finola. "How many fellows are we talking about?"

Shanahan paused, took another long drag of his cigar, and then puffed out a cloud of smoke. From the waver in his expression, he almost seemed to be debating whether to tell the truth or to lie. Finally he met Riley's gaze. "Ten."

"Ten?"

Kiernan released an exasperated sigh. "That doesn't include the two Da kicked out of the house when he found them trying to put their hands on Finola."

"So technically twelve?"

Shanahan turned to face the fireplace, leaving Kiernan to confirm with a nod.

"That can't be all that bad if you're counting back to when she first started courting—four, maybe five years ago?"

"Two years," Kiernan spoke again.

Twelve suitors in two years. Riley released a low whistle. "What's wrong with Finola?"

"Nothing is wrong with me!" she called.

Something *was* wrong. That was certain. Riley wasn't sure what it was. But he'd relish trying to figure it out . . . and figure her out.

"So. . . ?" Shanahan pivoted and raised his brow at Riley. "Think you want to give our Finola a go?"

All eyes were upon him expectantly, even Bellamy's.

Riley hesitated, not because he didn't want to give Finola a go. Sweet saints above, he wanted to give her more than a go. But if Finola had shunned twelve other suitors, how could he hope to have any success?

"To be perfectly honest with you, Riley"—Shanahan's shoulders deflated—"if this effort with the matchmaker doesn't work, I might be left with no choice but to send Finola to join the Sisters of Charity."

Turn Finola into a nun? Sure, she'd been enticing even in the black habit she'd been wearing on previous occasions. But after witnessing her descending the stairs tonight in that shimmering blue gown with the glow of the chandelier highlighting the red in her brown hair, she'd made him breathless with her beauty. It would be a real shame to hide such a treasure behind convent doors and baggy gowns for the rest of her life.

Not to mention that Finola wouldn't survive such a lonely

existence. He didn't know her well, but he'd seen enough of her personality to realize she needed people, flourished on helping others, and was much too lively for the quiet, contemplative life in the church.

Good thing he thrived on challenges. He stood and held out a hand to Shanahan.

The man's eyes filled with hope, and he clasped Riley's hand firmly. "Aye? Then we have a deal?"

"Consider this a match, Mr. Shanahan. When would you like to pluck the gander?"

◆ ◆ ◆ ◆ ◆ ◆ ◆ ◆

As Riley and Da finished settling on dates and times for their meetings, Finola rose from the settee and veered toward the stairway, ready to be done with the embarrassing ordeal.

"Wait, Finola." Mam followed after her and clutched her arm before she could get too far. "You need to say a proper good-bye to your future husband, that you do."

Future husband. Finola nearly shuddered at the words. But she took hope from her da's admission—if this effort at matchmaking didn't work, he would let her join the Sisters of Charity.

His words sent a charge of renewed determination through her. Her hard effort was paying off. It wouldn't be long now before she'd be able to get what she'd been working toward.

During the meeting with Da and Kiernan, she'd heard the surprise in Riley's tone and his questions as he learned about her history of failed courtships. He had even asked what was wrong with her. That meant going into the match, he would already be harboring doubts about her. Hopefully she'd be able to easily increase those doubts until he decided she wasn't the right woman for him.

Down the hallway, Madigan had stepped out of the dining room and was watching her, his eyes alight with curiosity. She

72

wanted to pull him aside as she had in the past and give him her usual instructions. But she'd have to wait for later when Riley was gone and her family busy with other matters.

She couldn't waste much time. She needed Madigan to collect information about Riley as quickly as possible, especially since Da and Riley were meeting at Oscar's Pub tomorrow to pluck the gander. If the negotiations went smoothly, then Riley would return in only three days' time for the celebratory dinner.

She had to be prepared by then.

Her mam guided her back around just as Riley and Da exited the parlor with Bellamy and Kiernan trailing.

At the sight of her, Riley stopped and watched her approach, his dark eyes sliding over her, pausing on her bare shoulders and then on the swell of her bust. Mam had made her wear a corset under the gown, and Enya had tied it in such a way that her curves were well displayed.

Finola was accustomed to Mam's encouragement to use her natural feminine wiles to snag a man. Highlighting her appearance might help to gain a man's attention in the short term. But Finola had made sure it was never enough.

As though realizing the focus of his attention, Riley jerked his sights back to her face, but he couldn't conceal the dark smolder in his eyes.

Aye, Riley Rafferty liked how she looked. He'd made no secret about that, not since the day he'd caught her changing in the horse stall.

What if she facilitated another incident, and he *just happened* to be at the wrong place at the wrong time as her da walked in? There had been the time when she'd staged an almost-kiss with one suitor just as her da had walked in the room. Her da had booted the fellow out and told him never to come back.

Now that she and Riley were all but betrothed, Da would

allow for some displays of affection, especially since they would be getting married before Shrove Tuesday, only five weeks away.

Even so, Da had high standards of chastity and always had strict rules regarding suitors. He still would keep a watchful eye on her—on them. Certainly she could arrange something with Riley to get him in trouble.

She wasn't proud of all her scheming. But in the end, everyone would realize she'd done the right thing by avoiding marriage and a family. She didn't deserve it, especially not a child of her own.

She held out a hand toward Riley. "Take you care now, Mr. Rafferty."

"Miss Shanahan." Riley took her hand, lifted it to his lips, and kissed her knuckles lightly.

As with earlier when he'd held her hand, she envisioned him kissing her bare skin, without the gloves in the way. And her breath swelled inside at the prospect.

When he backed away and lowered her hand, she expected his gaze to smolder again, but he turned with a nonchalance that took her off guard. As he said his good-byes to her parents and brother, she waited for him to slant another look her way or to give her a parting witty remark.

But as he strolled out of the house with Bellamy, he didn't look at her again.

As soon as the door closed and cut him off, she released a breath she hadn't known she was holding. She pressed a hand against her chest to ward off the strange desire to chase after him. . . . Not to see him again. Most certainly not. Only to warn him, because the truth was, she liked him enough that she didn't want to hurt him.

And if he persisted in pursuing her, she would end up hurting him one way or another.

All the more reason to put an end to this match as rapidly as possible. Tomorrow she'd send Madigan to gather information on Riley, especially regarding all the things he despised, loathed, and abhorred. Once she had an arsenal of ammunition, she'd be able to prepare for strategically ruining his feelings for her until he ran away and never looked back.

8

*A*t the sound of Madigan Shanahan's voice in the hallway outside his family's tenement, Riley paused, and
his pulse hammered a sudden and unsteady pace.

Had something happened to Finola?

Riley's mind jumped straight back to seeing her in the mud
struggling to escape as the oncoming hackney hurtled her way.
What if she'd fallen into harm's way again and this time had
gotten hurt?

Or maybe Madigan had come to relay a change of plans
regarding tonight's pluck-the-gander meeting with his father
at the pub. Surely Madigan would have delivered such news to
the wagon shop and not his parents' home.

With only an hour until the meeting, Riley had left work
early, gone to his room above the shop, and changed out of his
dusty work clothes into a suit. He'd left enough time to stop
by to see how his dad was faring.

Good thing he had.

"You'll tell me tomorrow?" Madigan's voice dropped low.

"I don't know" came a shy reply . . . from Lorette.

"You'll be doing me a really big favor," Madigan said.

"Then maybe I will."

Riley held himself motionless so he wouldn't miss a word of the conversation between his sister and Finola's brother.

What was this about? It didn't sound like Finola was hurt or that there was a change of plans for tonight's meeting.

"Thank you, Lorette." Madigan's tone turned almost breathy. "I always have taken a shine to you with how sweet and pretty you are."

Riley's muscles tensed. Did Madigan harbor feelings for Lorette? Was that why he was here? Riley guessed the lad was about the same age as Lorette. But they were both way too young to start liking each other. Way, way too young.

He started up the stairs, surprised the two hadn't heard the door open, but apparently they'd been too wrapped up in each other to pay attention to anything going on around them.

As he rounded the landing and made his way up the last set of steps, they came into view. Lorette was standing just outside the closed door of the apartment. And Madigan was leaning against the wall next to her much too closely.

At Riley's appearance, Madigan straightened, and his eyes rounded with surprise. From the way Lorette was gazing at Madigan and with the flush in her cheeks, it was obvious she was enamored. It was likely inevitable since Madigan was every bit as handsome as Finola was pretty.

Even so, Lorette was too young to have her head turned.

Riley crossed his arms and widened his stance. "Madigan."

"Hello, Riley."

"Nip along. Lorette's not allowed to have fellows come calling."

"Riley, he's not calling on me." Lorette wound her hands tightly in front of her, her flush deepening.

"Then why is he here?"

Lorette darted a glance at Madigan.

He winked at her, then sidled past Riley and began to trot down the stairs.

"Don't call on Lorette again, Madigan," Riley called after the lad.

Madigan paused upon the landing, his handsome features schooled into innocence. "I was just delivering a message from my mam inviting your whole family to eat the gander with us on Friday."

The lad was delivering more than a message from his mam. He was delivering flattery and charm. Riley should know, he'd once done the same thing, and in the process hadn't thought twice about asking for a favor in return.

He'd put his old ways behind him long ago, even before Helen died. But that didn't mean he couldn't recognize when someone else was using the techniques.

Madigan loped down the rest of the stairs. A moment later, the building door opened, then closed.

Lorette didn't move except to raise mortified eyes to Riley. "I'm sixteen, Riley. You have to cease treating me like a child."

She *was* still a child. At least in his mind. But he stopped himself from saying so. After living with four sisters, he'd learned to tame his tongue if he wanted any peace. "You're my little sister. And I'm just trying to protect you from a rogue like Madigan."

"He's not a rogue."

"Oh, that lad's a rogue if I ever met one."

"I think he's nice."

Riley snorted. "He's being nice because he wants something from you."

Lorette stiffened.

Riley examined her more closely, this time noting the way she wouldn't meet his gaze. Anger pricked at him. "What did he do? Try to kiss you?"

"No, Riley. No." Her voice fell to a whisper, and she still couldn't meet his gaze. "I might be naïve, but I'm not that easily swayed."

He released the tension inside and lowered his voice too. The walls were thin, and he didn't want to embarrass Lorette any more than he had to. "If he wasn't trying to steal a kiss, then what did he want?"

She stared at her boots.

"Be honest with me, Lorette."

Finally, she met his gaze, her eyes as guileless as always. "He says he needs to know all the things that make you angry and that you don't like."

What in the blazes? "Whyever would he want—?" Riley paused as understanding hit him. Madigan wasn't the one who needed to know. He was gathering the information for Finola.

Lorette's expression turned earnest. "It's only because Finola wants to learn as much as she can about you before your wedding. She sent Madigan to secretly find out."

"I see." Yes, indeed. He did see. In fact, everything was as clear as if a gust of wind had blown through him and cleared away the cobwebs. After puzzling over the conversation he'd had in the Shanahan parlor last night, now he knew exactly how Finola had managed to drive away twelve suitors in two years.

Finola Shanahan was as sly as a fox. That's how.

He almost smiled, but he was still too surprised to do anything but stand with his mouth open.

"You can't say anything to Finola." Lorette clutched his arm. "Madigan swore me to secrecy."

"Of course. Finola is only trying to ensure that I'm suitable for her." Bother it if she was. No, she was collecting information she could use to make him failed-suitor number thirteen.

"She doesn't want to trouble you or our family if the match isn't suitable."

"Right enough."

Wrong. Finola wanted to figure out what would send him running from her as fast as a hound with his head in a hornets' nest. The question was why? Why had she driven away her previous suitors, and why did she want to sabotage a match with him?

Several children exited a door nearby and noisily clomped past. He and Lorette paused their conversation, waiting for the group to descend the stairs and move out of earshot of their conversation.

He didn't know Finola well yet, but during the interactions he'd had with her so far, he'd sensed the potential for more developing between them. Surely he hadn't imagined the glances that indicated she'd been aware of him, of his presence.

Even last night, when he'd taken her hand in both greeting and farewell, she hadn't been able to hide her quick intake of breath or the slight tremble in her fingers, and he'd assumed she felt the undercurrent between them too.

From the first moment he'd met her, when she'd brushed him off and treated him like a little child, he'd known she was different from other women. That meant if he wanted to win her affection, he had to come up with a different approach.

And the truth was, he *did* want to win her affection. With every passing day, his desire to win her was only growing. But winning her would be a challenge. Finola Shanahan herself was a challenge, and he'd relish the chance to play this little game of hers.

As the door to the building closed behind the children, Lorette's eyes brimmed with sudden tears. "You're not sore with me, are you, Riley?"

"Now, now, sweet love, of course not." No one could ever be sore with Lorette, at least not for long. "Why don't I help you with a list for Madigan? Then we'll be able to give him the most . . . beneficial information."

"Are you sure?"

"I'm certain. We want to assist Finola in every way possible, so she can make the right decision, don't we?"

Lorette blinked away the glistening of tears and offered him

80

a tremulous smile. "She doesn't realize how lucky she is to have a man like you."

"We'll make certain she learns." He would indeed. "Let's find a piece of paper and pencil and get started with a list right away."

Lorette nodded and turned to open the door.

"The first thing you can add is that I don't like to hold hands."

Lorette paused, then shifted to look at him with raised brows. "You don't?"

He hesitated. He needed to be careful with how vehement he was with what he supposedly didn't like, or Lorette would suspect he was being disingenuous. And he didn't want Finola to guess the list was entirely fake either.

His mind scrambled for the best way to sound convincing, and he knew of only one way. "I'm not ready to be close to a woman . . . in that way . . ."

Lorette's face quickly flamed. "I'm sorry, Riley. I know it must be hard to imagine yourself . . ." Her voice trailed off with a hint of mortification.

A pang of guilt flashed through him. He was being deceitful to his sister and hated that he had to do so. But in this case, it was best to let her believe he wasn't eager for intimacy when in fact it had become all too clear over the past week since seeing Finola in her unmentionables that he was more than ready for it.

He dropped to a whisper again. "I'm doing this for Dad, because he wants me to find a wife." Even if it had become more than that now, the gentle reminder to Lorette would only make his list more believable.

"He's really happy with your willingness to get married, to be sure."

His dad had been more than a little thrilled with each of the updates regarding the plans for him to marry Finola. In some ways, the match had given his dad fresh energy and life, maybe had even contributed to his starting to feel better. Riley didn't want to consider how a failure to succeed with Finola would affect his dad's health for the worse.

All the more reason to thwart Finola before she thwarted him.

"Let's make sure to add no touching," he whispered as gravely as he could manage. "Especially of my hair."

Lorette gave a quick nod.

"And absolutely no kissing. That would be much too difficult to handle."

If Lorette's face could get any redder, she'd rival a flame itself.

"Hugging is out of the question," he added.

"This is going to be quite a list." Lorette's whisper was more of a squeak.

The guilt pushed up again, but he ignored it. "I'm sure Madigan will understand when you explain why. And since Finola's concerned about the hastiness of our union, I'm sure she'll be grateful that I want to take things very, very slow."

"Yes, you're right, Riley. And so thoughtful."

"No love letters or tokens of her affection either. That would be painful too. For now, it would be best if she treats me as a friend and nothing more."

"I agree. Building a friendship is important."

It *was* going to be quite the list when he finished. And he couldn't keep from smiling at the thought of what Finola would do when she saw it.

9

Finola pressed the folded slip of paper in her pocket and then let herself look more fully upon Riley, who sat at the opposite end of the dining room table from her.

He hadn't paid her much heed throughout the feast, using only the most formal of manners whenever he'd interacted. She hoped his politeness meant he was forgetting about their first unfortunate encounters and was trying to finally behave as a gentleman.

As with earlier in the week when he'd visited for the initial matchmaking meeting, he was attired in a white shirt underneath a vest and coat, and a cravat tied about the turned-up collar, accentuating his angular jaw and the other handsome lines of his face.

Just because she intended to foil the match didn't mean she couldn't appreciate his fine looks, the way his toasted blond hair curled up at the back of his neck and near his ears, the stretch of his coat across his broad shoulders, and even his muscular arms.

He wiped his hands on the linen napkin and placed it beside his plate as the servants finished clearing off the remains of their meal—roasted goose with bread stuffing, cabbage and potatoes with bacon, and honey-glazed carrots.

The cook entered the dining room carrying a silver tray laden with a traditional round cake made with dried fruit and spices.

Mam rose from her spot and motioned for the cook to set the cake on the nearby sideboard. "Time for the barmbrack."

Finola couldn't keep from releasing an exasperated sigh, one that drew Riley's attention. He peered at her through the glowing light of the candelabra at the center. "I take it you don't like barmbrack, Miss Shanahan?"

The polished oak dining room table had been set with their finest porcelain, polished silverware, crystal goblets, and spotless linen. The room, like the others in the spacious house, was lavishly decorated, the paneling and wallpaper complementing the black horsehair upholstery of the chairs. One wall contained an enormous mirror above a large black marble fireplace. The other wall held a large sideboard with another mirror.

"Oh, I like it well enough." Why did her pulse start to speed every time she had an exchange with him? "I just think the superstitions associated with it are silly."

"I admit, my family doesn't regard some of the old traditions." Riley was leaning back in his chair as relaxed as if he were completely at home. With his dad still recovering from the heart attack, his family had regretfully declined the invitation to join in eating the gander. Da had suggested having another celebratory supper closer to the wedding, one that hopefully Mr. Rafferty would be able to attend.

Finola knew what Da had left unsaid, that he didn't quite believe another supper would come, that the wedding plans would fall apart before then. Though she didn't want to disappoint him, she'd silently agreed the chances of having a second celebration were slim.

She fingered the sheet again in her pocket—the list Madigan had gathered with Riley's sister's help. When Finola had read it yesterday, she'd been more than a little shocked by the nature of the things Riley found disagreeable, so much so she questioned whether the list was true.

Once Madigan had explained that Riley was a widower, the list had taken on new meaning. And she'd finally understood why a heroic and popular man at the age of twenty-six hadn't yet been snatched up by an eager young woman, because he'd already once been snatched up by a woman named Helen.

Aye, Finola could admit she'd had Madigan inquire further into Riley's first marriage, and he hadn't discovered much except to report the rumors that it had been short and tumultuous.

According to Riley's sister, her brother had been opposed to remarriage. But shortly after his dad's heart attack, he reluctantly promised his dad that he would get married, particularly because he wanted to honor what he thought was his dad's dying wish. Only then had he agreed to meet with the matchmaker.

Now, here Riley was, honoring his dad's request. Even though William Rafferty was no longer at death's door, Riley intended to go through with the match. But he apparently wanted to do things "right" this time by building a friendship first and not focusing on the physical attraction.

His goals were noble, and under other circumstances she would have respected his solid plan. But her situation was anything but usual. If she had her way, this breakup would be the quickest yet. She might even be able to facilitate it tonight.

"The barmbrack cake is a fun tradition, Mr. Riley." Enya spoke from beside Finola. As one of the servants placed a freshly cut piece of cake in front of her, Enya twisted the porcelain plate around as though peering for one of the items within the cake's dark layers. "There's a ring hidden within."

"Tell me about it." Riley's gaze had already shifted away from Finola onto Enya.

"It's believed that whoever finds the ring hidden within the barmbrack will get married early." Attired in an emerald gown that highlighted her red hair, Enya was as vivacious as always. Tonight she'd transformed from an ancient Celtic goddess into a regal queen.

Finola had the strangest urge to be the one telling Riley about the tradition—but not because she'd didn't want Riley paying Enya attention. Enya would never be seriously interested in a man like Riley.

In fact, Enya had argued again earlier in the day with Mam about Bryan Haynes, this fight bringing her to tears. Afterward, she'd thrown herself across the bed she shared with Finola and lamented about the need for Mam and Da to accept all people and stop being so narrow-minded.

"Long ago," Enya continued, "the cake contained many other items beside the ring."

"Seems that eating the barmbrack must have been dangerous." Riley eyed his slice of cake. "At the very least it was a choking hazard."

"The items were small," Kiernan interjected from his chair beside Riley. The whole family was present around the massive table—Mam and Da each on an end. The boys sat in their usual spots on one side starting with Kiernan, then Madigan, and ending with Quinlan, who was thirteen and the youngest of the family.

Her baby sister, Ava, would have been the youngest . . . if she hadn't died that fateful day.

Of course there were two other siblings who'd succumbed to measles not long after Ava's passing. Mam had been devastated to lose them so close to her baby. Her grief had been agonizing to watch. So had her disappointment in failing to get pregnant month after month so she could replace the children she'd lost.

Mam's heartache had only made Ava's accident all the worse and had added to Finola's guilt, the guilt that still taunted her. Sometimes at night when she woke up to echoes of Ava's crying, she thought she could also hear Mam's.

On the opposite side of the table, Finola had her place as the oldest, with Enya in the middle and Zaira last. At nineteen, Zaira wasn't far behind Enya in drawing the attraction of the local young men. With Da's determination that his children get married in order by age, Zaira had complained she'd never have the chance to wed, or if she did, she'd already have one foot in the grave, especially because Finola was holding them all up.

Finola bit back a sigh. Maybe she should just run away to the convent. She'd contemplated that option on a few occasions. But she wanted to part ways with her parents on good terms. If she could make it past this last suitor, then she'd finally be able to go.

"Finola is wishing to get a thimble in her piece, that she is." Madigan spoke from around a forkful of cake.

"Thimble?" Riley asked.

"Whoever gets the thimble will end up a spinster," Madigan explained with a wink toward Finola, his expression filled with knowing mischief.

A moment later, Riley's gaze collided with hers. The dark blue was unreadable, almost stormy, with a power that swirled something low and tight inside her. She wasn't sure what it was, but his eyes, his looks, his charisma were dangerous. She could see how a woman could become charmed by him all too easily.

But not her. She'd remained strong through all the other suitors. She could do so with Riley, no matter how magnetic he might be.

She poked at her cake with her fork and pretended innocence. "Of course I don't want a thimble. But I suspect Mr. Rafferty might be hoping for the button of bachelorhood."

"And why would I be hoping for that?" Riley's tone was casual.

All eyes turned upon Riley, as though he had a secret he needed to divulge.

Finola wavered. Had she made a mistake in alluding to his reluctance to get remarried? Maybe she ought to keep that fact to herself for now. After all, if her da suspected any issues, maybe he would have Bellamy find a different man, and she'd have to go through the matchmaking process again . . . for the fourteenth time.

She lifted a forkful of cake to her mouth and took a bite only to clamp down on a metal band. She rolled it around, cleaning the cake from it before pulling it out. "No wee worries, everyone. I have the ring." She suspected Mam had marked the location of the ring and instructed the servant to deliver that particular portion directly to Finola.

The attention returned to her, and she held up the ring for everyone to see. It was a simple silver band without any elaborate decorations, nothing special. Even so, she had to make the most of the occasion to scare Riley.

She pushed her chair back from the table and stood. "Looks like Mr. Rafferty and I will be taking our vows early."

He didn't respond, but he was watching her along with the others, his expression once again unreadable.

"Before Shrove Tuesday." She started around the table toward his end, searching for any sign that the news displeased him.

His eyes only seemed to darken the closer she came, so by the time she stopped in front of him, the swirling had returned to her belly.

He didn't say anything, simply waited, his shoulders tense, his body motionless.

Somehow the air between them seemed heavy and warm. Was the heat coming from him? Or was it pulsing from her? In fact, the whole room had heated, as if a servant had started a blazing bonfire.

What was this about?

She needed to step away from the strange new sensations. But she couldn't. Not yet. She had to stick with her plans and do the first thing on the list in her pocket—hold his hand, right here, right now, in front of everyone.

But how could she? It was so personal and was perhaps crossing a boundary that shouldn't be crossed.

With all the other suitors, her scheming had been harmless. She'd sobbed all over the suitor who hadn't liked women who cry, pretended she wanted a dozen children and listed them by name for the suitor who'd been reluctant to have babies, and talked about all the trips on the Mississippi she wanted to take for the suitor who hated steamboats. She'd eaten raw fish around another man with a weak stomach so that he ended up retching. Madigan had helped her scare one fellow away with snakes and had dumped paint on another.

Aye, she'd conspired to no end. But it had been for the best. The men deserved a better wife than her.

Before she lost her nerve, she offered the ring to Riley. "I do believe this is our engagement ring. And it seems only fitting that you should be the one to put it on me."

Riley didn't take it from her. Instead, he lowered himself to one knee before her. He slipped his hand inside his coat pocket, and in the next moment, he held out a different ring—a traditional claddagh ring, a gold band with two hands clasping a heart topped with a dainty crown. The heart represented love, the hands friendship, and the crown loyalty.

It was delicate and beautiful, and her heart pattered faster at the sight of Riley down on his knee with the ring. If she'd ever once dreamed of getting engaged, she couldn't have asked for a more perfect moment than this.

"Miss Shanahan, I would be pleased if you would accept this ring as a token of our agreement to marry."

10

*R*iley knelt in front of her and peered up at her, his eyes containing only sincerity.

Finola couldn't look away.

Did he hope to move forward into a marriage that was represented by love, friendship, and loyalty? Maybe in spite of the reservations he'd expressed to his father, he intended to do his best with a second marriage.

It was noble of him. She had to admit, Riley Rafferty was a fine and decent man, regardless of the interesting way they'd met. At this moment, he made her want to forget about everything that had happened in the past with Ava and move forward with a new life. None of the other suitors had made her feel that way.

There was something about him that was different from any man she'd ever met. And, of course, she couldn't deny her attraction to him, which was also different from the other men who'd come calling.

If only she was a different woman—a worthier woman without such a stain on her conscience. . . .

Straightening her shoulders with resolve, she held out her hand so he would have no choice but to put the ring on, touching her in the process, the very thing he wanted to avoid.

Her conscience nagged her, as it had in the past, to talk again with her mam and da and explain her passion to enter the convent. But what if they disregarded her feelings the same way they did Enya's?

No, she had to stay strong for a wee bit longer and try to overwhelm Riley Rafferty with her physical affection. And if he didn't run away fast and scared, she'd have to plot another way to chase him off.

Riley stared at her hand for a moment, then took it in his. This time she wasn't wearing gloves and could feel the calluses on his palm. They were work roughened, the kind that belonged to a man accustomed to long hours of labor. And his fingers were warm.

She could sense her family watching and from the corners of her eyes could see her da looking on eagerly. If only he wasn't so intent on having each of his children walk in his footsteps and having the kind of life he'd carved out for himself. Aye, he only wanted to provide the best for them. But what if his idea of what was best wasn't best for her?

As Riley began to slip the ring over her finger, his thumb brushed against the length of her finger, as though preparing the way for the ring. It was such a soft caress and the slide of the ring so slow that she found herself holding her breath until it was in place. Even then she couldn't breathe as he raised her hand toward his mouth.

Was he planning to kiss her fingers again, as he had during his last visit?

His eyes met hers, and something within them spoke of both tenderness and strength, not unlike the day he'd rescued her from being hit by the hackney.

She couldn't move, couldn't object—although she knew she

should. She'd planned to be the one in control of their physical interactions. But she felt helpless to do anything but wait for him to finish.

His breath caressed her knuckles first. Then his lips touched her, feather-light, exquisite, sending tingles over her skin. He'd hardly just begun when he lowered her hand.

She didn't immediately move back, strangely unsatisfied and wishing he'd done something more, although she couldn't describe what.

He stood and put at least an arm's length of space between them but watched her expectantly.

She needed to acknowledge his kind gesture. "Thank you, Riley—Mr. Rafferty." She extended her hand and examined the ring. "It's beautiful, to be sure."

"It belonged to my mom."

She was curious to know more about his past, although learning about him might make parting ways difficult. She needed to be careful. It would be best not to invest any more in the relationship than was necessary.

Besides, he'd likely gotten down on one knee in front of Helen too and slipped this very ring on her finger.

A knot twisted inside at the image of Riley kissing another woman's hand. But just as quickly, she pivoted away from him and the image.

As she passed around the table behind her da, he clasped her arm and steered her back toward Riley. "The two of you need a wee bit of time to get to know each other. I suggest moving to the parlor."

Before she could protest, Kiernan and her da were directing Riley and her out of the dining room. Her da didn't release her arm until he'd walked her to the settee in the parlor and situated her there. Kiernan did the same with Riley, positioning him right next to her.

She started to scoot away. Her da had always prohibited her

from sitting directly beside a young man, had even required separate seats. But her da pressed her shoulder firmly to hold her in place. "You'll be married soon enough, Finola."

The insinuation brought a flush to her insides, leaving her speechless.

Da gave her arm a final squeeze before heading out the door with Kiernan on his heels. Once they were gone, she glanced around the room. No one was in sight.

Had her da not only given her permission to sit next to Riley, but also left her unchaperoned? He'd never before allowed it, had always required all his daughters to have a chaperone any time they entertained suitors.

She stared at the parlor entrance, waiting for him to come back through. Or at the very least to send one of her siblings to sit with Riley and her. She prayed he'd choose Madigan. Her younger brother hadn't stopped her from scheming with other suitors and certainly wouldn't tonight either.

But the mantel clock ticked loudly as the seconds passed and no one returned. Finally, Riley cleared his throat. "How was your charity work today?"

"It was good, to be sure." How was it possible she was still very much alone with Riley?

He reclined against the settee, stretching out a leg and resting one of his big hands on his other knee. He seemed comfortable enough, didn't appear to be nervous.

"Another steamer full of immigrants arrived today," he said. "I don't know where they'll all go since there's not a room available anywhere that I know of."

"They're having to live in crowded conditions, two and even three families per apartment." What should she do first from the list? Hold his hand, run her fingers through his hair, maybe rub his arm?

"I suspect the overcrowding will ease in the spring when a good number will head out to the West."

"Even if the overcrowding does ease at some point, 'tis maddening to go into their homes and find so many struggling to survive."

She didn't interact with many people—other than the Sisters of Charity—who cared about the problems of the immigrants as much as she did. The topic was too important not to give her full attention, so she temporarily put aside her plans to make Riley dislike her and instead found that she could carry on an intelligent conversation with him about the immigrants and their needs.

She lost track of the time as they discussed the many issues the immigrants were facing upon arrival in St. Louis, as well as in other big cities throughout America.

He talked about what he'd accomplish for the foreign newcomers if he was elected mayor, and she shared more about what she wished she could do for them if she had unlimited means. He had good ideas, but he also listened well to her, asking questions and forcing her to think about ramifications she hadn't considered before.

At some point, the conversation led to the immigrant stories of their parents.

Her da had left Ireland as a lad of eighteen. As a younger son of a well-to-do silk manufacturer, James Shanahan hadn't had much to look forward to in Ireland, where the land had already been divided up and distributed so there simply wasn't enough to go around. He'd decided to take his chances in America and had been among the early settlers to arrive in St. Louis. He'd used the little he'd brought with him to invest in land and sawmills. With his profits, he'd continued to buy more land in St. Louis and the surrounding area. Eventually he'd sold his sawmills and invested in iron.

Riley's dad had a similar story. He'd immigrated to Cleveland at sixteen years of age to help an uncle on his farm, but after arriving, he'd learned his uncle had died. Fortunately, a local wagonmaker had taken William Rafferty into his care and apprenticed him. It had taken him until he was thirty to become a master craftsman and save enough to open his own shop. By then, he'd been married with three children, including Riley, who'd been seven.

"Dad was always fascinated that Lewis and Clark began their exploration of the West in St. Louis." Riley leaned forward and braced his elbows on his knees. "My dad believed even more people would start their journeys west there and would need wagons. So he packed up our belongings, loaded them on a steamship, and we started down the Ohio River."

Something changed in Riley's voice, and Finola sat forward now too. "We made it all the way to the Mississippi when the steamboat had a boiler fire."

Finola guessed the direction his story was going, and her heart sank.

"We had no choice but to abandon ship or burn up with it." His back turned rigid. "Since it was spring, the current was swift and difficult to swim."

She had the sudden need to reach out and comfort him, to at least lay a hand on his back. But she forced herself to keep her hands in her lap.

A muscle ticked in his jaw. "My dad was only able to save one of us. Me."

"Holy mother, have mercy," she whispered. "I'm sorry, Riley, that I am."

He hung his head, and his shoulders slumped just a little, the pain of the loss clearly still as vivid for him as Ava's loss was for her.

"He dragged me out onto the shore and went back in for the rest of my family." Riley stared down at his tightly clasped hands. "But he was too late. We found my mom and younger brothers downriver later. They drowned."

She didn't know what to say to comfort him, guessed words

were inadequate to ease the ache inside, just as words had never eased the ache inside her.

She twisted the delicate claddagh ring he'd given her. He'd said it belonged to his mother, which meant it was special. She needed to give it back, tell him she couldn't take something that was so important to him. Not only didn't she deserve the beautiful ring, but wearing it was irreverent since she wasn't planning to keep it.

The hearth fire had dwindled so that now only small flames flickered, not enough to ward off the chill of the January evening, and she shivered.

At her motion, he straightened and turned his attention upon her. "You're cold."

"Only a wee bit—"

Before she could finish her sentence, Riley was already standing and striding toward the ornate wood box beside the hearth. While most of the rooms in the house were heated by coal stoves, the parlor still had the more elegant but less efficient wood-burning fireplace.

As he worked to stir the embers and add a few logs, she studied his profile, the angular edges, the hardness of his jaw, the ripple of muscles in his neck. Saint Riley of the Kerry Patch. He was strong, daring, and selfless.

She didn't know of anyone else who'd chance getting clobbered and run over by a team and hackney to rescue a careless woman stuck in the mud. But he'd done it and countless other good deeds.

What was becoming clearer with each encounter she had with Riley was that he was not an ordinary man. He was someone special.

Someone so special needed a woman who was equally special. And that woman was not her.

She glanced out the door to the entryway hallway. No one was in sight. She needed to put her ploys into effect before

96

Riley left for the evening. She didn't want him feeling close to her after their talking. She needed to push him away. And to do so, she had to move their relationship too quickly beyond the friendship he wanted to establish.

Hesitating but a moment longer, she stood, stuffed a hand into her pocket, and fingered the list that Madigan had brought home for her.

No kissing. No holding hands. No hugging. No running fingers up chest or arms. No massaging shoulders. No caressing of face. No combing fingers through hair. Basically, no physical contact.

But just thinking about the list again and all the things that were forbidden sent a tremor through her insides, one that made her want to try out each of the items, but not merely because Riley was against them.

Yet how could she when she had no experience enticing men? In spite of having twelve suitors over the past two years, she'd never done anything on Riley's list—except hug one time. She'd never purposefully stroked or kissed or hugged or massaged or any of the other things.

She had the sudden need to stop and fan herself. Instead, she approached Riley and didn't halt until she was standing right behind him. She hesitated a moment, then forced herself to do the deed. She skimmed a hand up the back of his vest, his coat discarded on the settee.

His muscles were unyielding beneath her touch, his body stiff, his shoulders straight. But he didn't resist, at least not yet.

Another tremor rippled through her, this one more delicious, giving her a burst of courage. She slid both arms around his middle so that her chest pressed into his back.

At the contact, he inhaled sharply.

Was she bothering him already?

She laid her head against him and tightened her hold.

He didn't move, likely didn't know what to think of her boldness. Perhaps he assumed she was comforting him after the heartache he'd shared. And aye, she did want to comfort him. But more than that, she wanted to end the match.

Drawing in a fortifying breath, she loosened her hands and skimmed one up his stomach until she reached his ribs. His muscles flexed beneath her touch—out of protest?

No doubt, any second he would turn her around, reprimand her, and tell her she was too forward for a man like him.

She grazed her other hand upward over his ribs and then back down. Except for another quick intake, he didn't move.

Her cheek rested against the silk of his vest, and she breathed in the faint spicy musk of his cologne. The warmth of his back, the hardness of his body, the rise and fall of his chest. Everything about him was powerful at this proximity.

For a reason she didn't understand, she simply wanted to bask in his nearness—and savor the pleasure twisting within her. But she made herself continue the charade, which was suddenly all too easy to do. Her fingers had gained a mind of their own and glided up one of his arms, starting at his wrist, his forearm, and then his bicep. Though his shirt formed a barrier, she could feel him tense the higher she went.

He was getting upset and would thrust her aside at any moment. If only the contact with him wasn't having such an enticing effect on her. She hadn't expected this reaction, but she couldn't deny that Riley Rafferty was a desirable man on so many different levels, including physically.

As she slid her hand to his shoulder, she waited for him to pull away, to put her at arm's length, and then to chastise her for being wanton. Because that's what she was doing, wasn't she? Being wanton.

Ach. She was taking this all too far. In fact, she shouldn't have even started this physical contact, shouldn't have considered it. What she should have done instead was send Madigan back to Riley's sister to get a different list, one that was simpler and easier.

With a huff of frustration, she released her hold on Riley and turned away, but in the next instant, he snagged one of her arms and pivoted her around so they were now facing each other.

His eyelids were lowered halfway. His wavy hair was tossed back rakishly. And his jaw was taut, his muscles rippling there. Why did he have to look so appealing?

"Finola Shanahan." His voice rumbled and made her stomach flip-flop. "Do you want to explain yourself and what you were just doing?"

"I intended to comfort you."

"Did you now?" His hands settled on her hips, sending her stomach into a whole series of flips. Before she could gain her balance, he drew her flush so suddenly that she toppled against him.

She grabbed on to both biceps, planning to push herself back. She needed to walk away. But as the muscular length of his torso pressed against her, heated longing swelled rapidly inside and surged along her nerve endings so that she didn't want to back away—couldn't back away.

The blue of his eyes was so dark it rivaled a deep, bottomless well. Was he angry at her for initiating the contact? If so, why was he holding her?

"Comfort?" His whisper was almost accusatory. "Is that all?"

She was one tiny step away from severing her relationship with him. All she had to do was stand on her toes and press her lips against his. He wouldn't be expecting it. And such a kiss would prove to him once and for all that she wasn't the woman for him.

"Well?" His whisper took on a harsher note.

Aye, he was getting mad. She needed to kiss him now. Without another moment of hesitation, she raised onto her toes and touched her lips to his. She wasn't sure what needed to happen next, had never even witnessed a kiss. But as she pressed a wee bit harder, something powerful pulled her in.

Part of it was his response. It wasn't the silence, stillness, or disappointment she'd expected. Instead, he lifted a hand to the back of her head, seemed to guide her closer, and angled in to fully capture her mouth with his.

His lips—so warm and tender—plied against hers, and she closed her eyes as a hundred different sensations coursed through her—sensations that were new and exciting and made her body come to life.

The pressure of his mouth somehow deepened, like he would devour her if he could. But at the same time, she could feel his restraint—not only in the kiss but in the banked power of his hand that was gliding down her head.

As his fingers moved to her neck, he didn't slow his descent. Instead, he skimmed her throat, the touch threatening to make her lose all conscious thought. When he reached her collar-bone above the neckline of her gown, she stopped breathing altogether.

With his mouth and his fingers wreaking havoc with her, she trembled with a wanting that frightened her. What was she doing?

More importantly, what was *he* doing? Why wasn't he storming off and telling her he never wanted to see her again?

She shoved against his chest.

He removed his hand from her collarbone, and his mouth against hers softened, although it continued to hold her captive.

She had to step away, but his scent and heat and body were so much more alluring than she'd imagined. And she simply wanted to linger.

But in the next instant, his lips against hers began to curl up into the beginning of a smile. Why was he smiling? That hadn't been the reaction she'd been seeking.

She let go of him and backed up.

Before she could retreat a safe distance, his hands dropped to her hips, spanning her waist on either side. And holy mother have mercy, she loved the pressure of each of his strong fingers, as if he was the master craftsman and she his workmanship. She could just imagine the way he commanded the tools and wood and iron he used every day and knew he would do the same with her.

As though reading every thought running rampant through her head, he started to draw her flush again, his smile quirking higher on one side almost arrogantly.

This time when she looked into his eyes, the blue had lightened, and his attention dropped to her mouth, his desire written blatantly all over his face.

He wasn't put off by kissing her in the least. In fact, he seemed rather pleased with himself, as if he were a cat who'd just swallowed the canary.

"Don't forget," he whispered. "You still need to massage my shoulders, caress my face, and comb your fingers through my hair."

At his quoting of the last three things on the list in her pocket, she gasped. Then she reached up and slapped him across the cheek.

11

*A*s Finola squirmed to free herself, this time Riley let her go. Even with a smarting cheek, his grin widened.

"Riley Rafferty, you're worse than a scoundrel." She stalked toward the settee and halted in front of it, cupping her hands over her cheeks.

They were an adorable pale pink. Her eyes were flashing. And her lips were still full and swollen from their kiss.

Their kiss. Sweet saints above. He wanted another one more than he wanted anything else. At this moment, he had great sympathy for Samson telling Delilah the secret of his strength. If kissing Delilah was anything like kissing Finola, then he was liable to end up a dead man just like Samson. Or he'd lose her, which at this point was looking like a worse alternative than death.

The truth was, the more he was with Finola, the more he wanted her. But the other truth was that she was doing everything she could to cut him out of her life, even going as far as initiating the things on the fake list Lorette had given Madigan.

All evening he'd been waiting for her to make her first move. He wondered how and when she'd find a way to try something, especially because Bellamy had warned Riley before the first visit to be on his best behavior and refrain from any display of physical attraction, that James Shanahan put great value on chastity before marriage.

That's why when Shanahan had settled Finola next to him on the settee and told her she'd be married soon, Riley had been more than a little surprised. When Shanahan had walked out of the room without a glance back, Riley had known then what Shanahan wasn't saying aloud—that he was giving Riley an opportunity to do whatever he needed to win and keep Finola, including stealing a kiss or two from her.

He'd done well all throughout dinner in curbing any hints of his attraction, had even refrained from picturing Finola in her unmentionables again. But once they'd come into the parlor, he'd been ready to finish the little game she'd started. He needed her to understand that though she might be cunning, he was too, and he would give back the same measure she doled out.

So he'd waited on the settee with her, had expected her to act right away. But he'd been pleasantly surprised she'd taken the time to talk with him and they had deep conversations about important things.

He wasn't sure why he'd opened up so readily about his family's move to St. Louis and how his mom and brothers had died. There was something about Finola. Maybe it was that same genuine caring spirit he'd noticed during their first interactions. Whatever it was, he liked it. And he felt comfortable sharing with her in a way he never had with Helen.

When he'd gone to stir the fire, he sensed a shift in her mood. That's when he'd known she was acting upon the list. As he listened to her soft tread draw nearer, he tried not to act too eager. But truthfully, the moment she glided her fingers over his back, he'd become thoroughly and completely addicted to her.

He hadn't been able to get enough of her touch, had wanted her hands to roam freely wherever they pleased, had been near to groaning by the time she blazed a trail to his shoulder. It hadn't taken long for her movements to become slower and hesitant. He'd known she was pulling away, too innocent to carry through with much more than a simple back hug and arm graze.

Whatever the case, before she could rush away, he'd stepped in and prodded her along, pulling her around and giving her access to more of him. It hadn't taken much more prompting for her to initiate the kiss. From the tentativeness of her touch, he suspected it was her first. And for a reason he couldn't explain, that thought pleased him immensely.

The question was, had she kissed him because she was attracted to him and found him irresistible? Or had she done so because she'd hoped to make him dislike her?

Either way, she opened up to him and let him kiss her back, and she liked the kiss enough that she hadn't ended it right away.

He smiled again just thinking of the way her fingers had tightened against his arms and the way she held her mouth to his for a moment longer than necessary.

Seeing his mirth, she glared at him, the blue of her eyes icy enough to freeze the river. "You're toying with me."

"*Me*? Toying with *you*?" He started across the room toward her. He wanted her again, and this time he intended to let her know that no matter what she might do to thwart the attraction between them, it wasn't going away.

As he drew nearer, her eyes widened. "What are you doing?"

"The question is, what are *you* doing?" He didn't stop.

"I'm not doing anything." She moved away from him until she bumped into the settee and tumbled backward onto it. "You're the one who gave my brother a list of falsehoods."

He towered above her. "You're the one who asked for the list."

"Aye, but you should have been truthful." As she peered up at him, the ice in her eyes melted, and her lips twitched with a faint smile, as though she was fully aware of the ridiculousness of her statement.

He leaned down, placed both hands on the back of the settee on either side of her. "Finola Shanahan, you're a corker."

Her pale face with all its delicate freckles softened, and she breathed in a sharp breath.

He was helpless but to drop his sights to her lips. Sweet saints above.

When her lips parted in readiness for another kiss, he knew then that he'd made his point. He'd let her know he was the one in control of the situation, that no matter what mischief she might try, he was up for the challenge.

One question remained unanswered, though. Why was she trying to drive away her suitors? Including him? He had to get to the bottom of the issue. Because the truth was, he didn't want to force a woman to marry him, even if the matchmaker, her family, and every blasted person in St. Louis approved of the match.

If she wasn't willing, he wouldn't do it. He'd pressured Helen into marrying him, and look how that had turned out.

"You know I like you and think you're beautiful," he whispered, holding himself above her and still boxing her in.

"You do?" Her reply was breathy, making her chest rise and fall much too enticingly.

"A blind fellow a mile away could see how attracted I am to you."

This time her lips almost reached a full smile. Almost, but not quite, as if she'd forgotten how to smile. Maybe he'd have to make it his goal to teach her how to smile again . . . if they stayed together.

Her gaze was riveted to his mouth, and the shimmering warmth in her eyes told him she was reliving their kiss.

Oh yes, he wanted to kiss her again . . . but first he had to make sure she was done fighting against the union and that she truly wanted to marry him.

"Tell me one thing," he whispered.

"What?" she whispered back.

"Do you plan to make this a regular habit?"

"Regular habit of what?"

"Finding out all the things I dislike so you can try to push me away?"

At his directness, her eyes widened.

Before she could respond, he plowed forward. "From the way you kissed me, it's obvious you like me too."

"Obvious?" She sidled past him and stood, bracing her fists on her hips and glowering at him once more. "You might be a charmer, but you shouldn't be surprised when you can't charm everyone."

He wanted more from her than clichéd answers, but he wasn't sure how far to push her.

Raised voices grew louder and closer outside the parlor.

"Stop right there, young lass," came James Shanahan's booming call. "This discussion isn't over."

"Yes it is! Talking to you and Mam about anything important is impossible. Im-poss-i-ble."

The voice belonged to Finola's younger sister Enya. The antagonism between the redhead and her parents had been clear all throughout the feasting, even though they'd obviously tried for Finola's sake to put aside their frustrations with one another and remain congenial.

But as with anything left to boil too long, their feelings were now bubbling up and flowing over the brim.

"You will not see that young man again," Shanahan said, his voice tinged with anger. "Do you understand?"

"You cannot control my life this way." The two were now standing in the hallway almost directly outside the parlor.

"I'm your father. And it's my God-given duty to protect you from making poor choices and to direct you to walk in the ways of the wise."

"I love him, Da." Enya's voice rang out passionately. "I want to marry him."

In the middle of the room, Finola stood immobile, her already-pale face turning paler, and her expression widening with clear mortification.

He wanted to tell her that she needn't be embarrassed by his witnessing a family squabble. His sisters had their fair share of obstinance from time to time.

But in the silence that settled out in the hallway, he bit back the words. Now was neither the time nor place to reassure her.

"You have to listen to your father, so." The new voice belonged to Mrs. Shanahan. It was calmer but no less firm. "His investigator is concerned—"

"You've investigated Bryan?" Enya's voice rose again.

"I investigate every suitor—"

"I know everything there is to know about him. He's told me all about his life, and he's a wonderful man."

"You haven't known him long enough to determine that." The trio was moving past the parlor and seemed to be headed down a hallway. A moment later they entered a room and a door closed. The now muted argument continued, but the worst of the storm seemed to have passed.

"I'm sorry you had to hear that." Finola had crossed to the doorway. Before she could make an effort to eavesdrop any further, Kiernan stepped through.

Had the young man been sitting in the front entryway all throughout his time with Finola, chaperoning from a distance? If so, he'd likely heard them talking about the kiss, maybe even heard them actually kissing. No doubt he'd report every detail to his father.

Finola ducked her head, as though she'd just realized the same.

In spite of the argument the Shanahans were having with their daughter just a few rooms away, Kiernan's expression contained a hopefulness that was directed at Riley. "Da wanted me to invite you to call on Finola again any night that you're free."

Finola's shoulders straightened as if she were resolving herself to another battle ahead. And although her face remained neutral, protest sparked in her eyes.

She didn't want him to come courting. Not tonight. Not tomorrow night. Not any night. Maybe she didn't make her wishes known as vocally as Enya, but she was certainly sending a message to her father regardless—she didn't want Riley or any other suitor.

Like Enya, did she have another man she already loved, one her father wouldn't accept?

Riley tossed aside the question. Surely Finola wouldn't have kissed him like she had if she was interested in someone else.

So what was it? The question echoed through his head again. What was preventing her from getting serious with any one fellow?

"You need to come again soon." Clearly Kiernan was accustomed to worrying after each suitor's visit. And it was no wonder. Finola was skilled at keeping men at arm's length.

Riley waited for Finola to give him some indication that she'd welcome him back, that he was different than the rest, that she would let him into her life. But she kept her focus on a swirling pattern on the carpet.

A strange knot of disappointment tied itself inside his gut. But at the same time, he knew he couldn't give up. Not yet, not when he'd hardly begun his attempts to win her over. He'd give their relationship until the end of January. That was a couple of weeks away. If he couldn't win Finola over by then, he'd admit defeat and call off the match. But until then, he had to rise to the challenge and do what every other man had failed to do—make Finola fall in love.

The problem was, he couldn't approach Finola with the usual ardor and accolades. He had to have a different plan of action.

And at the moment, he could think of only one way. "Since I'm officially running for mayor, I'll be very busy campaigning and won't have much time for paying calls."

Kiernan shook his head and began to frown.

At the same time, Finola's gaze darted to his. Did her expression contain a hint of disappointment? He wasn't sure. But he took courage from the small sign.

"Some friends have organized an office—a campaign headquarters of sorts—on First Street, not far from my father's wagon shop." As soon as he'd made his announcement to run for mayor, friends and businessmen had stopped by the shop in a constant stream, so that finally Big Jim had been the one to suggest getting an office, mainly so work on the wagons wasn't interrupted.

Although Riley directed his conversation toward Kiernan, he was watching Finola's face. "Finola is familiar with the struggles within the immigrant communities. Her astute ideas would be an asset to the campaign team—if she'd like to help with the election efforts. Tomorrow evening. After supper?"

Her eyes had lit up so that the blue was bright. Did that mean she liked his idea?

Kiernan rubbed his chin, studied Finola a moment, then shook his head. "I'm not sure what Da would say."

Finola's brows puckered. "I'll tell him I'm doing more charity work."

No, he didn't want her using any more of her underhanded methods, not with him and not with her parents. "I'm sure I could convince your father, if that's what you're worried about."

Kiernan nodded. "He wouldn't approve of Finola being among a crowd of men."

"We have a few other young women on the team. Besides, I'll be with her at all times."

Kiernan paused, as if calculating how much time Finola would get to spend with him.

"It would be an opportunity for Finola to get to know me better."

"Maybe it would be good then. I'll have our driver bring and pick her up."

Riley supposed he ought to be relieved that Kiernan wanted him to keep spending time with Finola. It meant that the family approved of him and would accept him. At least he hoped so.

"And what do you say, Finola?" Riley asked. "What would you like to do?"

"Aye, I'll do it, that I will." She lifted her chin and gave him one of her saucy looks, one that sent his pulse racing. "But, mind you, it won't be for you, Riley Rafferty. I'll do it because I care about the people."

He shrugged and then started out the parlor door. "Mind you, Finola Shanahan. Soon enough you'll be doing it because you care about me too." At least he hoped so.

She released a huff of exasperation.

At his approach, the silver-haired butler moved to open the front door.

Riley swiped up his coat and hat from the hallway coat tree. As tempted as he was to turn around and look at Finola one last time, he didn't want to give her the satisfaction of knowing just how much power she was gaining over his heart.

Instead, he whistled a merry Irish tune while inwardly praying that he wasn't already falling in love.

12

*F*inola stepped away from the carriage and approached Riley's campaign office, her heart giving an extra beat at the prospect of the evening ahead.

Not because she was getting to see Riley again. She was simply excited to participate in the campaign.

The light coming from the large front window spilled onto First Street, chasing away some of the darkness of the evening.

He'd asked her to join his campaign team. Her. He said she had *astute* ideas and would be an *asset*. And from the sincerity with which he'd spoken, she knew he hadn't been flattering her. He meant what he said.

That was the thing about Riley Rafferty. . . . He didn't mince words. His directness often took her by surprise, but she was finding that she liked being taken by surprise by him. And she liked his keen mind. He'd obviously figured out her scheming with Madigan and brilliantly schemed against her in return.

As she reached the arched entrance, the door opened wide, and warmth along with more light cascaded over her. And there stood Riley in the doorway, his smile and the stars in his eyes welcoming her. He was attired in a casual suit, but his hair was mussed, and a layer of stubble covered his jaw and chin.

She could admit she'd thought of him often since last evening's visit, even though she'd tried not to. She'd replayed the way he'd spun her around, fitted his hands on her waist, and tugged her body against his. Just the memory of it made her stomach flutter and her toes curl.

Then his kiss . . . the way his lips had captured her down to her very soul. And his words . . . *"I like you and think you're beautiful."*

Though she'd tried to scheme for another way to make Riley run from a relationship with her, the thoughts of the kiss and the words had crowded in and kept her from coming up with another idea.

Even now, she scrambled to think of how to alienate him, which was difficult to do with his overpowering muscular frame only a foot away.

"You came." His tone held a note of wonder.

"Is that okay?"

"I was hoping you would."

"You were?" She glanced beyond him to the busy interior, some people sitting at desks, several manning a small printing press, still others standing before a giant map of St. Louis tacked to the wall.

Through the light of the lanterns, cigar smoke cast a lazy haze over the room. But the energy and excitement within was palpable.

Riley was taking in her gown—or at least what showed beneath her cloak—the lovely pale green evening attire her mam had insisted she don before going out. The gown wasn't as fancy as the one she'd worn last night. But at the sight of another woman bustling about the office wearing a simple skirt and blouse, Finola guessed she was overdressed.

She held herself back. What was she doing here? Had she made a mistake in thinking she could do this?

Riley's gaze lifted, and appreciation widened his eyes. "You are just in time to join in the discussion about how to provide better medical care to the immigrants." He waved her inside.

As she stepped tentatively through the door, the scents of tobacco and ink circled around her and drew her in, whispering of all the possible ways they could make changes for the better.

"Everyone," Riley called over the hubbub. "I'd like to introduce you to Miss Shanahan. She's here to help with my campaign."

As the conversations around the room faded and all eyes focused on her, she held herself straight as a lady should.

For a moment, no one spoke.

A middle-aged priest, wearing his long black cassock, stepped away from the table. With spectacles low on a wide nose, he came forward and held out a hand to Finola.

She accepted the handshake, trying to draw strength from Riley's presence beside her.

"Welcome, Miss Shanahan. I'm Father O'Kirwin. I'm Riley's campaign manager."

As Riley introduced her to several more people on his team, soon they were all seated around a large central table. With the start of the discussion about the medical needs of the immigrants, she was surprised when Riley drew her into the conversation, asking her to share her firsthand experiences with the people she helped.

Before long, she was immersed in the lively conversation regarding not only the health problems but also the contributing factors, including the crowded homes, lack of nutritious food, unsanitary conditions, and more. All throughout, she grew more and more impressed by Riley's understanding of the issues, his passion for the people, and his vision to make changes.

"The schools are growing overcrowded too." Father O'Kirwin pushed up his glasses and pointed to a spot on the map on the northern edge of the Irish district. "I propose Riley offers to build a new one here."

Everyone nodded at another possible way to increase Riley's popularity.

Finola agreed it was a good idea, but surely if Riley was mayor, he could do so much more than build a school for the Irish. He could also work to provide education for all people, including the Black folks, who'd been sorely discriminated against by the law that was passed only two years earlier that outlawed schools for them in Missouri. "May I add that Riley should also work at allowing for the reopening of the Black schools in St. Louis?"

Around the table, silence descended so thoroughly that the argument and vulgarity of a group of youth outside on the street punctuated the office. The lantern hanging above the table cast a glow over the expressions that were now wary.

Had she said something disagreeable? Surely Riley was an abolitionist and all those on his campaign were against slavery. As heroic as he was for the downtrodden, he hadn't struck her as the type of man who would take the side of slavery, even though slavery was legal in Missouri.

She pivoted in her chair. Sitting beside her, Riley was staring at the sheet of notes in front of him.

A sick knot tied in her stomach. "Don't tell me your campaign is pro-slavery."

"We're not." Father O'Kirwin spoke from his spot across the table.

She breathed out her relief. Her da was a supporter of the abolitionist movement. Everyone knew where he stood on the issue of slavery. And she was proud of him, proud of what their family stood for, and she wouldn't change her stance for anyone.

Behind his spectacles, Father O'Kirwin's eyes turned solemn. "But you must know a large portion of our constituents among the Irish immigrants have no wish for the slaves to be free because they fear free Black folks will take away their jobs."

Finola had heard mention of such nonsense. "Even if that's true about the jobs—which it is not—one group cannot excuse the suffering of another because it makes life easier for them."

Grumbling began to resound around the table from some of the men. She'd obviously brought up a divisive issue.

"Regardless of what the constituents want," she continued, "Riley has to make it clear that he's against slavery."

Riley leaned in and murmured near her ear. "Could we speak privately about this?"

She hesitated. At the pleading look in his eyes, she nodded.

He led her to a dark corner of the room near the printing press, which was now idle. The others from the campaign had also risen and were gathering their coats and hats in readiness to leave.

"I assure you I am most adamantly opposed to slavery." Riley's voice was low and earnest.

"But . . . ?"

"As you can see, we don't have a consensus on how to handle the slavery issue among the campaign group. Thus, we've decided to not to bring it up."

"You do know that your silence on the matter speaks for itself?"

He palmed the back of his neck. "We need the votes of the poor immigrants."

A part of her understood his dilemma. After just one short meeting at his campaign office, her eyes had been opened to all the projects he and his team wanted to accomplish in St. Louis, particularly for the poor and the immigrants. Even so, they had to do what was right for all people.

She met Riley's gaze levelly. "If you compromise your stance against slavery in order to win votes, then you will lose your honor in the process."

"I won't be comprising."

"Then you'll be a coward."

115

Riley heaved an exasperated sigh. "It's much more complicated than you realize."

Before she could argue with him any further, the office door banged open.

"Saint Riley?" A ruddy-faced lad with a bloody nose and one eye nearly swollen shut scanned the office until his sights landed upon Riley. "The Bulldogs are fighting the Farrell Gang, and it's not going well for the Farrells."

"I'll be right there." Riley was already crossing the room to the coat tree.

Finola followed. There were many gangs all throughout the Kerry Patch and among other immigrant groups as well. Did Riley intervene often in their disputes?

As he swiped up his coat and began to shrug into it, his eyes held an apology. "Sorry I have to leave so quickly."

"What's wrong?"

"A gang of nativist fellas is stirring up trouble with the Farrells."

She'd heard of the nativists who opposed the influx of immigration, especially of Catholics, but she hadn't realized the nativists had resorted to fighting in the streets. The immigrants didn't need another problem added to all those they already faced.

Riley tugged on his hat as though he had every intention of racing off and breaking up the battle. "You'll go directly home?"

She glanced out the window, the streetlamp illuminating her family carriage. "Yes, my driver is waiting."

He was already pushing wide the door. "Good."

Before she could ask him more, he and the lad stepped outside.

"Be careful, Riley." Father O'Kirwin was frowning.

"I'll be fine," Riley called over his shoulder before the door closed and shut him from their view.

Father O'Kirwin shook his head, and worry creased his forehead. "Last time Riley split up a fight between two gangs, he came back with a black eye, busted lip, and three cracked ribs."

A strange sense of fear crowded up into Finola's throat. Saint Riley might be a champion to everyone in St. Louis, but he was putting himself in harm's way each time he rushed to the rescue—just as he had when he'd dashed into the street to save her.

Finola could only stare through the window into the night, a chill working its way up her spine. How could he plunge headlong into the most dangerous situations so impetuously?

She was the opposite. She preferred to use caution, liked everything to be ordered. Then she could maintain a measure of control. Perhaps that's why living in the convent appealed to her so much. The days, the hours, sometimes even the minutes were carefully controlled. There were very few surprises.

Which meant fewer chances to make more mistakes. Mistakes that were deadly . . .

With another shiver, she started toward the door. As much as she was growing to admire Riley Rafferty, he was too wild, too reckless, too rash—all qualities that were at odds with the life she wanted to lead.

She hadn't figured out a way to drive him away yet. But she would soon enough.

13

*F*inola's first waking thought was that Riley's lips were on hers again—soft and warm and delicious.

But in the next instant as her eyes popped open to the big bed she shared with Enya, she released a tight breath. No, not a breath of disappointment that she wasn't actually kissing Riley again. Instead, the tight breath was one of relief, wasn't it?

She shifted to her back and stared up at the speckled plaster ceiling. At the rate she kept reviewing the kiss, she would never forget about it. She was only searing it into her memory for the present age and in the one to come.

She lifted her pillow, clamped it over her face, and released a groan, hoping she wouldn't waken Enya. Thankfully, her sister was a heavy and late sleeper and rarely disturbed by the tossing and turning caused by the frequent nightmares of Ava.

At just the thought of the sweet, beautiful child, a baby's wail arose inside Finola's head, the familiar haunting one that taunted her for how careless, how irresponsible, and how self-ish she'd been. Her mam's words echoed the loudest of all, the words she'd screamed as she'd fallen to her knees beside her dead baby—*"Finola, what have you done?"*

"I'm sorry," Finola whispered into her pillow as she had so

often over the years. She wasn't sure if she was apologizing to Ava, to God, or to her mam. But she knew the apology would never be enough. Nothing would ever be enough to erase the tragedy and her guilt.

She pressed her hands to her ears to block out the wailing. But that never worked to ease the sound. It only continued to roll through her head in unending waves. No Hail Marys, no other prayers, no Scriptures, no songs, no reasoning ever helped.

There was only one thing that would end the torture. . . .

She slipped to the edge of the bed, sat up, and silently prayed, *I promise I'll go to the convent and spend my life working to make amends.*

As the vow rose to heaven, the crying faded until blessed silence returned.

With a heavy sigh, she turned and let her sights drift over Enya. . . .

Except Enya wasn't in bed.

Finola's pulse gave a startled jump.

Not only was Enya absent, but her side of the bed was smooth and unruffled, almost as if she hadn't slept at all. That couldn't be the case. Enya must have made her portion already—although, why would she do so today when she never bothered with it any other morning?

Several of Enya's drawers in the tall chest were open, and the wardrobe door stood wide. But surely that only meant Enya had already awoken and gotten ready without disturbing her.

But no, that couldn't be it either. There were plenty of nights when Finola didn't hear her sister climb into bed beside her. But at the early hour, Finola was always a light sleeper and would have heard Enya leaving. Unless she'd been too distracted by her dreams of Riley this morning?

But even as she scrambled to make excuses for Enya's absence, her heartbeat raced faster. Something wasn't right. She could feel it deep inside.

As she scanned the room to make sense of where Enya was, a folded slip of paper on the vanity table caught Finola's attention. She rose and padded across the room, the thick rug muting her steps but unable to soften the hard thudding in her chest.

The morning light coming in from the slits in the draperies showed that vanity table was half empty. . . . Enya's comb and brush and jewelry and powders and perfumes were gone.

Finola's fingers shook as she picked up the sheet and peeled it open to reveal Enya's handwriting. Quickly she moved to the window and thrust aside the drapery, letting light spill over the note, only a few lines long.

"Bryan has asked me to marry him. Da and Mam have refused to consider his offer and have left me with no choice but to run away with him. Please don't worry about me. I'll finally be happy. Love, Enya."

Finola sagged, and she groped for the edge of the vanity, knocking over several bottles of perfume before managing to lower herself to the cushioned bench.

As she stared at the letter, the ache inside swelled rapidly, and tears sprang to her eyes. "Oh, Enya, how could you?"

Finola had met Bryan only once when she and Enya had been shopping one afternoon after Christmas. Enya had dragged her into the store where he worked as a clerk and introduced her to him. He'd been dashing and handsome and witty. And he'd most definitely been enamored with Enya—like most men. At the time, Finola hadn't noticed anything about him that had caused her to be worried, but the courtship—if it could even be called that—had been short.

Even though Enya had made no secret over how frustrated she was with Da and Mam, Finola had never guessed her sister would defy them to this extent. It was one thing to express herself and plead with Da and Mam to listen, but it was another to reject everything they wanted and run away from home.

"If Da and Mam have concerns about Bryan Haynes, then

you need to listen to them. They're older and wiser and only want the best for your future." As soon as the whispered words had settled in the quiet of the room, Finola closed her eyes against the rebuke. Wasn't that what her parents wanted for her too? The best for her future?

Finola shook her head and blinked back the tears. Aye, she needed to listen to her parents—and respect them. And aye, they were older and wiser and only wanted the best for her too. But her situation was different from Enya's. Wasn't it?

She reread Enya's note several more times before pushing herself back to her feet. As much as she hated to be the one to deliver the terrible news to Da and Mam, she had to do so while there was still time to go after Enya and stop her.

As she crossed to the door and reached for her robe, she had the urge to go to Riley and tell him too. He was Saint Riley. Surely he would know what to do. More than that, she had the feeling he would listen and offer comfort. And at the moment, that was what she needed more than anything else.

14

*H*er parents were devastated to read Enya's letter and learn she'd run away. Her da convened in his study with his investigators. A short while later the fellows hurried out to find Enya and bring her back.

Then her da and mam waited in the study for news. After dressing, Finola joined them.

As the morning wore on without any updates, a visitor might have suspected that they'd received word Enya had died. Everyone, including the rest of her siblings, waited gravely for one of the investigators to return with a livid Enya in tow.

By midday, Da finally shoved up from his chair, his red hair mussed and his eyes filled with desperation. "Ach, I cannot sit around a single second longer." He strode out of the room with Kiernan hurrying after him, and several moments later the back door slammed behind them.

Finola had been holding Mam's hand, but she stood and paced to the window, familiar shame and guilt weighing heavily upon her. Although her da and mam hadn't said so, she suspected they were thinking she should have paid better attention and kept Enya from leaving. And they were right. If anyone could have stopped Enya, she should have been the one since they shared a room.

"Why don't I go to the convent and let the Sisters know what happened?" She also needed to inform them she wouldn't be going with them into the Kerry Patch to aid the immigrants— although she could send one of the servants to deliver the message in her stead.

Her mam was holding her head in her hands and didn't respond.

"They often hear news on their visits," Finola continued. "And even if they don't hear anything, they can ask around."

Mam gave an almost imperceptible nod, and Finola took that as permission to leave. Within minutes she was outside bundled in her coat and on her way to the Visitation Convent. The January day was typical for St. Louis, the temperature near to freezing and a frigid breeze blowing from the north, bringing clouds and the possibility of precipitation.

Usually she had her driver take her to the convent, laden with pots of soup and day-old bread from the various bakeries that donated the food. But her da didn't mind her walking the two blocks, which she did from time to time.

When she'd first started going with the Sisters, they'd only been visiting in the Kerry Patch once a week. But over recent months, as the conditions for the immigrants became more crowded, they'd increased their trips to three days.

As the unassuming brick building came into view, Finola picked up her pace. Visitation Convent wasn't large, nothing more than an old home that had been converted into a living space for the Sisters. It sat next to the seminary for young ladies, the one Finola had attended until she'd turned fourteen.

Even now, the small private school was in session, with a few of the educated nuns devoting themselves to teaching, while the others spent their days doing charity work.

Finola raced up the stone stairway to the convent entrance,

knocked softly, and then entered. The warmth and coziness of the home enveloped her as it always did whenever she stepped inside.

Standing in the front entry hallway, four sisters were in the process of donning capes and gloves and bonnets over their habits. At the sight of her, they halted.

"Finola, dear." Sister Anne, the oldest of the women, with a plump face and double chin, spoke first. "We didn't expect you today, dear."

"We heard about your sister," whispered Sister Catherine, a middle-aged nun who spoke in hushed tones. "And we've been praying ever since the news came our way."

"Thank you." Finola loved the prayerful example the Sisters provided, which was another reason why she wanted to join the convent—so she could spend more time in prayer and learn to deny herself worldly pleasures.

"Finola?" The Mother Superior stepped out of the library and into the hallway. Although a tiny woman, she exuded great strength and purpose, directing those under her supervision with a measure of firmness and kindness.

Finola had been only ten when the revered nun had asked her to come to her office after school. As Finola had stood trembling on the opposite side of the big desk, the Mother Superior had complimented her on her progress and encouraged her to consider joining the convent, telling her she had all the qualities that a Sister needed.

Later that day, when Finola relayed the Mother Superior's suggestion to Mam and Da, they'd only shaken their heads and muttered about how the Mother Superior certainly wanted Finola to join but for reasons that had more to do with the amplitude of her dowry than the quality of her character.

Even with her parents' skepticism, Finola hadn't been able to put the possibility out of her mind. The seed had been planted and had only grown over the years so that now it was ripe for harvesting—as the Mother Superior liked to say.

In fact, just before Christmas, the Mother Superior had pulled Finola aside and asked her to take the commitment more seriously, had even offered to communicate to her parents on her behalf. Finola had insisted she needed to be the one to talk to her da and mam about it and assured the Mother Superior that she would do so soon.

"I need to speak with Finola." The Mother Superior gave the four Sisters a nod, which sent them scurrying with their baskets down the hallway to the back exit of the building. They wouldn't have the soup from the Shanahan kitchen to take to the immigrants today. Nevertheless, they'd have the day-old bread to distribute.

As soon as the door closed behind the Sisters, the Mother Superior crossed to Finola, her hand outstretched.

Finola knelt and kissed the woman's hand, then rose and waited with eyes cast down for the nun to start the conversation.

"I received news that your father has called on the matchmaker on your behalf."

"Aye, he has." Finola wasn't surprised the Mother Superior had heard. Gossip in their Irish community spread quickly.

The revered nun was silent a moment. "Does this mean you've chosen not to join us after all?"

"No, Mother." Finola met the woman's gaze. "I am still planning to become a nun."

"But your father has already signed agreements for your match."

"I don't intend to go through with it." Even though her first efforts at pushing Riley away had failed, she wasn't giving up.

In fact, she'd gotten the idea to foil her suitors from the Mother Superior after she'd broached the subject of entering the convent to her parents for a second time a couple of years ago. When she'd told the Mother Superior that her parents wished for her to get married, the wise woman had encouraged Finola to seek ways to show her parents that she was more suited to become the bride of Christ instead of the bride of a man.

She'd tried to do so ever since.

"Have you entreated with your parents about the matter?" The Mother Superior gentled her voice as though talking with a child.

"My da said this is the last time he'll intervene, that if this suitor fails, then he'll allow me to enter the convent."

The Mother Superior pursed her lips. "Entering into service for God shouldn't be a last choice because all else fails. It should be the primary priority for a heart like yours who seeks to do the will of God."

Finola nodded. "Aye, I agree, that I do."

"The matchmaker rarely fails in making his matches."

"He hasn't had to make a match for a woman like me." Bellamy hadn't made *any* matches before, but even if Oscar had been arranging the match, she still would have ensured she was one of his failures.

"Very well, child. See that you accomplish what you need to soon." The Mother Superior spoke to her for several more minutes about the benefits of serving Christ—all the reasons Finola had heard a dozen times before.

After the Mother Superior's dismissal, Finola walked away from the convent with slow and uncertain steps. She'd hoped to find solace and peace among the ladies like she normally did. Instead, her guilt only weighed heavier. Guilt at not doing a better job in keeping Enya safe. And guilt in not yet succeeding in showing her parents that she was more qualified to be a nun than a wife and mother.

Yet, how could she persist in ruining the match with Riley

while Enya was gone? They were experiencing enough difficulty with Enya's waywardness, and Finola didn't want to add to their woes and heartache more than she already had.

Should she put a halt to the scheming during this crisis?

A chill crept into her hood and down her backbone, and she huddled within her thick wool coat, the trim of fur more for show than for warmth.

Aye, she wouldn't do anything to purposefully disrupt the match for a few days until Enya was found. Instead, she'd use the time to come up with new ideas for how to scare Riley away. If he didn't get himself killed first . . .

How had Riley fared last night in breaking up the gang fight? Had he ended up bruised and bloodied? Broken bones? Or worse?

She didn't want to care what had happened to Riley. But her heart began to speed anyway, and she couldn't control the overwhelming need to make sure he was okay.

As she neared the corner of Morgan, instead of crossing over to the next block, she turned east toward the river. She'd keep her visit short. Tell Riley she'd been in the area and was merely doing the neighborly thing in checking on him.

Even though a match was out of the question, he was, after all, a good man. And she didn't have to shun him.

The miles of riverfront were crowded with countless more steamboats, some coming, others going, black plumes puffing from the tall smokestacks. Stevedores and deckhands milled about among the passengers who were disembarking and would soon go to hotels, boardinghouses, or squeeze into tenements with friends or family who'd arrived before them.

The wind slapped against her as if to reprimand her, but she pushed onward, picking up her pace until she turned onto Front Street. Inwardly, she tried to convince herself to turn around and go directly back home without this detour. But her feet propelled her forward.

As she stepped into the open door that was wide enough for a vehicle, the clanking of tools against metal drifted in the breeze, and she hesitated. What was she doing here? After her conversation with the Mother Superior, this was the last place she should be, giving Riley the idea that she was encouraging their relationship.

She'd make this stop quick—inquire after his well-being and then go on her way.

The workshop was spacious and filled with wagons in various stages of construction. Tall windows along the front and back of the shop provided plenty of natural light. Like the door, they were open, probably to allow ventilation for the dust and smoke that hung in the air.

And the heat. She could feel the increase in temperature even at the door. Against the back wall, a double forge burned brightly with a large vent tube hanging above it and a coal box dug into the ground near the water tank. In front of the forge, an anvil rested on a timber block, and a well-organized tool table seemed positioned for maximum benefit to all the workers.

The many workers. Who had ceased their hammering, sanding, sawing, and painting to stare at her.

She scanned their faces, searching for just one. But among the sweaty countenances, she didn't see the man she needed. Aye, she needed him, and she didn't want to think about that admission too closely.

A bulky man with hunched shoulders and glistening ebony skin stood at a worktable, a wheel in front of him, with only a few of the spokes inserted. He wiped his forehead with a bandana before he shifted and looked across the workshop. "Rafferty."

She followed the man's gaze to a bench underneath one of the rear windows. And there was Riley. He straddled the bench, holding a part of the wagon she couldn't even begin to name, and he seemed to be screwing in metal rods.

He wore an off-white cotton shirt with both sleeves rolled up past his elbows. Faded red suspenders held up his trousers and stretched taut over his shoulders. He was hatless, his wavy blond hair disheveled, likely from the heat and the hard work. He didn't appear to be harmed in any way from the gang fight.

He was focused intently on the task before him, his biceps bulging with the effort of twisting in the rods. Not even the call of his name drew him from his task, allowing her the chance to admire his profile. A layer of scruff covered his jaw and cheek, giving him a rugged look, one that was every bit as handsome as the clean-shaven gentleman he'd been the night he shared supper with her family.

Now, at the sight of him again, this man who'd kissed her and shaken the foundation of everything she thought she knew, she was overwhelmed with a load of feelings she couldn't begin to name.

"Rafferty," the man called again. "Your woman's here."

Your woman? As if she already belonged to Riley? She supposed in the minds of everyone else, she did already belong to Riley Rafferty. After all, Da and Riley had signed the bindings the night of their meeting at Oscar's Pub. With Da's solicitor presiding over the paperwork, they'd sealed the match with the legal agreements that spelled out her dowry.

Even so, she wasn't sure she liked the term of being *his woman*. But it seemed to finally gain Riley's attention. His head snapped up and swung toward the door. As his gaze landed upon her, he hopped up, his eyes finding hers.

Something about his expression, his warmth, openness, kindness, and compassion shot straight to her heart and brought swift tears to the surface.

His brow immediately wrinkled, and he started toward her with his long stride.

She hadn't meant to show him her distress, had only wanted to ask him how he was doing before going on her way. But now that she was here and with him looking at her with such concern, the weight of all her burdens was almost too much to bear.

As he stopped in front of her, he gently took her arm, his eyes worried. "Finola, what's wrong?"

"I'm fine." She managed to get the words out.

"No, something's amiss."

She glanced around, and he did the same. The other workers were still idle and watching her interaction with Riley.

He began to tug her out the door. "Come on. We'll go someplace private." He led her outside, the bitter wind once again slapping at her, reminding her that she shouldn't have come.

She'd have to set the boundaries again later. But for now, she wanted—needed—to tell him about Enya.

He rounded the building and directed her into an alley. From the bins of coal, stacks of wood on pallets, and crates of iron, she guessed they were at the back of the wagon shop. He reached for a closed door, opened it, and then pulled her inside after him.

Paint cans, buckets, handles, and more filled the floor-to-ceiling shelves of what appeared to be a supply closet.

He started to close the door but then left it open halfway—no doubt to allow for light since the closet didn't have any windows. Then he gently grasped both of her upper arms. "Something happened."

He wasn't asking a question. Instead he was giving her the opportunity to tell him everything.

She tried to speak, but emotion clogged her throat. And at that moment, she realized why she'd really come. Because deep inside, she'd known he'd care about all she was going through. Because she wanted him to hold her and feel that rare sense of safety and security she'd felt the day he'd rescued her.

Without waiting for an invitation, she leaned against him and rested her head against his chest.

15

$\mathcal{F}$inola had come to him and was touching him.

Was she playing another game with him today?

He didn't think so. Even if she was, he didn't care. He wrapped his arms around her, heedless of anything else but the need to feel her close.

She slipped her arms around his torso, too, and released a shuddering breath.

He tugged back the hood of her cloak to find her hair styled in a simple braided knot. He had the sudden urge to take out her pins and let her hair unravel in his fingers. But instead, he brushed a hand over the back of her hair and tucked her head under his chin.

She nuzzled against him, relaxing there as if she was finally where she wanted to be.

A sense of satisfaction pulsed through him at the thought that Finola Shanahan had wanted to be with him. With whatever was wrong, she'd wanted his support.

As if the sight of her beautiful body that day in the livery hadn't been enough to awaken him to his needs, the physical contact with her when he'd kissed her had brought him fully alive. Now his every dream and waking moment had been filled with her, the taste of her mouth, the feel of her body, the brush of her fingers over his skin. Even last night at the campaign office, sitting beside her at the table, he'd been all too aware of her every move and every breath.

But the other truth became clearer the more time he spent with her. As much as he wanted this match with Finola, he refused to push her into marriage. She had to come to him freely, or he wouldn't do it at all.

This was a good sign, wasn't it? Even with the uncertainty and newness of their relationship, she'd sought him out, upset about something and needing his comfort.

He pressed his nose into her hair and breathed her in. He didn't know much about women's perfumes or lotions or soaps. But she had a light, flowery scent that reminded him of summer.

He wanted to brush his lips over her hair, but he held himself back. He couldn't get distracted by his attraction to her, had to focus on her needs and not his.

Resting his cheek on her head, he held her gently, sensing a change in the tautness of her limbs as well as a relaxing in her body.

Long moments later, she expelled another sigh, this one even and calm. "Thank you, Riley," she whispered, finally pulling back.

"You're welcome." He didn't know exactly why she was thanking him, maybe for being there for her in her moment of distress. He didn't want to break the connection, but he couldn't hang on to her like the lovesick fool he was turning in to. He reluctantly let go and took a step away from her.

She didn't meet his gaze, almost as if she was embarrassed by the encounter.

"Are you doing better?" he asked.

She hesitated, then peeked up at him through her long lashes. "Enya ran away from home last night to marry Bryan Haynes."

After the argument between Enya and her parents that he'd overheard the other night, he wasn't surprised by the news.

"She left me a note telling me I shouldn't worry about her, that she'll be happy."

He could only guess how upset James Shanahan was by this turn of events. It was clear the man loved his children and wanted them to each have secure and happy futures. No doubt he was doing everything he could to find Enya and keep her from marrying a man of questionable character.

Riley's muscles tensed with the need to do something. Should he offer to help with the search?

The details rushed from Finola, and with each word she spoke, he could see her stiffening and growing more tense, until at last her eyes welled with tears again.

"Now, now, sweet love." He dropped his tone to the soothing one he used for his sisters when they were getting emotional. "Why the tears?"

"I should have stopped her, Riley." The admission came out a low, broken whisper. "If I'd been awake or if I'd been paying better attention—"

He cut her off with a finger to her lips. "Listen, even if you'd stayed awake all night and stood guard over her, she still would have found a way to sneak out."

"But I could have awakened Da, and he would have stopped her." A tear spilled over and slid down her cheek.

He swiped at it with his thumb, trying not to notice the smoothness of her skin. "Enya's a smart girl, and she would have gotten past your father too."

Finola held his gaze as though his words were like a rope saving her from drowning.

"You're not to blame for Enya's actions."

"I could have done more, to be sure."

"Are your parents blaming you? If so, that's not fair."

"They haven't said anything."

"Good. Because then I'd have to go over and tell them to stop being daft, blathering idiots."

Her eyes rounded, but the tears were gone. "You wouldn't dare do such a thing."

"Watch me." He made a move as though he intended to go.

She grabbed his arm. "Riley Rafferty, you'll not be doing anything of the sort."

He smiled. "Are you worried about what would happen to me, Finola?"

"Not a wee bit."

He let his smile widen. "I think you are."

She just shook her head, but she was fighting back a smile.

He wanted to see her smile, knew it would be beautiful.

But she ducked her head, and her expression turned serious again. What else could he say or do to make her see she wasn't at fault, that Enya was a grown woman who'd made her own choice?

"Any ideas of where she went?"

For a few minutes, she shared all that she knew about Bryan, how he'd recently moved to St. Louis, was working as a clerk for a local merchant, and had plans to open his own business soon. Enya had met him at a party during the Christmas season and had obviously fallen for him quickly.

Riley stuffed his hands into his pockets to keep from reaching for Finola. "How about if I head out around town and check with the connections I have to see if they've heard anything about Enya or seen her?"

"No, Riley. That's too much, and you have your work."

"I don't mind."

"I didn't come here to make you feel like you have to get involved."

Oh, he wanted to get involved with her in every way possible. But he bit back the overzealous words and shrugged.

At the same time, she bumped the shelf behind her, and an old axle wobbled.

He reached past her to steady the item and keep it from falling on her. As he did so, his body brushed against hers. Instead of backing away, as her version of a proper *gentleman* would, he made a show of situating the axle, pushing it away from the edge, leaning against her even more. He couldn't seem to help himself.

It wasn't much contact, but it was enough to draw a soft intake from her.

At the sound of her reaction and the tantalizing feel of her body, every inch of his flesh that touched hers heated with sharp need, just like it had the night of the kiss. He closed his eyes and let his chin graze her cheek. Sweet saints above, Finola Shanahan would be his undoing.

He paused with his mouth by her ear.

She drew in another breath, this one quicker and sharper.

She was like a fire burning down a building. And he was walking straight into the flames. The pain of a failed marriage with Helen had been enough. If he wasn't careful, he would get hurt again, maybe even incinerated.

Opening his eyes, he took a step back. Her lashes had fallen, her cheeks were flushed, and her mouth had parted just slightly as if she'd been hoping he'd kiss her.

The inferno inside him flared hotter. Bother it. He wanted to kiss her again. But he couldn't. He had to wait until he knew for certain she was willing to marry him and wasn't doing everything in her power to get out of matrimony.

"I know you didn't come here to get me involved in the search." Even with his resolve, he couldn't keep from teasing her. "You came because you wanted me to kiss you again."

Her eyes flew wide, and she raised a hand as though to slap his cheek but stopped midway. "I didn't come here to kiss you, so I didn't. And you'll mind your manners not to say so." She gave a huff and pushed past him out of the storage closet.

He followed on her heels, and when they were out into the alley, he clasped her arm, halting her from running away from him.

As she faced him, the sass was back in her blue eyes, and she lifted her dimpled chin. "For your information, I was in the area and stopped by to see how you fared after the fight last night."

"So you were worried about me, were you now?"

"No, I was checking to see if you were dead or alive. I didn't want to send Madigan to uncover your dislikes—the real ones this time—if you were dead."

He grinned. "Go ahead. Send him. I'll give him another list."

"Maybe I will."

Heavy flakes of snow had begun to fall, so he reached for her hood and gently raised it over her head. As he lowered his hand, he let himself graze a patch of freckles on her cheek. "I know why you came to me, Finola." He kept his voice low, wanting her to know he was done with the fun and games. "You came because you know I'll do anything to help you." She started to shake her head, but he finished before she could interrupt. "And if you didn't know it, now you do."

She remained quiet. In spite of her hood, a snowflake fell onto the tip of her nose.

He wiped it away.

She cast her sights to the gravel of the alley.

"Will you be going with the Sisters of Charity into the Kerry Patch today?"

"No, I'm staying with Mam. She needs me."

"Would you let me come with you next time you go?"

Her gaze darted up to his. "Why?"

"I'd like to hear directly from the people what they need." He didn't have to do it for his campaign since his popularity was soaring—even more so now that he'd signed the papers making the match with Finola official. He'd gained Shanahan's support along with his influence among the wealthy community of St. Louis. Even so, Riley wanted to accompany her and truly did want to meet more people.

"Let me go with you tomorrow," he insisted, "or whenever you next go. I promise I'll help and won't get in your way."

She hesitated, then after a moment nodded. "Alright. You can come. But this is serious business, and I won't be having you distracting me from serving the poor folks."

"I can't help it if my good looks and charm distract you."

She narrowed her eyes at him.

He laughed.

She spun on her heels and began to walk away, but not before he saw her lips twitch.

With a warmth he wanted to hang on to forever, he watched her until she disappeared around the corner—not caring that he was staring or that she could turn and catch him in the act.

16

$\mathscr{F}$inola scooped the last spoonful of broth into Mary's mouth and at the same time brushed limp hair from the young woman's forehead. "There, now."

From the thin pallet upon the floor of the crowded apartment, Mary tried for a smile. "You're an angel, so." She reached out a bony hand, a tattered blanket falling away to reveal her skeletal arm.

Finola sat back on her heels and took the hand, a familiar helplessness stealing through her. "I wish I could do more for you and your family."

The dank air held the stench of unwashed bodies and excrement. With the broken window patched with boards, a lone candle cast its grave light over the room, the pile of soiled clothing serving as a bed for the emaciated children, holes in the sooty walls stuffed with old newspapers, a mound of refuse in an unoccupied corner.

"You're doing grand." Mary's tired gaze shifted past the clusters of other families to the open door. "And your man is grand too, so he is."

Finola glanced to where Riley stood in the hallway outside the apartment with a group of men surrounding him. He held one of Mary's little boys on his shoulders. The tyke was wearing Riley's hat and sucking on one of the peppermint sticks Riley had distributed among the children.

Riley had crossed his arms over the child's legs to hold him in place, which only served to highlight his muscles and remind her of those arms surrounding her yesterday in the little closet behind the wagon shop.

Her heart sputtered with fresh warmth, as it did every time she thought about his embrace. Why did each encounter with Riley Rafferty have to rattle her down to her bones?

His expression was intense, almost severe now, as he listened to the men air their many complaints. After the past hours of accompanying her from one apartment to the next in the worst of the tenements, she'd expected him to look tired. She could admit she was. But after each visit, he only seemed to gain energy.

"You'll be married soon?" Mary's question was raspy and followed by a fit of coughing that shook the woman's frail body. Mary, her husband, and five children had arrived in St. Louis two months ago, carrying one bag with all their worldly possessions. Like most of the other immigrants, they were severely malnourished.

Mary had gotten sick on the passage over, on what were becoming known as the "coffin ships." Finola had heard enough tales of the vessels to know that Mary, in her weakened condition, had been fortunate to survive the crowded, disease-ridden voyage. The trouble was, she hadn't regained her strength and was growing weaker with each passing day.

Perhaps if she had a sanitary place to stay with better nourishment, she might be doing better. But this building, unlike the tenements the Shanahan's owned, was drafty and dirty.

"Thought you were a nun, so I did," Mary continued the conversation. "Didn't know you have such a fine fellow as Saint Riley himself."

"'Tis but a recent match."

Riley had been at her house this morning meeting with Da before she'd descended for breakfast. Apparently, he'd spent the better part of yesterday afternoon searching for Bryan Haynes and had come to report his findings.

When the two had finished their meeting, she pretended not to show an interest in Riley. But he explained that he'd gained her da's permission to accompany her into the Kerry Patch and she had no need of the Sisters if he was along.

Riley hadn't made any mention of her visit to him at the wagon shop, for which she was grateful. Her da didn't approve of her traveling to the waterfront unaccompanied. And she didn't want to burden him any further, not with how distraught he still was over Enya's disappearance.

She and Riley had loaded several large pots of Cook's soup into a cart and then passed by a bakery for the day-old loaves. During their time together, he didn't bring up their embrace. Instead, he shared with her all the details he'd learned about Bryan Haynes, namely that the fellow hadn't shown up to work and was last seen getting on a steamboat heading north. No one could verify if he'd been with a woman, but he'd purchased two tickets, which seemed to be confirmation that Enya had gone with him, and only God in heaven above knew where.

"He sure does have eyes for you, so." Mary turned her attention back on Riley, straining her neck to get a better view.

"Now don't be imagining such things, Mary. 'Tis a practical match. That's all." Actually, there would be no match. But Mary didn't need to know that.

Finola admired Riley's strong profile again. More than his handsomeness, she appreciated how he genuinely cared about the people and their concerns. He cared enough that he'd decided to run for mayor—not out of personal ambition or gain. He was doing it because he truly wanted to make changes for the better.

From what she'd learned at the campaign office, he was competing against an alderman who was wealthier and more powerful, as well as a judge who'd earned a reputation for his fair and honest dealings. Both men were friends of the family. And they would be difficult to beat.

If anyone could do it, Riley Rafferty could . . . but not if he took a stand against slavery.

She'd continued to contemplate Riley's dilemma if he spoke out against slavery—namely losing the votes of the Irish immigrants. And if he lost those votes, he'd surely lose the election and then not be able to make a difference in anyone's lives, neither the Irish nor the Black folks.

Even though she understood the quandary, she still couldn't excuse him. Every person against slavery had to do their part and make their voices heard, otherwise how would they ever bring about changes? The truth was, as Saint Riley of the Kerry Patch, Riley had a big voice and could make a difference by educating the Irish immigrants about the evils of slavery and addressing their fears about St. Louis not having enough work for everyone.

"The matchmaker clearly made a perfect match, so he did." Mary's voice held a note of humor.

Perfect match? Hardly. Bellamy might have believed he'd made a perfect match, but he'd realize soon enough that he had a long way to go in learning how to be a matchmaker.

"You cannot keep your eyes off him either."

Riley chose that moment to glance her way. At the sight of her staring at him, he quirked one of his brows. She dropped her sights back to Mary. That man didn't need any more flattery filling his head. He was already revered everywhere he went by young and old alike. And if she paid him even a wee bit of attention, he'd mistake it for interest and tease her to no end.

A short while later, he carried the supply bag down to the cart waiting outside the tenement, with only empty pots remaining.

They'd given away all the food and distributed the few coats and shoes and blankets that some of the parishes had started collecting and saving after she'd approached them earlier in the winter about doing so.

The thin layer of snow that had fallen yesterday had already melted and given way to more mud on the street. With the busy traffic passing by in the late afternoon, she made sure to tiptoe carefully around the cart, not wishing to give herself or Riley a repeat of his rescue.

He situated the bag in the back, then helped her up onto the seat. "Do you mind if we swing by the campaign office before I take you home?"

His gloved hand lingered around hers as he peered up and waited for her response. A part of her didn't want her time with him to come to an end. But another part urged her not to spend any more time with him than she absolutely needed to.

At a carriage hurtling past them, Riley's attention shifted. And in the next moment, he released her and was chasing after the vehicle. He leapt through the mud as if it was solid ground, his feet pounding hard and his arms straining to latch on to the carriage.

A young lady inside was banging against the door, her expression filled with horror as she stared down the street behind her.

Finola followed her gaze to a man rubbing his hatless head and sitting in the mud as vehicles passed him by. The coachman had fallen off, perhaps after bumping over one of the large holes in the street. Now the carriage with its occupant was racing away, the horses apparently having been spooked by the incident.

Riley ran faster, sidestepped as a wagon nearly hit him, and then launched himself forward.

"Holy mother, have mercy." Finola could only hold her breath as Riley fumbled for a handhold. When he grasped a railing more firmly and found a spot for his foot, she allowed herself one shaky breath before she held it again.

As the carriage rolled down the street ever faster, it jostled over more holes, throwing Riley hard against the door. But even as he watched the horses and the road ahead, he climbed steadily to the bench. Just as the team careened he lunged for the reins.

With half his body now hanging off the seat and the carriage wheels rising off the ground on one side, Finola released a cry of alarm. If the vehicle tipped over, he'd be crushed and badly hurt, if not killed.

Regardless of the imminent danger, Riley wrapped the reins around his gloved hands and called out commands to the horses. In the next instant, the wheels slammed back to the ground, rocking the carriage and jolting Riley. He strained to hold on, finally drawing the horses to a halt.

People had poured from businesses and tenements. Some were leaning out of open windows. The traffic had come to a standstill—as it had the day Riley had rescued her. And as Riley hopped down, a chorus of cheering, whistling, and clapping greeted him.

He didn't seem to notice, was too busy opening the door and checking on the occupant.

The woman, upon descending, threw her arms around Riley and then kissed him directly on the mouth.

The kiss didn't last long, and Riley was already stepping away from the woman before she could do anything more. Even so, a strange indignance swelled within Finola. How dare that woman kiss Riley so freely? Surely she knew Riley was matched. Even if she didn't, a kiss was much too brazen.

A moment later, the coachman, who was limp-running, reached the carriage. Riley questioned the driver before helping him up onto his seat and then assisting the lady back into the conveyance.

As the carriage continued on its way, much slower and more cautiously, Riley finally turned. His sights came to rest on Finola first. His brows were furrowed as his gaze took her in on the wagon bench where he'd left her.

Only then did she realize she was clutching her cloak with both fists and that her pulse was racing.

As he started down the street toward her, he accepted the well-wishes and back thumps from his many admirers. But he didn't stop until he reached the wagon, his eyes dark with concern. "How are you getting on? You look pale."

He was thinking about her well-being right at this moment?

She released a long, tight breath. "Aye, Riley Rafferty, why do you think I'm pale? You almost got yourself killed, and in the process nearly sent me to an early grave."

He climbed up onto the bench. "Is that your way of letting me know you were worried about me?"

"As worried as every other man, woman, and child watching you." Actually, she was petrified and could hardly move.

He gathered the reins and flicked them, nudging the roan mare forward.

She hadn't yet released her grip on her cloak, and her heart hadn't returned to its normal pace. She wasn't sure it ever would.

"Just admit it, Finola. You were worried you'd lose me." He tossed her an easy smile, one that made him far too handsome, even though he was splattered with mud.

Regardless of his physical appeal, he was too daring for a woman like her who wanted a simple, quiet life.

"You can say it." His tone contained a playful arrogance, one she was beginning to like in spite of knowing she shouldn't.

"Say what?"

"That you don't want to lose me."

During their time together today, she hadn't thought once about how she could drive him away, and clearly he knew it. "You seemed to enjoy the kiss with the woman you just rescued.

Maybe you'd like a match with her instead." Actually, she hadn't been able to tell if he liked it or not. Had he?

He stared straight ahead, but his grin widened. "You're jealous."

"Jealous?" She scoffed. "Why would I be jealous?"

"Because you want me all for yourself."

"I'm not falling in line to worship you the way all the other women do."

"Is that a fact?"

"'Tis a fact."

He slid her a sideways glance, one with brows cocked that said he knew her defenses against him were crumbling.

But the truth was, even if she lowered her resistance to him once in a while, she was still planning to dissolve their match after Enya was found and her parents weren't so overwhelmed with their runaway daughter. As much as Finola was beginning to like Riley, her place was in the convent, where her life would be regimented and all her guilt would finally go away.

A call from the tenement across the street drew his attention. Several men, including the doctor, were exiting the building and now crossing toward Riley.

He tipped up the brim of his hat, stopped the cart, and waited for them.

Their expressions were grave as they approached. Finola had seen that look before during her visits. And it usually meant someone had died.

The doctor was the first to reach Riley. He glanced around as though he was afraid of anyone else hearing and lowered his voice. "I regret to inform you, we have our first death from cholera in the city." The doctor nodded toward the tenement across the street.

Cholera. At the dreaded word, Riley tensed.

He hopped down, helped Finola off the wagon, and together they followed the doctor into the dingy tenement, which was as filthy and run-down as the one they'd just been in. The stench of feces, however, was worse.

As the doctor and other men covered their noses with handkerchiefs, she did the same, although it only helped a little.

They descended into the lower level, darker and more dismal than the apartments on the upper levels. And dank. The chill in the air rivaled the stench.

Finola had been too young in the early 1830s to remember the cholera epidemic in St. Louis when hundreds had died. But she'd heard the reports of the recent cholera outbreaks in Europe, killing thousands upon thousands of people so quickly that the healthy couldn't keep up with the burials and were dumping bodies into mass graves and rivers.

With so many immigrants coming into St. Louis, she'd suspected it would only be a matter of time before the unstoppable disease came to the city, especially because the immigrants were talking about how cholera had devastated New Orleans and Vicksburg.

Now, as she peeked into the room and took in the pale, almost blue, lifeless form with sunken eyes, stiff limbs, and skin that was abnormally wrinkled, she couldn't keep from trembling. Another man lay listlessly on the floor nearby the corpse, and he was vomiting violently into a basin.

Aye, she'd heard the tales. First came the vomiting, then the bowel discharges and abdominal pain, until the skin became blue and wrinkled. After intense suffering, the person often died within a day, sometimes sooner.

No one knew how the "Blue Death" spread, but most believed it was passed in the very air they breathed, especially the putrid fumes emitted from rotting matter.

Finola pressed her handkerchief closer to her mouth and nose, praying she would keep from inhaling the dangerous vapors. They stayed inside only a moment longer before retreating to the street.

Once outside, she gulped in breaths of air. Even if it, too, was rank with the stench of sewage and coal smoke and flesh from the nearby slaughterhouses, it was better than what was inside the tenement.

For a short while, Riley conversed with the doctor and the other men about ways to contain the disease so they wouldn't have an outbreak. Already several families were sick in the Kerry Patch. And there were likely other cases they didn't know about.

As she and Riley went on their way, the gravity of what they'd witnessed overshadowed everything else, and they rode in silence. Riley finally spoke. "There's much to be done in the tenements to prevent the spread."

"Aye, to be sure. We'll visit every day and do what we can." She didn't realize she'd included Riley in her plans until after the words emerged.

He nodded as though it was natural for them to make plans to work together to stop the spread of the illness. "Will the Sisters of Charity be willing to help more often?"

"Of that I have no doubt."

She believed, as the Sisters did, that God's people couldn't hide or cower when it came time to assist those in need—the sick, the hungry, the destitute. No matter the risk to themselves, the Sisters were always the first to serve. She wanted to follow their example.

"You were good with the immigrants today." Riley's voice held admiration.

"So were you."

"Then you agree that we make a great team?"

She agreed, but she hesitated to say so, didn't want him to think their relationship was progressing. Because it wasn't. It had to stay firmly where it was—a partnership to help the immigrants.

"Admit it." His voice hinted at playfulness, as if he was trying to lighten the moment.

"Admit what?"

"That we work well together and make a great team."

"Okay." She heaved an exaggerated sigh. "You're right."

The muscles in his arm flexed as he directed the team toward First Street. Her thoughts flew back to the night in the sitting room when she'd approached him from behind and glided her hands over his arm. The remembrance of his sinewy flesh sent sudden heat spilling through her. How had she dared to be so bold?

"Take your time looking." His tone dropped low and was filled with invitation.

She stared straight ahead, her cheeks flushing.

He chuckled.

Riley Rafferty was going to make her crazy . . . crazy about him. And she couldn't let that happen. Not in the least.

17

"Where are you taking me, Riley?" Finola asked from beside him on the bench of the Dennett gig.

It was a fine piece of workmanship, one he was proud of. He'd spent most of his free time over the past year building the lightweight two-wheeled carriage that was pulled by one horse. While he'd maintained the three-spring suspension, he'd tweaked the design so the body was sleeker and slimmer and the wheels slightly smaller, allowing it to go faster.

Over the past week, Big Jim had helped him paint it a light blue late at night when he finished the other work awaiting him. When Big Jim said it matched the color of Finola Shanahan's eyes, Riley denied it. Maybe he hadn't purposefully picked out a paint color to match her eyes, but it had happened. And he guessed he'd probably paint everything light blue for the rest of his life if he could.

He chanced a glance her way only to find those wide, beautiful blue eyes watching him expectantly.

"You have to wait and see."

With her fur-lined hood pulled up and secured by a scarf, her face was hardly visible. But her eyes . . . they were mesmerizing, always drawing him in and gripping his heart harder, so that with every passing day he needed her more. He found himself restless and distracted and out of sorts until he arrived with the buckboard at her home. Only then did his world seem to come into focus and the day truly begin.

They'd spent the past week with the same routine—heading into the Kerry Patch and visiting the newly arrived immigrants, warning them of cholera, and giving out advice for how to avoid it. She'd gone with him to his campaign office one evening, but they'd only ended up arguing about the slavery issue again.

Of course he hated slavery. Abhorred it, especially after Big Jim had told him his story about being torn apart from his wife and young infant and sold to a new slave master. Big Jim had tried to visit his wife one weekend and had been accused of attempting to escape. His new master had beaten him until he'd almost died, leaving his shoulders permanently hunched. The scars on Big Jim's back were difficult to look at, and Riley couldn't imagine the suffering the gentlehearted man had experienced during the beating.

After hearing about the battered slave's woodworking abilities, William Rafferty had been the one to purchase Big Jim at the slave market at the front of the capital building. He'd promptly given the man his freedom and then offered him a job in the wagon shop.

It turned out Big Jim was incredibly smart and dexterous and became a master wagonmaker in half the time it took other apprentices and journeymen. He'd been working and living at the shop ever since and rarely left the safe confines except to go to church on Sundays and visit with the pastor's family.

Big Jim never talked about his wife and child. And Riley hadn't wanted to bring up the painful past, although his dad had once told him that he believed the woman and child had been sold downriver.

Whatever the case, Riley hadn't wanted to argue with Finola about the slavery issue. He already felt guilty enough for not taking a stand against it with his campaign. But almost everyone—Father O'Kirwin in particular—had told him that his private beliefs about slavery didn't need to play a role in this election, especially when so much was at stake.

Today, on their day of rest, he wanted to spend time with just Finola, without worrying about the election or having constant interruptions.

Not that he hadn't enjoyed the time working with her. He'd meant what he said about them being a good team. He'd loved every moment with her. She had a deep compassion for the immigrants, her kindness knew no bounds, and she was never timid and always willing to do the filthiest and humblest of tasks.

Although he was getting to see the treasure she was both inside and out, he hadn't had any opportunities to work on winning her affection. Oh sure, they'd had brief connections—her hand brushing his when passing him something, or his lingering when helping her down from the wagon.

Even so, he could sense she was still holding herself back. When he'd spoken with Bellamy after mass earlier in the day, the young matchmaker had suggested that Riley get her away from the busyness and distractions of everything else and spend time with just her.

Her father had privately confided the past evening that none of the previous twelve suitors had lasted more than two days. Shanahan had pumped Riley's hand and congratulated him for remaining with Finola longer than two weeks. Riley guessed that was why Shanahan had allowed Finola to continue to visit in the Kerry Patch despite the cholera outbreak—because he was still anxious about Finola making a mess of the match.

The three-week deadline Riley had given himself for winning her was fast approaching. But for a reason he couldn't explain, he felt almost as precarious in his relationship with her now as he had at the beginning.

Today he wanted the chance to change that, wanted to make

sure she was growing to care about him too, wanted to make sure she was secure in their match.

"Not much longer now." The temperatures had dipped below freezing over the past week, and the wind was bitter so that the usual mud was hard, allowing the gig to clip along at a decent pace.

Everyone was hoping the drop in temperatures and the cold winds would drive the foul air from St. Louis and carry away the cholera. But it seemed every day they got word of more families contracting the disease.

In fact, when Riley had swung by his family's tenement earlier, his dad suggested the possibility of leaving the city limits and heading out to the country. Eleanor had a brother who lived on a farm, and he'd offered to have them come stay with him until the threat of cholera had passed. Riley had encouraged them to go, even though his dad was improving and gaining strength with every passing day.

Shanahan had talked of sending his family out of the city too. But the disease hadn't spread into the wealthier districts. Of course, Shanahan had heard no word from Enya. He was still searching for his wayward daughter, but so far, every clue had led to a dead end.

As Riley turned the corner onto Lafayette Avenue on the outskirts of town, Finola sat forward, her gloved hands gripping the seat near his thigh under the heavy woolen blanket spread across her lap and across the foot warmer he'd situated by her boots.

He wanted to reach down and hold her hand. Did he dare slip his arm around her and pull her into the crook of his body?

He'd put off any blatant advances, not wanting to scare her. He'd been patient, giving her the chance to become comfortable with him, giving them both the opportunity to get to know one another. But maybe it was time to stop being so cautious now that she didn't seem to be fighting against the match anymore.

As the park came into view ahead, he slowed the gig. The assortment of maples, locusts, birch, and other trees were gray and bare, but he could pretend they weren't still in the busy, dirty city and were instead in an oasis, where the appetite of progress hadn't yet devoured the natural beauty.

He maneuvered the gig into the line of other parked vehicles. Then he motioned toward several lads, and one of them bounded over, eager to earn a few pennies for tending to the horse and watching over the gig.

A moment later, Riley was leading Finola along a path to the pond, a bag slung over his shoulder. As the trees thinned and the frozen water came into view, she halted and her eyes brightened. "Ice-skating?"

"After working hard all week, we deserve an afternoon of fun, don't we?" He stood beside her, watching her take in the dozen or more skaters sliding around on the ice.

Her breath came out frozen and white, and for the first time since he'd met her, she gave him a full smile.

His heart nearly stopped beating at the sight of it. He wanted to forget all about ice-skating and stare at her the rest of the afternoon. But she didn't give him the chance. She grabbed his arm and hurried him to the edge of the pond.

At her excitement, he was relieved Zaira had been honest with him when he'd asked her to tell him some of Finola's favorite activities. He could admit he'd been worried that Zaira might be working for Finola the same as Madigan to provide Riley with a false list.

It didn't take long for them to put on the skates he'd tucked away in the bag, and soon they were racing around the pond, dodging other couples as well as children eager to take advantage of the frozen waterway.

Finola's cheeks and nose quickly turned rosy. Her eyes sparkled, and she was more animated than he'd ever seen her, as if she'd left behind a burden on the shore and was floating free.

"I haven't been ice-skating yet this winter." She shuffled along expertly beside him.

He wasn't half bad himself, although he hadn't put on skates in a long time. Not since Helen.

"And mostly we skate at places closer to home," she continued. "I think I've only been out here a time or two when I was very young."

"It doesn't freeze quite as well as the smaller ponds." Ahead, the deeper western part was blocked off with several posts and signs that said *Keep Off*.

She'd tossed back her hood, and the soft afternoon light fell across her hair, bringing the red strands to life. The hint of her smile still lingered, especially in her eyes.

"You should smile more often." He'd slowed his speed to match hers.

Her expression turned grave once again, and she peered ahead with a somberness and seriousness he'd noted often in her countenance since meeting her.

What had happened to bring her sorrow? There was still so much about her he wanted to know. "Will you tell me why you so rarely smile?"

She picked up her pace, moving ahead of him.

Before she could get too far, he reached for her hand, only intending to keep her from getting away. But as soon as his gloved hand wrapped around her mittened one, he tightened the hold, deciding he didn't want to let go.

She attempted to tug her hand free, but he gripped her more firmly and pressed his shoulder against hers.

"Let me guess," he said, as unwilling to let the topic go as he was her hand. "You were jilted by your first love, and ever since, you've resented men."

She released a scoffing sound. "Of course not."

"Then you haven't ever been in love?" He held his breath as he waited for her answer, not quite sure why he cared.

"Riley Rafferty, 'tis none of your business. But if you must know, then no, I've never fancied myself to be in love with any man."

"Good."

She focused on the ice and the path they were taking. But the hint of a smile was back in her expression. The hint was enough for now. But someday soon, he wanted all of her and all of her smile. He just hoped she'd be willing to give it.

They skated for a while before he led her to a bench and retrieved two mugs and a jug from his bag. The apple cider had been hot when they'd left her house and was now lukewarm, but her expression seemed contented as they sipped and talked.

When the cold forced them up and into action, they skated again, this time for warmth. As he reached for her hand, she darted forward, not giving him the chance to capture it.

A pang of disappointment shot through his chest, until she glanced at him over her shoulder. Her gaze challenged him—almost dared him—to try to catch her.

His pulse raced forward before he could make his feet do so. She wasn't rejecting him. She was flirting with him, wasn't she?

He gave her a few more strides to gain a lead before starting after her.

She peeked at him before increasing her speed.

At the chase, a thrill wound through him. Was that why Bellamy had paired him with her? Had the matchmaker known he'd relish the pursuit?

His longer legs easily began to close the distance.

The breeze twisted loose strands of her hair and turned her cheeks even rosier. She wasn't smiling, but her expression contained pleasure, even happiness.

His own happiness swelled. He could get used to spending his life chasing after her and winning her anew each day.

"I took you for a fast skater." She threw the playful taunt at him.

156

"I can catch you if I want to." He tossed a taunt back.

She shook her head and tried to accelerate. But she was already going as fast as she could.

In several easy moves, he slid behind her and wrapped his arms around her waist. She held herself stiffly for only an instant before relaxing.

Slowing to a crawl and careful to keep their skates from tangling, he drew back her against his chest. They'd reached a secluded spot without many skaters, and suddenly all he could think about was having more of her.

Without further thought, he bent into the span of her neck showing above the cloak where her scarf had fallen away. He brushed his nose there, breathing in her unique floral scent.

At the graze, her hands slipped over his. He half-expected her to try to pry herself free, but she pulled his arms tighter, as if she didn't want him to let go.

Her acquiescence chased away the voice of caution. Without a second thought, he pressed his lips behind her ear. The scent, the satin, the softness—she was as addictive as she had been from the moment he'd met her.

She angled her head, clearly giving him permission to kiss her again.

He intended to take it. This time, he grazed her neck lower, brushing his nose first before letting himself taste her skin.

At his light kiss, she inhaled sharply.

The sound of her pleasure unleashed the need he'd been holding back, and it coursed in hot waves through his veins. He'd never experienced such intensity before, and it left him breathless. It was almost as if every other woman he'd been with, including Helen, had been a counterfeit to Finola.

He wished he could go on kissing her. The very thought sent his heart into a weightless fall of its own, one he didn't want to fight, but one he needed to if he needed any hope of respecting her chastity until after they were married.

As if sensing the direction of his desire, she squirmed and broke free. Though he wanted to speed after her again and kiss her lips and never come up for air, he forced himself to wait, trying to cool off.

From the moment he'd rescued Finola Shanahan that day in the mud, it was almost as if she'd taken his heart captive. And now it was hers.

He didn't want it back. But he wanted hers in return. He could only pray she was getting closer to giving it to him.

18

*F*inola gripped the seat of the park bench to keep from bending closer to Riley as he knelt in front of her and unlaced her skate. The magnetism of his presence, one glance at his handsome profile, even the pressure of his fingers through her skate shifted the air in her lungs, making each breath feel heavy.

She'd been aware of him all throughout their skating expedition, from the ride to the pond to their drinking of the apple cider and everything in between. But somehow, since the moment he'd chased her and wrapped his arms around her from behind, she'd been intensely attuned to him and his every move.

They'd only skated for a little while after that. He hadn't touched her or made a move to kiss her again, but the air had remained charged with something she couldn't begin to name. Attraction? Desire? Need?

The very remembrance of his lips caressing her neck sent a pleasurable shudder through her.

"I kept you out too long." His voice was tinged with worry. He obviously thought her shudder was from the cold and didn't realize it was one of desire. For him.

"I'm fine." Was she fine, though? Because the more time she spent with him, the more she wanted to forget all about her vow and the need to stay away from having a husband and children so that she didn't hurt anyone else.

He tugged off the first skate and then began unlacing the second.

She shouldn't have gone skating with him, should have told him she needed a day to rest at home. But when he'd suggested taking a ride in his new gig, she hadn't been able to say no. Riley Rafferty was one persuasive man, and his charm difficult to resist.

Besides, her da had asked her to take the outing, and with how haggard he'd become since Enya's disappearance, she wanted to make him happy instead of causing him more grief.

Which was why she was still avoiding putting an end to the match with Riley. But she had to soon. Not only was Shrove Tuesday drawing ever nearer, but she wasn't being fair to Riley. Although today was the first time he'd initiated physical contact with her, she'd sensed his interest and his attraction every single day, and she couldn't drag out their relationship any longer.

She had to put distance back between them for the rest of their time together. She drew in a breath and then forced formality to her tone. "Thank you for taking me skating."

"I'm glad we could go." His fingers on her laces stalled, and shadows fell over his features. "It's been a few years since I've gone."

Why had it been a few years, and why did the remembrance of past skating make him sad? Her thoughts whirred for an answer and landed on only one. "You came skating here with your wife, didn't you?" Her question came out tentative, and she prayed she wasn't overstepping herself by bringing up such a tender topic.

He picked at a knot in her laces. "I proposed marriage to her here."

"It must be hard to be back since it holds special memories." Her resolution from only moments ago to keep her distance from Riley evaporated all too easily. She couldn't ignore him while he was being vulnerable in sharing something about his wife, could she?

"She told me no."

"What? She did?"

"I got down on one knee in the middle of the pond and asked her to be my wife. She skated away without a word."

Apparently, the place held only painful memories. "I'm sorry for asking, Riley."

"She wasn't as enthusiastic about marriage as I was." Although he tried for a note of humor, the pain was still there nonetheless.

Finola couldn't remember ever seeing Helen with Riley. In fact, she couldn't picture Helen at all. Maybe she'd never met the woman. What had she been like?

"Obviously, I didn't take no for an answer." He stared back toward the pond. "I spent the rest of the time while we skated trying to convince her of all the reasons why we should get married. A week later, she finally agreed."

"She loved you enough to marry you in spite of her reservations?"

"No. She discovered she was with child."

"Oh my." Finola flushed at the implications.

Riley bowed his head. "I'm not proud of what happened, and I think the guilt is probably what drove me to propose. Even so, I shouldn't have pushed her into the marriage."

Riley had shared intimacies with another woman. A woman who had become his wife. The idea of him kissing and touching anyone else sent a twinge of protest through her. "Did you love her?" As soon as the question was out, she shook her head. "Of course you did. And 'tis none of my business, to be sure."

His felt hat was tipped sideways, and she had the urge to straighten it. More than that, she wanted to take it off and drag her fingers through his hair.

As soon as the urge flitted through her head, she clasped her hands together tightly to keep from doing something so impulsive . . . and possessive.

Finally he lifted his head and let her see the tragedy in the depths of his eyes. "I thought I loved her," he whispered. "But after we were married, I could see my selfishness for what it was. If I'd truly cared about her, I wouldn't have pressured her so much, would have considered her needs and not just my own."

Finola guessed he was referring to the physical intimacy in his first marriage. Yes, indeed, he was an experienced man, but he hadn't taken advantage of her, had been quite respectful. Even today, he could have easily turned their passionate moment on the pond into something more. He could have twisted her around and kissed her more ardently. She most likely wouldn't have resisted if he had.

As if reading her mind, his attention dropped to her mouth. Blatant desire darkened his eyes. She wanted to let him kiss her again. God alone knew how much she did. But she couldn't. She'd just chastised herself to be fair to Riley and not to give him false hope.

He swallowed hard and then tore his gaze away, finally unlacing the knot on her skate as if he couldn't make his fingers work fast enough.

Had he read her hesitancy? Or was he attempting to respect her chastity in a way he hadn't done with Helen?

Whatever the case, the moment was too intense.

Doing her best to ignore the ripple of tension that seemed

to be tugging her to lose herself in him, she slipped her feet into her boots.

At a loud cracking and popping behind them followed by screaming, Riley was up and on his feet in an instant. Still wearing his skates, he spun, and before Finola could even assess what the problem was, he sprinted across the ice toward the direction of the *Keep Off* sign.

On the other side of the blocked-off portion of the pond, a boy had fallen through the ice. His head was visible above the surface of the water. He was trying to grab on to the edge of the ice and pull himself up, but with each heft, he broke away more ice and floundered in the water.

A group of three other boys stood a short distance away, having crossed the barrier too. They were staring at their friend and then down at the ice beneath them, their faces filled with fear. How long before it cracked under them?

Riley called out to the boys, "One at a time, inch back toward the shore!"

The boys hesitated and looked at their friend who was pale and frozen, his movements growing more desperate as he struggled to stay above water.

"I'll go after him," Riley shouted. "You just get off the ice."

"No." The word slipped out before Finola could control her reaction, and she cupped a hand over her mouth to keep from protesting further. Even so, more objection welled up so swiftly she thought she might be sick to her stomach.

She couldn't let Riley skate onto the dangerous ice. He was heavier than the children. He'd break the weak layer for certain.

But how could he do anything less than attempt to rescue the drowning lad? Nothing would stop him. He was brave and strong, and it would do no good to try to convince him otherwise.

Other skaters were now congregating along the edge of the

blocked-off area, calling out suggestions for ways to save the boy without causing more harm to anyone.

Surely with all of them working together, Riley wouldn't have to do it alone and put himself into so much danger.

But instead of stopping and consulting with the others, Riley grabbed the rope barrier along with the sign and dragged it with him toward the boy, all the while unraveling the rope from the post.

Finola's chest seized, and she couldn't breathe. What was he doing? Why wasn't he taking the offers of help? Or at the very least, moving forward with more caution?

At a dozen paces from the boy, the ice began to crack beneath Riley's skates, and he finally slowed. Without a moment of hesitation, he tossed the rope. It landed directly in front of the boy, splashing in the water.

"Grab on," Riley called, his voice as calm as though he were giving instructions to one of his campaign workers.

The boy, his face frozen with terror, fumbled with the rope for a moment but latched on.

Riley lowered himself to his knees and began to haul against the rope, tugging the boy up out of the water. But the lad lost his grip and plunged back into the pond, spluttering and coughing. His hands, though mittened, were likely frozen and unable to cooperate.

Again, without any indecision, Riley flattened himself onto his belly and crept forward.

Finola wanted to close her eyes and block out the unfolding disaster, but she could only stare with growing horror.

"Hold up your arm!" Riley called to the boy as he neared the water.

Before the boy could do as instructed, the ice cracked all around Riley, and he disappeared beneath the surface. The momentum of the crashing ice took the boy down too.

More shouts rang out from those along the edge of the danger area. Finola was too frightened to release the scream building in her chest or to utter the briefest of prayers, not even a Hail Mary.

Another man began to creep cautiously out toward Riley and the boy. But before he could get far, Riley's head popped above the water, his hat gone. He hoisted the boy in one arm and swam toward the edge of the ice with the other, angling toward a patch that didn't appear to have any cracks.

As he reached the solid area, he spoke to the boy. Finola couldn't make out Riley's words, but the lad nodded, and in the next instant Riley was thrusting him up and out of the water onto the ice.

"Now roll," Riley called.

The boy was sluggish but managed to roll several feet.

"Again." Riley was grasping the ice with both hands, his skin ashen, his wet hair now dark and flattened to his head.

The boy managed to move a few more feet.

"One more time." Icy water dribbled down Riley's face, his attention focused on the boy.

Everyone had stopped to watch, and this time the boy made it far enough away from open water that one of the other men stretched out, grabbed him, and pulled him to safety.

As soon as the boy was well away from the gaping hole, Riley wiggled his way up onto the ice and was only halfway out of the water when it broke again. He slipped back under and didn't come up as quickly this time. When he surfaced, he seemed slower, weaker.

He was starting to freeze to death. It wouldn't be long before his body shut down, and he lost the ability to save himself.

Riley began to swim toward the rim of the ice again.

Someone else had to venture out and rescue him. As if coming to the same conclusion, several men started toward him.

"No," Riley called. "Don't come any closer."

The men halted and exchanged glances. Did they intend to listen to Riley's foolishness and let him die?

Well, they might, but she wouldn't.

Finola's boots weren't laced, but she stepped onto the pond and started toward Riley. Without her skates, her feet slipped and slid, but she raced as fast as she could, her heart thundering like a dozen racehorses.

She might not have the strength to haul him out of the water. And she might very well fall through, cracking ice for herself. But she couldn't stand back and watch him drown, no matter what he said.

Swallowing the fear—and taste of bile—rising in her throat, she shouted out, "I'll go! I'm lightweight and can make it."

At the sound of her call, Riley shook his head. "Don't let her come out here. Please!" The desperation in Riley's tone made her pause but a moment before pushing onward.

She sidestepped several men and crossed over onto the thinning ice.

"Finola Shanahan, you stop now. Do you hear me?" Riley roared, his eyes widening with terror. In all his rescues, she'd never once witnessed his terror. She guessed he was only wanting to protect her from danger, was afraid of something happening to her.

Even so, she couldn't cower away from trying to help him. As she took another tentative step, he growled and hefted himself out of the water. As the ice crumbled around him again, he threw himself away from the edge and toward the shore, scrambling to stay one step ahead of the disappearing solidness beneath his body.

Finally, the cracking stopped. Riley glanced at the ice around him as though to make certain he'd arrived on solid ground. With his garments and coat dripping and his skates soaked through, he likely weighed twice as much or even triple what he normally did. But he slogged forward, this time making a direct line toward Finola, the scowl still in place, his eyes as dark as a starless night.

With shaking legs, she took several steps back, retreating into the safe area of the pond. As he reached her and was finally well away from the danger, she collapsed to her knees, then bent over and retched onto the ice.

19

*E*ven though Finola wasn't the one who'd gotten wet, she couldn't stop shivering no matter how hard she tried.

"Add more coal to the fire," Riley instructed one of his apprentices. Then with a frown creasing his forehead, he wrapped another blanket around her.

"You need it more than I do." From her spot on the workbench in front of the forge, she tried to wiggle out of it and hand it back to Riley, but he draped it over her shoulders again.

"I'm fine now, Finola." Gently, he tucked the blanket around her tighter. "I'm dry and changed and plenty warm."

Finola nodded but shuddered again, especially as she relived the drive back from the pond to the wagon shop, with Riley's body shaking and his teeth chattering the whole way. She'd never prayed harder and was relieved the gig could go fast.

Big Jim must have heard their frantic pace, and he'd met them out front. He'd whisked Riley up to his apartment above the workshop and helped divest him of his wet garments and don warm clothing.

Now Big Jim was sitting nearby at another bench, tapping

a piece of metal into an arched shape. She'd seen him the previous time she'd been in the wagon shop. He was taller than most men—or would have been if he'd straightened to his full height. Instead, his shoulders were always stooped so that his head hung low.

A couple of apprentices lingered in the workshop, trying to be useful. They also lived in the rooms upstairs, and Riley had sent them down to give her blankets and tend the fires while he changed.

By the time Riley had returned to the workshop, her body was no longer cold. The trouble was that her heart was still icy, and she wasn't sure it would thaw.

As he stood in front of her, she examined him, needing to reassure herself, as she had already several times, that he was alive and unharmed. His hair was damp, but it was combed away from his forehead. His skin was paler than usual, but the ruddiness of his sun-browned face was returning.

"You're sure your fingers and toes will survive?" Her gaze shifted to his big hands.

He wiggled his fingers. "Look, there's nothing to worry about."

She released a taut breath, but it ended on another shiver.

Riley's brow furrowed before he nodded at Big Jim. "Would you mind giving us a few minutes alone?"

Big Jim paused in the tapping and smoothed a hand over the metal arch. "You think that's a good idea?"

"I'm a different man than I was three years ago."

"But you're still a man, ain't you?"

At the nature of the conversation, mortification pushed Finola up to her feet. After all that Riley had revealed about Helen, she knew exactly what Big Jim was referring to. "Please don't trouble yourself with leaving." She addressed Big Jim. "I need to be on my way home anyway."

Riley held out a hand as though to stop her. "No, not yet—"

"I'll walk." She didn't want to impose on Riley for a ride, not after the ordeal he'd just gone through. And it was getting too late now to work in the campaign office, not that he'd been eager to have her there after their disagreement over the slavery issue.

"Of course you'll not be walking this late, especially by yourself." Riley dropped onto the bench, tugged on her arm, making her lose her balance so she toppled onto his lap. "I'll be the one taking you after you spend a few more minutes warming yourself."

She tried to hop up and off his lap, but he snaked an arm around her waist and pinned her in place.

"Riley Rafferty." She pushed against his chest, but at the ridge of muscles flexing beneath her hand, she paused. "Whatever are you doing?"

Riley shot Big Jim a narrowed look. "Since my friend insists on staying to be my chaperone, I figure I might as well take full advantage of the situation."

The very idea that she was touching and sitting in so provocative a position sent more heat to her limbs. The graze of his fingers at her hip, the nearness of his mouth to her neck, the warm invitation in his eyes. Big Jim didn't only have to worry about Riley needing a chaperone. She clearly had wayward thoughts and needed one too.

Her face was much too close to Riley's, near enough to see the thick stubble that had formed over his face and jaw. Her fingers itched to brush over it, feel the scratchiness, and remind herself that he was alive. He was here.

But he'd almost died. . . .

"I need to go, Riley," she whispered, torn with the desire to remain with him but also unable to deny the urgency that had been building since she'd watched him nearly die—the urgency to get away and never see him again.

What was becoming clear was that she'd started to care

about him too much, so much that the prospect of losing him had nearly devastated her out there on the pond. If she cared about him this much now, after knowing him for such a short time, her feelings would only grow the longer she was with him.

She wouldn't be able to survive day after day watching him push himself to the brink of death, waking up every morning and wondering if the day would be his last.

She already knew how quickly life could end, in a blink, without any way to bring that life back. She'd experienced that with Ava, and she couldn't go through it again. That's exactly why the convent was the right place for her. It was a safe place and would give her a safe future.

Riley was the complete opposite of that.

He didn't make any effort to release her, his brow furrowing deeper. Did he sense her hesitation? Was he afraid that if he let her go, she'd retreat from him forever?

Doing so would be best for both of them.

"Please, let's not drag this out." She forced herself to speak the words.

His intense gaze took her in a moment longer, then he expelled a taut breath, his shoulders slumping. "I'm giving you a ride."

"That's not necessary. . . ."

But he was already setting her down and heading for the door. The gig was still parked outside where he'd left it. As he settled her into the seat, his expression remained grave. But he didn't say anything until they were on their way. "It's more than just the cold bothering you, isn't it?"

"Aye." The evening darkness was broken by the few street lanterns that had already been lit, but she wanted to stay hidden in the shadows.

"You're upset about the danger on the ice. About me falling in."

"Of course I am. It was a dangerous stunt, and you almost drowned."

"But I didn't."

"It was close."

"And yet, here I am."

"Don't be daft, Riley. You can't keep wrestling with death and hope to escape its clutches forever."

"Someone needs to be a hero."

"It doesn't always have to be you."

He shrugged.

She wasn't being rational about the matter. Of course, like all his other rescues, she didn't expect him to stand back, do nothing, and watch someone die. But why did he have to rush in time after time so recklessly? Almost as if he didn't really value his life.

Whatever the case, she had to cut him out of her life now. Tonight. If she let their relationship continue, it would get harder, and she'd hurt him even more.

If only she'd stuck with her plan to alienate him sooner like she had with the other suitors instead of spending so much time with him.

He didn't know it, but he'd given her the perfect way to send him running. He'd all but admitted he didn't want to have the same kind of marriage he'd had with Helen, that this time he wanted a willing wife.

Once he knew she wasn't willing, he'd realize they weren't meant to be together.

A part of her resisted saying anything, but she forced herself to say the words that would end her match with Riley. "You told me earlier that you regret your selfishness with Helen and for pushing her too far, especially into marriage."

He shot her a questioning glance. "I meant what I told Big Jim. I'm a changed man. And I'm trying not to pressure you."

"Aye, I have no doubt you're a changed man."

"I haven't kissed you again, even though I've wanted to."

His admission sent pleasure dancing across her skin. Even so, she absolutely could not admit she'd thought about kissing him again too. That would destroy her argument, one she needed to be solid.

"Even without, um—kissing—there's still pressure."

He glanced around to the businesses they were passing, many of the window fronts lit, people still loitering on the plank walkway. Then he leaned in and lowered his voice. "I'm using every ounce of self-control I have to keep my hands and thoughts in line. But I'm not perfect, Finola, especially because you're a desirable woman."

If he kept saying things like that, he would crack through the last of her resistance. She had to take control of the conversation, or they'd arrive at her home, and she'd be out of time to tell him the truth.

The truth. It would set her free from him. She knew it would.

But that meant she had to gather the courage to tell him about her aspirations to join the convent and why it was important to her. He'd already proven to be a good listener. But would he listen to this? Especially when her parents hadn't?

She had to try. It was her last hope of gaining the life she wanted.

"When I was growing up, I went to a private school for girls run by the Sisters of Charity." A lump crowded into her throat, threatening to clog her airway. She swallowed it and forced out the words she needed to say. "I loved it, and the Sisters loved me, and I dreamed of one day growing up and living with them there."

"As a nun?"

"Aye. But Mam needed my help to watch the younger children. So I stopped going to school and stayed home."

"Did you miss school?"

No one had ever asked her that before. Everyone had just assumed she'd do her duty as the oldest daughter and assist her mam with the young ones. During those weeks after she'd given up school, how had she felt? "I think mostly I missed the encouragement of the nuns. But I didn't miss it too keenly because I was so busy. Then Ava was born and became my world."

Finola had fed and changed and soothed the baby. She'd rocked her to sleep. She'd even gotten up at night with her. She'd never loved anyone more than she'd loved Ava.

As though sensing the tragic nature of the tale, Riley reached across the seat and took her hand. She needed to pull away, but the reassurance and comfort in his touch gave her the courage to keep going.

"Ava died not long after her first birthday."

Riley's fingers squeezed hers. "Let me guess. You blame yourself for the death?"

A familiar chill crept through her. The image of her baby sister's smiling chubby face with her blond-red curls flashed into the forefront of her memory. Finola could even picture kissing Ava's sweet cheek before setting her down on the floor that day in the upstairs nursery after changing the little girl's nappy.

"Be an angel," Finola had crooned as she picked up the tangled doily and her needle. "And play nicely." She'd been working at pulling out stitches all morning, and somehow the fine white thread had gotten twisted. She only needed a few more moments to unravel the tangles.

Through the open window, she could hear Mam and the other little ones outside in the yard. And Enya was playing the piano in the front parlor.

Finola let her gaze dart to Ava, who had crawled over to her basket of toys and begun to empty them all one by one.

174

Ava spoke a few words of gibberish, then sat back and clapped her hands.

Finola smiled at the sweet baby and earned a happy smile, one that showed all her gums and the couple of front teeth that had come in already.

"You're my wee angel, that you are." Finola returned her attention to her stitching. The delicate threads were tangled worse than she'd realized. And one section was knotted particularly tight. She prodded and poked at it, twisting the needle in, wiggling it, loosening the knot. If she didn't disentangle it, she'd have to snip the thread. She'd had to do that before, but then she'd have loose threads to worry about tucking away.

After long moments of trying, the thread finally came free, but then another knot formed, and she started to work on that one.

At Ava's babbling, Finola pricked her finger with the needle and glanced up. "What's wrong, my wee one?"

The basket of toys was empty, and the spot Ava had been sitting in was empty too.

Finola scanned the nursery but saw no sign of the baby. But the door leading into the hallway was open. . . .

"Ava?" Finola dropped the doily and sprang forward. Her heart lurched too.

At one year of age, Ava had just started crawling, and Mam had said to be careful not to let the baby out of her sight, had warned of all the dangers that an infant could get into. And now those dangers flashed through Finola's mind as she raced into the hallway.

Where had the baby gone?

As Finola glanced around frantically, she caught sight of Ava at the top of the long marble stairway that led down to the front entryway.

"Ava, angel. Stop!" Finola's cry echoed in the hallway. But

she was too late. Ava disappeared over the edge. A frightened wail was followed by endless thumping.

And then silence . . . ghastly silence.

Finola ran to the edge of the stairway and then down the stairs, desperate to get to the baby. Ava lay on her back, staring up at the chandelier with unseeing eyes, her neck twisted at an odd angle.

Finola hadn't realized she was screaming until her mam burst through the front door. Mam took in the scene in one glance and rushed to the baby. She fell to her knees and pressed trembling hands to the baby's mouth and chest.

"Holy Mary, have mercy." Mam's eyes filled with tears. "Finola, what have you done?"

"Finola, what have you done?" Those words echoed in Finola's head again as they had many times over the years since Ava's death.

Riley was waiting for her explanation. And he deserved it.

"I blame myself because I *am* to blame. I was supposed to be watching my sister at all times. But I got distracted, and when I next turned around, she was gone." Finola sat tensely, waiting for him to pull away, for disgust to flash across his face, or for his muscles to stiffen.

But he did none of those things. He lifted a hand to her chin, forcing her head around so that she was looking at him. His eyes were dark and serious. "It sounds like an accident."

Everyone had told her Ava's death had been just an accident, that the curious baby could have taken a tumble down the steps even if Mam had been the one watching her. But Finola knew better. Mam wouldn't have turned her back on the baby. Mam would have noticed Ava crawling out of the room sooner. Mam would have reached her in time.

Finola shook her head, sliding away from Riley's gentle touch and slipping her hand from his. "I'll always hold myself responsible for her death. I'll never forget about it and never forgive myself."

"Finola, sweet love." His voice was soft, beckoning, even pleading.

She stared down at her lap, couldn't afford to see anything in his eyes that might dissuade her from doing what she needed to. With a deep breath, she pushed onward with the words that would cut him out of her life. "I always knew I wanted to go into service, become a Sister of Charity. But after Ava died, I vowed that I would."

Silence settled between them, and it was only then that she realized they'd already reached her home, and the gig was now parked in front. The windows were all dark, which was unusual for a winter night. The traffic, too, seemed lighter, as if the world knew the seriousness of the conversation she was having with Riley and had decided to give them privacy.

After a moment, he finally spoke. "I take it your parents don't approve of your vow and your decision to become a nun?"

"They don't know about my vow. And even if they did, they've never believed I should give myself over to the church."

"Of course. Why else would they have pushed twelve—now thirteen—suitors on you if they supported your vow." This time his voice held a note of bitterness, even defeat.

"I wanted them to conclude for themselves that I wasn't suited for marriage and children."

"And if I walk away, you finally have the chance to show them."

"Aye." She'd been more honest with Riley than she had been with anyone else. Her plan to drive him away was working. Why, then, was misery poking at her heart?

He was silent, this time for long minutes. The noises of the evening sifted around them—the distant call of a newsboy, the blast of a late-arriving steamship, the clanking of a carriage passing on a cross street.

She chanced a peek his way to see that his brow was furrowed above troubled eyes. The muscles in his jaw were rigid. His grip on the reins was tight.

"Please say something," she whispered, unable to keep the despair from her voice.

He stared straight ahead. "After meeting me, after what we've shared, can you honestly tell me you still want to become a nun?"

Could she? She couldn't deny how much she cared about Riley. Their feelings had formed so quickly. The intensity of their connection had taken her by surprise. And her attraction to him was embarrassingly strong.

But she'd put all her energy into keeping men at arm's length for so long that she didn't know any other way. Even if the breakup hurt Riley in the short term, he'd soon get over her. The matchmaker could find him another woman, one who wasn't riddled with ghosts of past mistakes.

Besides, Riley deserved a woman who would love every aspect of him, even the part that was reckless and dangerous. He needed a woman who wouldn't cringe in fear of death every time he made one of his rescues but would instead encourage him to be the hero he was born to be.

And the biggest reason of all? Riley should have a woman who would be willing to give him a family of his own. "I don't want to have any babies, Riley. After what happened, I wouldn't be a good mother—"

"That's not true."

"I'd never be able to let my child out of my sight and would worry constantly—"

"Sometimes tragedies happen, but they don't have to determine the course of our lives." Even as he spoke, his words lacked the conviction and passion of a man who believed what he was saying.

She'd already learned over recent years that the only way

to find peace was by making reparation for her sin. Service. Prayer. Solitude. And now, in denying herself this relationship with Riley, maybe God would know that she was truly sorry. Maybe one day Ava would know it and forgive her from heaven.

Riley lapsed into a silence so heavy and thick, it weighed upon her, crushing her, until she could hardly breathe. Finally, he lowered his head. "I'm tempted to pressure you to change your mind. I want to argue with you and force you to see reason."

Like he'd done with Helen. Even though he didn't say the words, they lingered in the air between them anyway.

"But I won't do it."

Her throat tightened. Should she tell him to fight for her? That she needed his rescuing, but this time from herself?

She bit her lip to keep from speaking. She couldn't offer him any hope when she had none.

"So this is it?" His voice was raw with anguish. "We agree to part ways?"

She nodded.

"Then say it, Finola." In the darkness of the evening, his handsome face was taut and his eyes nearly black.

"Say what?"

"That you don't care for me and don't want to be with me. If you say it, I'll walk away and never bother you again."

Tears sprang to her eyes, and she rapidly blinked them back. She couldn't let him think she had regrets even though she did.

"Say it," he demanded harshly.

A sob pushed up, and she fought for a breath. Then she forced out the final words, the ones that would make him leave her and sever all connections. "I don't care for you and don't want to be with you."

She didn't wait for him to reply. Instead, she climbed out of the gig and practically ran across the flagstone path to the front door, unable to keep the tears from rolling down her cheeks any longer.

She didn't look back at him, didn't want him to see her crying, didn't want to see the pain etched in his expression and know that she'd put it there.

As she reached for the front door handle, Winston swung it wide and stepped aside for her to enter, obviously having been watching her interaction with Riley, perhaps tasked by Da or Kiernan to report to them with details.

Tonight there would be no tales of stolen kisses or shared intimacy or even flirty conversations. No, the only tales to report were of sadness. And if Winston didn't know it yet, he would from the tears streaking her face.

As he moved to close the door, she almost reached out to stop him, had the urge to rush back outside and tell Riley she'd made a mistake. But the servant seemed in a hurry. As he turned to her, only then did she notice the absolute stillness and silence of the house.

"There is a case of cholera in the neighborhood." Winston spoke gravely. "And your father has taken the rest of the family and staff away, out of the city to the country house to escape the disease."

Finola's knees shook, not from the news of the cholera spreading. As bad as that was, all she could think about was Riley riding away and never returning.

"Your father waited as long as he could for you to come home." The servant glanced out the half-moon glass at the top of the door, likely watching Riley's departure. "He would like you to pack your bags and be ready to leave first thing tomorrow morning."

She swiped at the tears on her cheeks, but more fell to replace them. She couldn't leave the city. Couldn't leave Riley.

But that's exactly what she'd done already.

Before she could throw open the door and chase after him,

she forced her way toward the stairway and raced up them as fast as her feet could carry her. She barely reached her bedroom before the sobs escaped. As she flung herself across the bed, she released the torrent. She'd not only broken his heart. She'd broken hers too.

20

*R*iley pushed his way through the crowded pub, his eyes on only one man. Bellamy McKenna. He didn't greet anyone else and didn't even stop to acknowledge the slaps of congratulations for rescuing the lad who'd fallen through the ice.

"Bellamy!" he bellowed above the racket.

The swarthy-skinned, dark-haired man was behind the bar counter in his usual spot, pouring drinks and making sure the establishment ran smoothly while Oscar sat at his back table surrounded on all sides by men waiting to talk to him, not only about making matches but also for advice. Those in any kind of trouble sought him out for his words of wisdom.

Riley crammed a hand into his hair. Should he seek out Oscar first for advice on how to handle Finola's rejection? Maybe the fellow would be able to tell him how to stop his chest from feeling like it had been ripped out by a bear and clawed into tiny pieces. His entire body burned. His head pounded. And his throat ached with the need to rage with the storm of emotions ravaging him.

"Bellamy!" he roared louder.

This time the younger matchmaker glanced up and gave him a nod while he finished pouring a shot of Irish whiskey.

Riley shoved through the throng the last few steps to the bar counter, staggering as if he'd already guzzled several pints. The men seated on the stools called out welcomes to him and moved aside good-naturedly, among them old Georgie McGuire with his mostly toothless grin and pale red cowlick sticking on end.

But tonight, Riley couldn't muster any cheer in response. Instead, he pounded a fist on the counter, causing glasses and bottles to rattle. "Bellamy."

Georgie pounded his hand on the counter too. "Bellamy, Saint Riley is calling for you."

Bellamy crossed his arms casually and then quirked one of his brows. "Riley Rafferty, my name hasn't changed in all the three times you've used it since walking in the door. If you be wanting something, just spit it out, why don't you?"

"Yes, I want something!" He thumped his fist again, and this time the patrons grew quiet, clearly sensing his inner turmoil. Either that or he had a face like a bulldog licking pickle juice off a nettle.

He wouldn't be surprised if it was both cases. After waiting outside the Shanahan residence for way longer than he should have, praying that Finola would come to her senses, rush out, and tell him she'd been wrong, he'd swallowed the lump the size of a boiled cabbage in his throat. He'd driven around trying to figure out what to do. But all the while, he'd only grown more agitated and confused and frantic.

By the end of the driving, all he'd been able to think about was that he had to find a way to convince Finola to marry him. But he didn't want to pressure her the way he had with Helen.

Finola's aspiration might be noble. Serving God was good and right and worthy. But she didn't have to become a nun to do it. She could keep on going to the Kerry Patch and aiding the immigrants. And once Riley became mayor, they could work together putting all their plans into place—plans for better garbage disposal, effective sewage system, cleaner streets, safer housing, and more.

Becoming a nun was just an excuse to escape her past. Probably because she was running away from her fears of all that had happened with her little sister. And he needed Bellamy to nip over to her place and tell her exactly that and that she didn't belong in the convent.

"Finola Shanahan doesn't want to marry me." As he spoke the words, the truth of them hit him with the force of a wagon hauling twelve thousand pounds of cargo. She didn't want him. She never had. And she'd made that abundantly clear from the start with all her efforts to ruin their relationship.

Georgie peered up at him, his expression growing somber. "What a cryin' shame."

"I'm staggered, that I am," said another of the patrons.

"Take you care now, Saint Riley," someone else called.

"Oh, aye, naturally she'll be having hesitations." Bellamy cut into the comments as he poured another drink, and the eyes of all the men at the bar swung to the young matchmaker. "But I didn't take you for the kind of man who let a few wee hesitations hold him back."

The men shifted rounded gazes back to Riley.

"Few wee hesitations?" Riley knuckled his eyes to ward off the pain building in his head. "No, Bellamy. She's dumped a whole steamboat full of hesitations on me."

"Is that a fact now?"

"Yes, and I need you to go talk some sense into her. Tonight. Right away."

The men, almost in unison, returned their gazes to Bellamy and waited, watching him expectantly. Bellamy finished corking the whiskey bottle then slid the glass of amber liquid toward Riley.

"Most women don't want the matchmaker coming to do the

dirty work after a row. They want the man himself to show up and make amends."

"We didn't have a row." At least not the way Bellamy was insinuating. "She told me she didn't care about me and didn't want to be with me."

Another round of sympathy erupted among the men at the counter, which rapidly turned into unwanted counsel, Georgie's the loudest of all. "There's no profit in plowing the same furrow twice. Find a new field for sowing your oats."

Bellamy's brow lifted, and his dark eyes seemed to be challenging Riley. But challenging him how? To take the advice and go make amends? Or listen to Georgie and the others and find someone new?

Why did he have to care about women who didn't love him in return? Maybe he was better off cutting ideas of love and marriage out of his life as he had before his dad's heart attack.

His dad certainly wasn't falling off the perch any longer. He was firmly holding on and didn't need his dying wish fulfilled since he wasn't going anywhere anytime soon.

"I'll hang up my hat and call it quits." Riley picked up the glass of whiskey and raised it. "Who needs a woman, anyway?"

His question was met by the men with the quiet of a morgue, and Georgie's wide grin disappeared.

Riley tipped back the glass and sank the whole thing in one swallow. As the liquid burned down his throat to his stomach, bitterness burned a trail right along with it. He could blather until he was blue in the face about not wanting a woman, but the fact was, he wouldn't fool any of these fellows, least of all himself.

After he'd allowed himself to die right alongside Helen, Finola Shanahan had brought him back to life, and there was no denying that. He was more than good and ready for a woman. In fact, he was embarrassed to admit just how good and ready he was.

"Fine." He wiped his sleeve across his mouth. "Fine. I admit. I'm needing a wife."

At his comment, the men nodded, and their comments came swiftly. Again, Georgie piped up the loudest. "Right enough. A bird can't fly with one wing."

Riley shoved his empty glass away. Yes, he longed for sizzling touches and soul-wrenching kisses. But he also wanted deep conversations, fun companionship, and common goals. He wanted someone to live for besides himself. He wanted love and laughter and life. He wanted everything he'd had with Finola.

Could he have that with someone else? He met Bellamy's gaze again. "Can you find me another woman just like Finola?"

Before Bellamy could answer, Georgie nodded his head like a cork bobbing in a barrel. "Daniel Allen is still looking for a match for his daughter. Bets might have the personality of a bag of hammers, but she's as sweet as pudding."

"She's also got big hands," one of the other men commented.

"And strong arms," said another.

Riley wasn't sure what big hands and strong arms had to do with being a good wife, but before he could say anything more, other men in the pub chimed in with suggestions of additional women. And soon he was being guided into a chair at the back table with Oscar, interviewing prospective fathers-in-law.

The din of laughter and coarse joking, the haze of tobacco smoke, and the polishing off of another drink, this one a Guinness, had Riley's head throbbing even more, so much more that the heat of the room became suffocating.

At one point, Riley caught Bellamy's eye across the room. Bellamy's expression lacked the usual mirth, was instead filled with censure, possibly even disappointment.

Riley shrugged. Maybe he was letting Bellamy down. But it was partially Bellamy's fault for guaranteeing Finola was the only one Riley would want and none other. Even if that had been true, clearly Bellamy hadn't counted on Finola not reciprocating.

But if Finola didn't want him, then he'd show her that other women liked him, women he didn't have to work so hard to convince to give him a chance, women who would eagerly marry him, women who would be honored to be with him.

He'd prove to her—and himself—that he was above crawling back to her and groveling at her feet. He wouldn't go to her and draw her into his arms and kiss away the furrow in her brow and get her to change her mind.

He was done with her. And that was all there was to it.

Releasing a tight breath, Riley tried to give his attention to the next big fellow, Daniel Allen, who'd apparently rushed to the pub the moment he'd gotten word that Saint Riley was back on the bidding block.

But Riley could hardly focus on the details of the dowry Daniel was promising to give him with Bets. Oscar seemed to think Daniel's offer was the best yet. As the two men finagled over the dowry, their voices rose until Riley's head felt like it was being beaten by an anvil.

His chest ached, and his body was suddenly exhausted. The events of the day were finally catching up to him so that all he wanted to do was drop into bed and sleep.

"What do you say, Riley Rafferty?" As Oscar started to chug his pint of stout, his bloodshot eyes above his purplish nose watched Riley expectantly.

Riley was past ready to be done with the matchmaking for the night. "I'll think on it."

"Then tomorrow night, you'll go meet Bets. When you're done, you stop by the pub." Oscar slapped the thick leather book in front of him. "After that, I'll sign your name with the match in my ledger and make it official."

Daniel beamed at Riley. "Bets will be thrilled."

Riley only felt dead rotten inside, but he nodded anyway.

Oscar set his glass down forcefully before sitting back in his chair. "Don't think on it too hard, Riley. I always say: You young people can't be too finicky. Marriage will take work whether it's one woman or another."

Riley had the sudden urge to stand up and shout out his protest. But he swallowed the words. He had to do this. It would keep him from going back to Finola.

Even so, what was he doing? Why was he considering a union to Bets Allen when the only woman he wanted was a petite beauty with the prettiest brown hair, the brightest blue eyes, and an adorable dimple in her chin. And her freckles. He could lose himself in those freckles.

She was the sassiest woman he'd ever met, didn't care about impressing him, and he loved that about her. But she was also the sweetest person he knew, genuinely caring about people with no consideration to herself.

Had he just made a mistake in giving hope to Daniel Allen and Bets that he could be a match?

His gut began to toss and turn, and he had the sudden feeling he was about to be sick.

As the bile began to rise at the back of his throat, he shoved his way through the men. Swallowing hard, he stumbled toward the rear door, past Bellamy's sister Jenny and her husband, who ran the kitchen. Riley managed to hold it inside until he stumbled out into the alley. Once there, he hunched over and vomited until he'd emptied the contents of his stomach.

Resting his hands on his knees, he remained bent, a wave of dizziness assaulting him again. A cold breeze blew against his face, but it couldn't take away the heat radiating from his skin. Or the rolling in his stomach.

The nausea rose again swiftly, and he retched into the half-frozen mud.

He'd only had a couple of drinks, not enough to make him sick. Maybe this rejection from Finola was getting to him more than he wanted to admit. Because that's what it was. Rejection. He'd tried to win her over, had thought he was making progress, thought she was beginning to trust him and envision what life could be like with him.

But neither his efforts nor his affection had been enough. Maybe he'd moved too quickly, been overly intense with his ardor. Maybe he should have been more patient with her. Maybe he shouldn't have pushed her to admit she cared for him.

Bother it. What in the blazes had he done?

With a groan, he spit out the bitterness of the bile on his tongue. When he'd started out today with her in the gig, he'd been so full of hope. This wasn't how he'd pictured he'd end the day. A broken man in a back alley.

Another spasm started to twist his innards. He had nothing left to expel, but he retched again anyway, this one so violent, he nearly collapsed.

A hand on his shoulder steadied him.

He pulled in a deep breath and pushed himself up, not wanting anyone to see him in his desperate state.

Bellamy stood beside him, gripping his arm. "What's going on here, Riley?" As several other men started to approach, Bellamy waved them away.

Riley closed his eyes. "I love her, Bellamy."

"I know." Bellamy's answer was gentle.

Riley waited for the matchmaker to rebuke him for refusing to trust him and giving up on Finola and turning to Oscar. But Bellamy only squeezed his arm.

"I've never loved another woman the same way I love her." Since he was confessing, he might as well tell Bellamy the whole truth. He hadn't known just how much he loved her until he spoke the words. "And I've lost her."

"Nothing is ever lost unless you let it be."

"What does that mean?" He was too weak, too dizzy, too tired to solve Bellamy's riddles.

"Win her back." Bellamy's tone remained sincere, and his eyes brimmed with encouragement.

Riley wanted to hang on to Bellamy's instructions and the reassurance, and for just a moment he had the sense that Bellamy was an ally. Maybe with a little more experience, the young man would make a good matchmaker after all.

"Listen now, Riley. I picked you for Finola Shanahan because I believed you out of any other man could break through her defenses and win her heart."

Riley pressed his fist into the painful spasm in his gut. "No offense, my friend, but you were wrong."

"I also picked you because of all the men I knew, you would have the courage and determination to fight for her."

The pain in his stomach started to double him over. "That's where you're also wrong, Bellamy. I already fought to keep one woman. And all my fighting only drove her to a watery grave."

Before Bellamy could respond, Riley made a dash for the privy. When he stumbled out a short while later, Bellamy was leaning against the back of the pub waiting for him.

The matchmaker's expression said that he'd already guessed what was ailing Riley. "Bother it." Riley paused, weak and shaking. "I've got cholera."

21

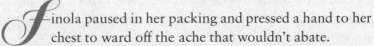

*F*inola paused in her packing and pressed a hand to her chest to ward off the ache that wouldn't abate.

She sat back on her heels and fought against the taunting in her mind. This time it wasn't a baby's cry echoing there. It was Riley's anguished words at their parting. *"Say it. Say that you don't care for me and don't want to be with me. If you say it, I'll walk away and never come back."*

She'd said it even though she hadn't meant it because she needed him to break things off between them. Aye, it was exactly the ploy she'd been waiting for, the one thing that would drive him away.

And it worked.

He left and hadn't returned. Not during the two days since he'd ridden away.

She glanced at the slant of the winter sunshine that filtered past the draperies. It was already well past noon, the time Winston had planned to leave for the country, and she still wasn't ready.

Winston had wanted to leave yesterday, but she had convinced him to let her have one more day, making the case that she couldn't simply disappear without explaining to the Sisters of Charity as well as the immigrants where she was going.

Winston hadn't been pleased about the delay, but he'd allowed it. She suspected he'd done so because he was anxious for Riley to return and didn't want to have to explain to her da the match had failed.

And what about her? Had she been procrastinating with the hope Riley would show up and plead with her to marry him anyway? And if he did, what would she do?

She fingered the claddagh ring she'd forgotten to give back to him. She ought to take it off. But she hadn't been able to make herself do so. Not yet.

"No, Finola Shanahan." She snatched one of her shawls from the bed and tossed it on top of the other garments in the trunk. "You made a vow to enter the convent, and you'll be keeping your vows, that you will."

When her da found out about the broken match, he'd be disappointed, to be sure. But he'd also realize she was a hopeless cause, and he'd have no choice but to allow her to join the Sisters of Charity. If she was lucky, he'd even be the one to suggest it, and she wouldn't have to bring up the subject for herself.

And aye, she still wanted to join the Sisters of Charity. She wouldn't abandon the women there or the plans she'd made. Even if she started to have second thoughts—which she wouldn't—she couldn't forget that Riley deserved a better wife and mother of his children than her. She had to do this for him.

At a sudden and heavy banging against the front door of the mansion, Finola bolted up, and her heart began to tap erratic rhythm. Not many would knock so forcefully.

But Riley would. If he was anxious to see her . . .

Although he'd said he'd stay away, maybe he wanted her enough to make another effort to work things out between them. Maybe he'd come because in spite of her confession, he'd decided none of her mistakes mattered, that he loved her enough to leave them in the past, that he was willing to accept her shortcomings, that he wanted to build a future with her anyway.

With her chest constricting, she picked up the heavy skirt of her day dress and ran across the room, desperate to answer the door before Winston did. By the time she reached the bottom of the steps and was racing across the front entryway, the butler was already there and opening the door.

Breathless, she halted, her muscles tightening with a need she didn't understand.

"Is Finola here?" came a man's voice from the front veranda. "I heard she's still in the city."

It took her only a moment to recognize the voice belonged to Bellamy McKenna. Why had he come? Had Riley sent the matchmaker in his stead to plead with her? Or maybe Bellamy was there to formally dissolve the match. After all, agreements had been officially signed. Maybe they had to be officially un-signed.

But did she really want to go through with unsigning any documents right now?

Winston opened the door wider.

"This is urgent." Bellamy's voice was grave.

What reason did the young matchmaker have to be so grave unless something had happened to Riley?

Her heart picked up its pace again, and she strode forward, sidling past Winston.

At the sight of her, Bellamy expelled a breath. "Thank Mary, Joseph, and Jesus." His garments were disheveled, as though he'd slept in them. And he was hatless, his dark hair a mass of messy waves.

"What's this urgent news you have for me, Bellamy?"

"'Tis Riley." His expression was more serious than she'd ever seen. Something was wrong.

"What happened?"

"Riley has cholera and is sick and weak in bed."

Cholera? Her knees buckled.

Bellamy shot out an arm and caught her.

"No, please, no." She clutched him.

"I'm afraid so, Finola. The doctor has already been and gone a couple of times." Bellamy's brows furrowed above his dark eyes, which were absent of any mirth.

With Oscar's Pub the center of the latest gossip among the Irish of St. Louis, he'd no doubt already heard about her breaking the match with Riley. And he'd probably also learned about her imminent leaving of St. Louis.

So why had he come over to deliver the news? Did he think she cared enough about Riley even after their parting ways that she'd want to say good-bye? If so, Bellamy knew her well. Even if the prospect of seeing Riley on his deathbed was frightening, she couldn't stay away.

What if there was more she could do to save his life?

She reached for her cloak from the coat-tree, only to have Winston clear his throat. "Miss Shanahan, your father will be expecting you to leave the city this afternoon."

"Another hour or so of delay won't matter, Winston." She tossed the garment around her shoulders.

"But 'tis the cholera, miss. I don't think your father would be approving of you going anywhere near it."

"She can stay in the hallway," Bellamy offered. "No need to go into Riley's room."

"I should think not." Winston's eyes rounded, as though he were scandalized by the mention of such a possibility.

She wasn't about to make Winston or Bellamy any promises about staying out of Riley's room. She'd never let illness or disease stop her from visiting sick immigrants. She most certainly wouldn't let anything stop her from seeing and helping Riley today. But if she said so, both the butler and Bellamy would forbid her from going.

Without another word, she stepped outside and headed directly for the gig parked in front of the house. Riley's gig.

"Remain out of his room, Miss Shanahan." Winston's worried command followed after her. "And be home in one hour."

She ought to tell him she would do exactly as he said, but she climbed up onto the bench and gave him a nod, which was her way of acknowledging that she heard him, not that she intended to follow his instructions. It wasn't her fault if he couldn't tell the difference.

On the ride over to the wagon shop, Bellamy relayed the events of the previous two days, indicating that Riley had started getting sick while he'd been at the pub two nights ago. Bellamy had driven him back to the workshop and then fetched the doctor.

Big Jim had stayed with Riley for most of the time he'd been sick, but then a messenger had arrived just this morning with the news that Big Jim's pastor friend was sick. Since Bellamy had been there at the time checking on how Riley was faring, he'd offered to stay for a short while and find someone else to help Riley in Big Jim's place.

"The doctor is with him now, so he is." Bellamy drove the gig as fast as Riley had on their way home from skating, and Finola clung to the seat to keep from toppling out as they approached the wagon shop.

"What about Riley's family?"

"Riley asked me not to be telling them he's sick. They were planning to leave the city today, and he doesn't want them remaining behind on account of him."

"We need to inform them, Bellamy. They deserve to say good-bye more than I do."

"He loves them and is wanting to keep them safe, especially since his father is still weak."

"That makes sense. But mind you, they're going to be sorely disappointed." Not many survived cholera. They'd be much more than disappointed if he passed away. They'd be devastated.

Everyone in the Kerry Patch would be shocked and saddened to lose Riley.

She had the feeling Riley would disapprove of her exposing herself to the illness too . . . if he knew about it. "You didn't tell him you were coming to get me?"

"He'll probably be too sick to notice." This time Bellamy didn't meet her gaze, focused instead on the entrance of the workshop ahead. "But I know you were starting to care about him."

"I won't deny he's the first man I've liked."

"He's the first man to withstand your wiles."

"What wiles?"

Bellamy shot her a sideways look. "I'm no fool, Finola. I think you're pushing Riley away even though you don't want to."

It wouldn't hurt to admit what she'd done . . . now that Riley was sick and could very well die. "After I shared my desire to enter the convent, Riley decided he didn't want to manipulate me into a union the same way he did his first wife."

"I've been puzzling how you persuaded a determined man like Riley Rafferty to walk away from you." Bellamy halted the gig in front of the shop. "Now the mystery is solved."

"I'm just sorry I ruined your first match and got you off to a poor start."

"You're a clever girl." Bellamy started to get down. "But let's get one thing straight. You're not cleverer than me."

When he tossed a smile her way, she released the tension that had been building during their conversation, relieved that he wasn't taking her severing the match with Riley too personally. Even though he'd failed with them, hopefully that wouldn't prevent others from seeking him out and trusting him.

As she climbed down from the gig and followed him to a side

stairway on the outside of the building that led to the rooms above the wagon shop, the silence from inside was eerie.

"Where is everyone?" she asked, following him up the steps.

"Big Jim sent the apprentices to stay at a nearby livery, hoping to keep them safe."

The riverfront was as busy as always with steamboats coming and going. And Front Street was still teeming with people but also with the fleets of drays, mule-drawn wagons that formed a steady stream of traffic to and from the waterfront.

Clearly, the growing spread of cholera wasn't holding most people at bay.

It wouldn't hold her back either, especially with Riley. After all, as a woman on the verge of entering a life of service, she was duty bound to provide aid to the sick no matter the consequence to herself.

Maybe he'd object to her being here because he was hurt after their parting. She wouldn't blame him if he didn't want to see her again. Even so, she wouldn't be easily swayed from tending to him.

They entered into a narrow hallway with several doors on either side, their footsteps on the plank floor tapping an ominous rhythm.

Bellamy led her to a far room, and as he stepped in, he motioned for her to keep to the hallway.

She held back, her chest tightening with the need to find an excuse that would take her into the room.

"Thank you for staying, Doctor." Bellamy and the doctor stood in front of the bed and blocked her view of Riley. All she could see were his legs stretched out underneath a blanket, motionless.

Was she too late?

"I've done all I can to make him comfortable." The doctor spoke in a hushed tone as he reached for his bag. "Now there's not much more to be doing."

Finola bit back frustrated words and tried not to show her impatience. Already her mind had been at work trying to remember everything the Sisters had said about the last cholera outbreak in St. Louis. A few of them had come to St. Louis specifically to provide aid to the suffering and dying.

They'd indicated they'd saved many people with their methods, including getting their patients to drink large amounts of a liquid containing sugar and salt.

As the doctor exited the room, he nodded at her, his aged face haggard with both despair and exhaustion. Even though she had a dozen questions, she swallowed them, sparing the poor man a delay when there were likely many more suffering people he needed to tend.

Besides, now that she had a full view of Riley, her attention had shifted to his face. His eyes were closed and his face pale and lifeless.

"Holy mother, have mercy," she whispered, pressing trembling fingers against her mouth and blinking back sudden tears.

How was it that just two days ago he was skating with vigor and strength, and less than forty-eight hours later he was lying at death's door?

A wave of despair crashed through her. She clutched the doorframe to keep from sinking to the floor.

Bellamy was at her side in an instant, holding her up. "You need to sit." He stretched for the chair positioned next to the bed and dragged it into the hallway. Then he guided her to it.

She had no intention of sitting in the hallway, but she allowed Bellamy to assist her into the chair until she could come up with a plan for getting into Riley's room and staying with him.

At least Riley's skin wasn't blue yet. Surely that was a positive sign that he still had time to recover. "Can you help me find a supply of salt and sugar? I'd like to give Riley a liquid the Sisters concoct when treating cholera patients."

Bellamy rummaged around the first room and located small

containers of both. It wasn't enough, but she joined him in the kitchen-like room and mixed equal parts into a pan of water she brought to a boil on the cast-iron stove.

From outside Riley's room, she instructed Bellamy on how to rouse Riley and get him to drink the sugar-salt water solution. Riley woke in a haze, hardly having enough energy to lift his head. But Bellamy managed to coerce Riley into taking several sips.

She forced herself not to rush in and take over. If she tried, Bellamy would likely drive her right back home. Instead, when Bellamy finished, she convinced him to make a trip to a nearby general store to purchase more sugar and salt. As he dashed off, he warned her that he'd only be gone a short while and that she shouldn't go into Riley's room unless she absolutely really needed to.

The moment she heard the gig pull away, she went directly in. She absolutely had to be by Riley's side. It was the truth. And she wouldn't let anything keep her from him.

22

She lifted the tin cup to Riley's mouth again and simultaneously raised his head. Though he didn't open his eyes or respond to her, she slowly and steadily made him drink the remainder of the liquid.

She was just finishing when Bellamy returned. At the sight of her at Riley's side, he only shook his head. Thankfully, he didn't demand that she leave.

He helped her make more of the solution, and when she insisted on being the one to give it to Riley, he didn't object, clearly realizing that she'd had more success in getting their patient to ingest the liquid than he had. And when he made mention of the need to go out and find another person to take Big Jim's place in caring for Riley, she'd claimed she would do it and that they needed no one else.

Bellamy only quirked a brow. And when she asked him to deliver the word to her family's butler to leave for the country house without her, he argued with her for a few moments before sighing and acquiescing.

He left to carry out her instructions, as well as to attend to his duties at the pub. Evening was settling when he returned, and she refrained from asking him about Winston's reaction to her decision to stay, knowing her da would discover what she'd done and would come to collect her soon enough.

For a short while, Bellamy assisted her in fetching and boiling water, making more solution, and tending to Riley's more personal needs. Riley awoke once when Bellamy was with him. But he didn't notice her presence, which was for the best. He was certainly doing better; his color was returning, and he didn't seem to be in any pain.

At the very least, she could watch over him tonight, continue to spoon-feed her concoction, and then be on her way in the morning.

As if hearing her unspoken thought, Bellamy stepped up to the brass footboard. The light from the lantern on the side table cast a warm glow over the sparsely furnished room. "I'll be gone for a wee bit to find someone to sit with Riley through the night."

"I said I'll be doing it, so I will."

"And stay with Riley unchaperoned?"

She waved a hand at Riley's prostrate form. "Why would we need a chaperone under these circumstances? Riley's too sick to notice me here. And if he wakes, he'll be angry and send me on my way."

"True enough." Bellamy stared at Riley as though he was seeing inside Riley's head.

Was Bellamy agreeing that Riley would be angry because of the breakup or because she'd exposed herself to cholera?

"I'll draw more water for you and bring it up so you won't be needing to go out."

"Thank you, Bellamy." She didn't think she'd need to give Riley much more of the sugar-salt water, but she might as well have extra water at her disposal just in case. If she should need to fetch water, she'd discovered earlier that the closest pump was down the street, and she didn't want to leave Riley alone any longer than was necessary.

Bellamy made short work of going after the water. Upon his return, his footsteps clomped heavily down the hallway, but then he halted suddenly and released a soft groan.

Was Bellamy getting sick now? She shook her head firmly, as if her silent protest could somehow prevent it.

At another groan, she jumped from the chair she'd positioned back at Riley's bedside and strode out of the room.

"Bellamy, is everything alright?" The moment she stepped out of the room, he stumbled, then tripped. As he did so, the full pail in his hand tilted, and water flew directly toward her. She had no time to duck or dodge out of the way. A deluge splashed against her chest and ran down the length of her gown. Icy-cold water.

She sucked in a sharp breath as it drenched her and made contact with her skin.

Bellamy straightened himself and then looked from the pail to her gown and back. "Guess I'm more tired than I realized and getting clumsy."

She held her arms wide. Her gown was more than just a little wet. It was uncomfortably so. But what did that matter if Bellamy was sick now too?

She searched his face for signs of his distress. His skin was its natural swarthy color, his shoulders edged with strength, his body exuded energy. The only thing different was the glimmer in his eyes. Was he finding mirth in her predicament?

What if he'd planned to splash her with water in order to force her to leave Riley's apartment and return home? He'd assume she'd want to change garments. But once home, he'd make certain she stayed there for the night to ensure that she was safe and secure.

"I know what you're up to, Bellamy McKenna." She fisted her hands on her hips.

"Oh, aye, do you now?" His eyes narrowed enough for her to know he was hiding something and that she was right.

"You made up the groaning to get me out here so you could toss water on me purposefully."

"Is that a fact?"

"'Tis one if I ever saw so."

"And whyever would I be wanting to toss water on you *purposefully?*"

"Because you don't think I should be staying here overnight with Riley, and you're trying to send me home."

"Oh?" His brows shot up.

Had she guessed wrong? She hesitated.

He dropped his sights to her wet gown, which was growing increasingly cold. "Naturally you have no choice but to go home."

"I do have a choice, and I'll be staying here."

"Not in a wet garment, you won't. And dontcha be telling me you're planning to take it off."

She held out the soggy skirt. Aye, that's what she'd do. She'd take off the gown. "I'll lay it out in front of the stove. By morning it'll be dry enough to don."

Bellamy pursed his lips and shook his head.

She lifted her chin and glared at him. "You know nothing will happen. Besides, my whole family is away, and the gossipmongers won't have to know I didn't come home for the night."

He cocked his head as though contemplating the situation.

"Besides, I can wrap up in a blanket so I'm not indecent."

"You'll have to promise to stay here in the apartment and not go out."

"I promise." She'd promise anything at this point, so long as Bellamy didn't force her to leave. Not yet. Not until she could see for herself that Riley was better.

Bellamy hesitated. "If you're sure?"

"I'm sure."

He bowed his head. Were his lips twitching with a smile? It was hard to tell in the dimness of the hallway.

She stared at him as he strode away, trying to figure him out.

When he reached the door, he paused. "I'll be back with the doctor in the morning."

"What time?"

"Early."

"I'll be sure to be ready."

"See that you are." With that, he closed the door behind him.

For a moment, she stood unmoving, the icy water rolling down her legs into her stockings and shoes so that now she stood in a puddle.

Had she made the right choice in staying with Riley for the night? Even though he was suffering from cholera and nearly unconscious, it was inappropriate for a single woman like her to tend to him. Only nuns or married women assisted men who were sick.

What would her da and mam think if they discovered her indiscretion? Or the Mother Superior?

Finola pressed a hand to her heart to calm the sudden racing. They wouldn't need to find out, would they? Besides, she wasn't doing anything wrong. In fact, everyone ought to thank her for saving their hero, Saint Riley of the Kerry Patch.

But she was alone with him. . . .

She took a hesitant step toward the exit. It wasn't too late to run after Bellamy and tell him to take her home.

But this would be her last night with Riley.

She inhaled to steady her conflicting emotions. He was sick. Nothing would happen. She needed to take the opportunity as the gift it was—the chance to spend a final few hours with him before they went their separate ways forever.

With her mind made up, she began extricating herself from her wet garments. Getting out of the tight gown was more difficult than she'd expected. She wriggled and squirmed until the layers pooled around her feet, soaking in the rest of the water on the hallway floor. Her chemise and underdrawers were wet too, but she didn't dare take them off.

As she rubbed her hands over her bare arms, her mind traveled back to the day Riley had caught her changing in the livery stable in the same state of undress.

She glanced to the bedroom, half-expecting him to be out of bed, leaning against the doorframe, and watching her with a smolder in his blue eyes.

A delicious tremor shimmered across her skin.

"Finola Shanahan." She gave herself a mental shake. "You're done with Riley Rafferty and need to put such thoughts far from your mind."

With a huff, she gathered up her gown and took it to the room that served as a kitchen. The cast-iron stove was still warm, the coals inside glowing. But it would need to be much hotter if she had any hope of drying the clothing by the time Bellamy returned in the morning with the doctor.

She opened the coal bin beside the stove to find only a shovelful of the black lumps inside. She'd have to make do with what was left for now and search around later for more. After adding the rest of the coals to the stove and draping her gown over one of the chairs close by, she started her search for a blanket.

Now that she was wet and unclothed, she was growing all too aware that the upstairs apartments were drafty and cold, especially because the rooms all relied upon the one stove in the kitchen-like room for heat.

Shivering and rubbing her arms for warmth, she rummaged around Riley's room for another blanket. But other than a chest of drawers with his work clothing and a wardrobe containing fancier garments, he had very few possessions, and the only blankets were those covering him.

She didn't want to invade the privacy of the other men who lived in the apartments, but a quick peek into each of their rooms showed their beds stripped bare. Had the men taken their linens with them? With the chill of winter, she supposed they had need of the warmth at night no matter where they might be staying.

As she returned to Riley's room, her teeth were chattering. Although she would have much preferred a blanket to warm herself, she was left with no choice but to use Riley's clothing. Carefully, she sorted through his drawers until she found a flannel shirt, trousers, and thick wool stockings. Because her undergarments were still wet, she discarded them before donning his clothing. The shirt dropped to her knees, and she had to roll over the waist and legs of the trousers, cinching the waist by tying a knot in the material.

Even though she looked ridiculous, she had no other options, especially because she couldn't find her cloak anywhere. Had she left it in the gig?

It didn't take long for the meager coal supplies to dwindle down to but a few embers and the temperature in the apartment to drop.

Finally, she tiptoed out of the apartment and down to the workshop, intending to bring back enough coal to last her through the night. To her dismay, the doors were all locked.

For a brief moment, she considered knocking on a neighboring door. But with a glance down at her scandalous attire, she shook her head and made her way back upstairs. Once there, she searched through each room again, but to no avail.

As she dropped into the chair beside Riley's bed, she sighed out her frustration and draped two more shirts over her body like blankets.

She should have taken more care before Bellamy left to ensure she had everything she needed. But she'd been the one to insist on staying when he'd wanted her to leave. This wasn't his fault. He'd tried to make her see reason, and she hadn't listened.

She still had hours to go before dawn, and already she was chilled and shivering and her toes were frozen, despite Riley's wool stockings. Her whole body would form into a block of ice before the night was through.

"Now, Finola," she chastised herself. "It won't be too terrible."

The lamp on the nightstand flickered and cast a warm glow over Riley's face, the stubble thicker and rougher after having gone without a shave. He finally looked as though he was sleeping peacefully.

He took up most of the double bed, but there was a slim margin of space beside him.

Not that she would get into bed with him. Never in a hundred years. In fact, just thinking about it sent mortification pumping through her. But if she scooted nearer, she could tuck her feet under the blankets for more warmth.

Before she could talk herself out of doing it, she wedged the chair beside the bed, then tentatively slid her feet under the covers. He was wearing only his underdrawers and an undershirt. She hadn't meant to peek, but at the time she'd been too worried to consider the state of his undress, had only thought about his survival.

But now . . .

She shivered again but not from the cold. This time it was from the realization that her feet were mere inches from his solid chest.

She watched Riley's face for any signs that he was aware of what she was doing. But he didn't budge except the rhythmic up and down of his chest with his breathing.

Maybe this sleeping arrangement would work. And maybe she wouldn't freeze to death after all.

She snuggled under the pile of shirts and curled her legs under the blankets. Although she only meant to rest her eyes and keep her ears open for Riley's needs, the past two restless nights and the long day of worrying about Riley caught up with her. Within minutes, she fell into an exhausted slumber.

23

*R*iley stretched and waited for the pain in his stomach to double him over. But strangely the terrible cramps never came.

Was he dead? With as miserable as he'd been, he'd felt like he was dying.

He shifted, feeling a mattress beneath him, covers above him, and a body curled against him.

His eyes flew open. A low flame in a nearby lamp revealed his room above the workshop. The memories rushed back—Bellamy driving him home in his gig and dragging him up to his bed.

Big Jim had been there during the worst of his sickness, trying to get him to drink water, his worried face hovering above Riley's. The doctor had come a couple of times. And Riley thought he'd also seen Finola. But surely he'd only been dreaming.

The body moved, snuggling deeper into him.

He froze, and his sights shot to the head resting against him.

Waves of hair cascaded all around, covering his chest, his arm, the blankets. Brown hair that was tinted with red just like

Finola's. A body that was small, slender, and curvy just like Finola's. Freckled skin that was just like Finola's.

Was this Finola? Or was he living out his deepest fantasy?

His gaze darted around the room, and he tried to formulate a coherent thought. But his attention went straight back to Finola as if she were a magnet that he was powerless to resist.

Did he want to resist? A small part of his brain warned him he needed to, that he had no right to this beautiful woman. But another part of him shoved aside all rational thought. If this was a dream, he wanted to be fully present. And if it wasn't a dream, he'd worry about the repercussions later.

He didn't know what had transpired to bring her there, but he was holding her, his arms wrapped around her, all of her soft curves pressed against him.

One of her hands rested on his bicep. The other was draped across his hip. How was she daring to touch him so familiarly?

Covers were piled over them both, keeping them warm. But his nose, his forehead, even his cheeks were cold, the temperature in his room close to the freezing mark. Internally, he felt as well as if he'd never been sick. Maybe a little weak and hungry, but his cholera was clearly gone. He'd survived.

And sweet saints above. He really was in bed with Finola.

A surge of heat flared in his gut—deep heat like a hot underground wellspring that couldn't be contained. It started to flow through his veins, searing him so that he wanted to draw her even closer, let his body cover hers, and kiss her until they were both delirious.

He swallowed hard and fought to control himself. As eager and ready as he was to show her how much he adored her, he had to go slow with her, had to go slow for himself.

With the softest brush of his fingers, he shifted several strands of her hair away from her neck. Then he grazed a line there, skimming just the tips of his fingers.

At his touch, she released a soft sigh, one that bathed his

neck and made him aware of how near her face was to his. Mere inches. Her freckled cheeks, her long lashes, her sweet lips pressed together and almost touching his chin.

He was in heaven. In fact, this was better than heaven.

Ever so gently again, he let himself draw another line over her skin, before he tucked a strand behind her ear.

She shifted nearer, her curves grazing him first before her lips made contact with his chin. She huddled against him, the barest contact leaving him suddenly breathless and aching with need.

He was going to kiss her. He wasn't strong enough not to.

Bending in, he laid a kiss against her cheek, then closed his eyes, relishing the softness and warmth and scent of her but forcing himself not to go any further.

As though sensing his restraint, her fingers circled around his bicep and tightened, and she arched into him just enough for him to know she was willing. Willing for what, he didn't exactly know. But he wanted to find out.

He only had to shift a little to reach her mouth. And in the next instant, he covered her lips completely. Like a forge blast to the flames, fire and heat and light exploded to life.

Her response was nearly immediate. Even though her inexperience and innocence was clear, she tested his lips with a fervor that told him she was eager for this connection too. Eager to share the intimacy. Eager for him.

She desired him, and that thought was like a bellows, pumping longing through him. He wanted Finola Shanahan more than he wanted anything or anyone.

He rolled just slightly, enough that he was leaning on her and able to press into the kiss with more power and all the passion coursing through him. With his hands splayed at her hips, he slid his knee between hers, wanting to get closer, wanting to tangle their bodies.

But at the feel of her bare leg brushing his bare leg, he froze. Was she unclothed? Was he?

Full wakefulness slammed into him with the force of a dam breaking. The current swept him back to the night after he'd taken her ice-skating when she'd told him she didn't care about him and never wanted to see him again.

He'd ridden away from her home believing he'd lost the woman he loved. What had changed? And how had they ended up in bed? Naked?

She stopped kissing him. As her eyes popped open, her gaze darted first to him, the bed, and then herself. The haziness of sleep in her expression rapidly evaporated, and she gasped and began to scramble away.

He snaked out an arm and caught her wrist. "Wait."

She was partially suspended above him, looking down at him. The covers had fallen away enough to reveal that he wasn't entirely naked after all but was wearing his undergarments. She, on the other hand, seemed to be attired in one of his flannel shirts and a pair of his trousers that had bunched up to her knees.

Before he could make sense of their situation, voices resounded in the hallway, and in the next moment, someone was stepping into his room. Actually, several people were entering and conversing among themselves.

At the sight of the two of them in bed together with Finola all but lying on top of him, the voices came to an abrupt halt.

"What's wrong?" came Bellamy's voice, as he sidled into the room behind the others, followed by several more men—mostly from Riley's campaign committee. Had someone decided they needed a meeting this morning? And if so, why?

"What in the blazes," Riley muttered. "I don't think we have enough people in my room. Why don't we invite a few others?"

"Dontcha worry one wee bit," Bellamy said with a grin. "More folks are on their way now that news of your recovery from cholera has spread."

Finola threw back the blankets even farther and started to

scramble out from underneath, but as she took in the sight of herself wearing his clothing, she drew the covers back and lay down stiffly beside him.

It was too late. He'd gotten a peek of his shirt askew, revealing her bare shoulder. But so had every other person in the room, and that realization formed a hard knot in his gut. He didn't want anyone else viewing what was his.

Was she his? Did he still have a claim on her?

Embarrassment was etched into her delicate features. She clearly hadn't expected to have half the city of St. Louis show up in his bedroom either.

For a few chaotic moments, Riley insisted that everyone leave. When Bellamy and Father O'Kirwin were the only two remaining, Bellamy closed the door and leaned casually against it.

His eyes were asking the same question that was running through Riley's mind: how had Finola ended up in bed with him? From her shocked reaction when she'd awoken in his arms, she obviously hadn't expected to be with him any more than he had with her.

What had happened during the night to bring them together this way?

Bellamy rubbed at his arms over his coat and then blew into his hands. "'Tis cold enough up here to freeze the whiskers off a cat."

"Aye, that it is." Father O'Kirwin's tone was as righteous and zealous as if he'd been standing in the pulpit at mass.

Riley could only stare at the two. Why in the name of the blessed virgin was his campaign manager here?

"Finola, I thought you intended to keep the fire going." Bellamy's eyes held a glimmer of mischief.

"You left me with an empty coal bin, so you did, Bellamy McKenna." She shuddered.

Without thinking, Riley tucked the covers around her more firmly.

Although she didn't try to extricate herself from the bed again, she tossed him a glare, one that told him his touching her was only making them look all the guiltier.

The fact was, their situation was already incriminating enough. Nothing could make it worse.

Father O'Kirwin stepped up to the bed and peered down his wide nose through spectacles at Finola, his brows furrowing together into a straight line. "Is it possible you decided to let the stove die so you'd have an excuse to get into bed with Riley Rafferty?"

She released an indignant huff. "No, I never did. I was cold, and I stuck my legs under the covers to get warm. I didn't mean to end up next to him."

"If you were so cold, why did you get undressed?"

"Bellamy spilled water on my gown, and I had to take it off."

Bellamy spilled water on her? Riley studied the young matchmaker's face again.

He shrugged and avoided meeting Riley's eyes. "I was bringing Finola more water just in case she needed to make additional amounts of her remedy."

"And you just happened to spill it on her?"

Bellamy nodded. "I insisted that she go home, but she wanted to stay."

Finola ducked her head, her cheeks turning pink.

This was interesting news. Finola had wanted to stay with him? To take care of him? Because she'd been worried?

Father O'Kirwin glanced at Bellamy, and the matchmaker gave him a nod as though to continue. But continue what?

"Finola Shanahan." Father O'Kirwin's voice dropped. "From the looks of things, you mishandled this situation. If you realized your mistake and wanted Riley back, you should have said so instead of staying the night with him like this."

Finola's eyes widened, the mortification in them growing. "I did no such thing. I vow it."

"Then why are you in bed with him?"

"I couldn't find any other blankets."

No blankets? Riley raised a brow at Bellamy, but the fellow had leaned into Father O'Kirwin and was whispering with him—more like *scheming* with him.

If Bellamy had arranged for the lack of coal and spilling of water, had he taken all the blankets from the apartments too? As part of a plan to get Finola and him back together?

"Seems to me Riley has plenty of other garments you could have used for warmth." The priest nodded at the pile of discarded clothing on the floor by the bedside chair.

Finola glanced at the clothing too, then expelled a tight breath. "I had no choice—"

"We always have a choice." Father O'Kirwin folded his hands over the large wooden cross necklace he wore over his cassock.

"I put on Riley's clothing to stay warm, but I was still cold, so I tucked my legs under the covers, 'tis all."

The priest *tsk*ed. "Doesn't look like that's all you tucked under the covers, lass."

"I must have crawled into bed at some point, though I don't remember doing it, so I don't." With each word of protest, Finola scooted farther back against him, as though attempting to escape from the priest's overbearing presence. She clearly wasn't mindful of what she was doing, but he was keenly aware that her backside was pressing into him, her slender shoulders all the way down to her feet and everything in between.

For a moment he could think of nothing else but the soft curves and how they fit so well against him. His muscles tightened with the need to skim his hands over every inch of her.

Father O'Kirwin was watching him through narrowed eyes as though reading the direction of his thoughts. "This situation is indecent and unacceptable."

"Aye, to be sure." Bellamy nodded but seemed to be fighting to smother a smile.

"I'll not be putting all the blame on Finola for the indecencies here," Father O'Kirwin continued, now turning his holy wrath upon Riley. "I have no doubt you woke up, saw Finola sitting in the chair, and decided to take advantage of the situation."

No doubt about it. Bellamy had orchestrated the events of the past night to put them into a compromising situation. Bellamy probably thought he was helping, especially after Riley's heartbroken confession outside the pub that he loved Finola.

Even so, the inquisition was unfair to Finola and making her uncomfortable. He had to put an end to it for her sake. Besides, while she might have ended up in bed with him due to Bellamy's underhanded methods, she'd made it clear the other night that she didn't love him or want him.

Riley sighed with what he knew he had to do. "Listen, as sweet as Finola is, I wouldn't take advantage of her. In truth, if I'd been conscious that Finola was anywhere near me, I would have sent her home and not risked exposing her to cholera." He'd been too sick and exhausted to truly understand what was going on. At least until he'd awoken and found her in his arms.

If he'd been a stronger man, a gentleman, even less of a rogue, he wouldn't have kissed her this morning. But he'd been too caught up in his feelings, had plunged forward with no thought to the repercussions. Repercussions to her. To him. To their families.

And he had also told Daniel Allen he'd think about a match with Bets.

He didn't remember much about his time in the pub with Oscar that night Finola had rejected him. But he suspected his hurt had driven him to consider Oscar's offer more than anything else. It was clear he couldn't simply jump into a new relationship and plan for marriage, not when he had so many feelings for Finola.

"Ach, what's done is done now, Riley," Bellamy said. "And we can't be changing it. Not that you truly want to."

Bellamy was right as usual. Riley had enjoyed every single second of his encounter with Finola in his bed. And if he went back in time and had the chance to re-do things, he'd probably kiss her again, maybe even try to make it last longer.

Bellamy's gaze lost all humor and turned intense. "You've made a mess of Finola's good reputation, that you have. And now you have to do whatever it takes to repair it."

Bother it. Bellamy was right again. The moment he'd realized Finola was in his bed, he should have jumped out. By staying, he'd put Finola's reputation in the community at risk. He didn't want to harm her in any way. But the tongues would start to wag about them, likely already were among the folks congregated out in the hallway.

Had Bellamy orchestrated that too? Had he purposefully shown up this early, hoping to catch them together in bed? And had he intentionally brought along enough witnesses to rival the heavenly hosts?

As though sensing Riley's unasked questions, Bellamy turned his gaze to the ceiling.

"You'll be marrying this lass, today." Father O'Kirwin pulled out his prayer book, clearly planning to start the wedding ceremony right then and there. "And I won't be taking no for an answer."

Riley thought the situation couldn't get worse. But apparently it could.

24

*G*et married? Today? Finola pushed up from the bed, heedless of the cover falling away and revealing her in Riley's oversized clothing.

The moment Father O'Kirwin and Bellamy glanced at her and then looked quickly away, Finola took in her state of attire to find that several buttons had come undone, and the shirt was slipping precariously close to the edge of her shoulder again.

Holy mother, have mercy. Would the humiliation never end?

She scrambled to start buttoning the shirt but couldn't make her fingers work fast enough. She didn't want them watching her buttoning herself anyway, so she threw herself down beside Riley and jerked the cover back over herself, trying to hold her body far enough away from him so she wasn't touching him . . . because every time her body made contact with his, her thoughts shifted to him, to the hard, lean length of his torso, the warmth of his presence, the solidness of his muscles.

She never should have stayed the night. At the very least, she should have remained in the chair instead of putting her legs under the covers. She guessed that as she'd fallen asleep and gotten colder, she'd inadvertently burrowed more and more under the covers until she'd ended up in Riley's bed altogether.

Whatever the case, she couldn't marry Riley. That was completely out of the question. No matter how this situation appeared to everyone else, she had to make them understand nothing had happened between Riley and her.

Except the kiss . . . One innocent little kiss. Or maybe not so innocent or little.

Flutters started again in her stomach. Only minutes ago, he'd been holding and kissing her as if he never intended to stop. She nearly closed her eyes again at the memory of the way he'd gently caressed her and then fused his mouth to hers in a kiss that defied reality.

Even though she'd been half asleep and thought she was dreaming, the kiss had been powerful enough to awaken every nerve, every muscle, and every inch of her skin to his touch. It was as if her body had been unconscious and had been brought back to life. Now she ached for more of him—needed more of him—to stay alive.

"Father O'Kirwin," Riley said, his voice too close behind her, warming her neck and sending shivers over her back. "Getting married today is a bit rash, don't you think?"

"After what I've witnessed here this morn, 'tis not rash at all, Riley Rafferty. Not at all." Father O'Kirwin opened his prayer book. "What would be rash is not marrying this lass and righting the wrong you've done."

"We didn't do much, Father," Riley insisted. "Just a little—"

Father O'Kirwin coughed. "I don't think Bellamy or myself need to hear the details of your time together."

"There aren't any details," Finola blurted. "We accidentally kissed. That's all."

"Accidentally?" Riley's voice dropped. "There wasn't anything accidental from my perspective."

A flush warmed her face. "We were half asleep, so we were, and didn't rightly know what we were doing."

"I knew."

"Oh, aye." Bellamy cut in. "A heart follows what it knows. Clear enough as a summer day that the two of your hearts want each other."

It didn't matter how much her heart wanted Riley. Her head was in control, and it was telling her she needed to put an end to the conversation about marriage. She'd already cut things off with Riley once. She'd simply have to figure out how to do so again.

"From what I heard, Finola got the barmbrack ring in her piece of cake." Bellamy spoke with all seriousness, as if the old custom actually had meaning. "And everyone knows that the person who gets the barmbrack ring will marry early."

Father O'Kirwin was paging through his prayer book. "So now that we have that settled, let us begin." He smoothed down a page, then made the sign of the cross. "In the name of the Father, and of the Son, and of the Holy Ghost. Amen."

As she fumbled to finish buttoning the shirt, she stiffened, panic bubbling up. This wasn't happening, was it? She had to stop the priest. Now.

Behind her, Riley touched her arm lightly and sighed. "No. We're not getting married." The bed began to shift as he crawled off the other side.

Was he saying no because he sensed her hesitation or because he didn't want to marry her anymore?

Inwardly, she chastised herself for even caring. He was putting an end to their predicament, and that was all that mattered.

As he stepped around the bed, he didn't seem the least disturbed that he was wearing only his undershirt and underdrawers. His sculpted muscles and defined torso were on full display—broad back and chest, bulging arms, and corded legs.

All that gorgeousness had been pressed against her only moments ago, and suddenly without him there beside her, she felt small and alone. Aye, she could admit she wanted him to crawl back in and wrap his arms around her. But that was only because the room was still so cold.

"No," Riley said again as he approached his chest of drawers. "Finola doesn't want the match. She made that clear."

"Dontcha be worrying." Bellamy glanced at Father O'Kirwin and nodded. "She's wanting you as much as you do her."

Did she? Even if so, Bellamy shouldn't be saying such things. "Bellamy McKenna, you're a conniving weasel."

"I'm just telling the truth, is all."

"The truth is"—Riley rummaged through a drawer—"Finola is here because you orchestrated it and not because she chose it."

Father O'Kirwin remained at the bedside with the prayer book open. "If you don't marry her, then you'll forfeit winning the election."

Riley didn't respond as he pulled out a shirt and began stuffing his arms in, with his back facing them, as though that somehow gave him a measure of privacy.

She'd never watched a man get dressed, and somehow the intimate act was more sensual than she'd realized.

Obviously sensing her perusal, he cast her a glance over his shoulder.

She forced her attention to Father O'Kirwin. "There's no need for Riley to forfeit. He's already ahead of the other two candidates, and he's pulling ahead more every day."

"He'll lose every inch of ground and then some when word of his indiscretion spreads." Father O'Kirwin's eyes held a gravity that Finola couldn't ignore.

Riley shrugged. "We'll explain what happened—"

"And you'll lose James Shanahan's support," Bellamy added.

"My da isn't that kind of man. He won't stop helping Riley just because our match is called off."

"He may choose to distance himself from the scandal." Father O'Kirwin met Riley's gaze levelly. "Even if not, you'll still lose most of the wealthy and influential men he brought over to support you. They won't give a flying hoot about you if you're not aligned with James Shanahan."

"They're not so shallow as that," she protested.

Father O'Kirwin shot her an impatient look, one that said she didn't know anything about politics.

Was he right? She swallowed against the anxiety rising in her throat. She hadn't really given much thought to the dowry agreement between her da and Riley. But Riley had become the front-runner in the election only after word of his match to her had become public knowledge. Aye, the connection to her da and his fortune was important to his winning.

"The match was mutually beneficial, Finola." Bellamy was watching her as though attempting to read her mind. "If you keep trying to wiggle your way out of it, not only does Riley stand to lose the election, but your da stands to lose the steel contract with Rafferty Wagon Company."

"Steel contract?"

"Rafferty Wagon Company agreed to purchase all the steel for their wagons from your da. Such an agreement stands to benefit your da's business. He's already got plans to expand his facilities. It'll give him a bigger name and help him gain national recognition."

She swallowed the growing trepidation. "I didn't know."

"Oh, aye," Bellamy continued. "We didn't want to be worrying you about the details of the match."

The reality of all that was at stake was suddenly clear. If she persisted in foiling the marriage to Riley, he would lose the election and her da would lose the chance for his ironworks to become a national name.

"None of that matters." Riley had opened another drawer, pulled out a pair of trousers, and was hopping into one leg.

"It does matter." Father O'Kirwin glared at Riley over the top of his spectacles. "You can't disregard the hard work that I and countless other volunteers have put into your campaign.

It just wouldn't be fair to all the people who believe in you and want you to win."

Riley stuck his foot into the other leg of his trousers, his movements strong and swift. As he finished with his trousers, he leaned against the chest of drawers and bowed his head, clearly taking the two men's words to heart. Discouragement seemed to weigh on him and slump his shoulders. Discouragement she'd caused.

An ache welled up inside, one that had been there since the day Ava had died. Aye, she'd vowed to enter the convent and do penance for killing her sister. But could she do penance a different way?

"Finola and I aren't getting married." Riley finally spoke.

"What, then?" Bellamy didn't seem quite as ruffled as Father O'Kirwin and was handling everything with his usual calmness. "Do you plan to go through with the possible match you talked about with Oscar the other night?"

"Match?" The word squeaked out before Finola could catch it. Did Riley have another woman lined up to take her place?

"Oh, aye," Bellamy answered. "Riley was doing his best to ease the sting of your rejection and so thought another match would take his mind off it, so he did."

Riley narrowed his eyes at Bellamy in warning.

Bellamy didn't bother to glance Riley's way and instead kept his focus upon Finola. "He's thinking about taking up a match with Daniel Allen's daughter Bets."

Finola sifted the name through her mind, but it wasn't familiar. Even so, she couldn't keep from disliking the woman. Was she someone Riley knew? A woman he'd once admired? Perhaps a beautiful and charming young lady who would give him the love and life he deserved . . . unlike her.

Was Bellamy right that Riley had sought out Oscar to ease the sting of her rejection? Whatever the reason, Riley was obviously not moping over her. "You moved on quickly." Her statement came out laced with accusation, although she knew it wasn't fair to Riley. He had every right to move on quickly, slowly, or otherwise.

Riley hadn't yet buttoned his shirt, was in the process of strapping suspenders over his shoulders. "I haven't moved on, Finola. That should be obvious enough after this morning. And Bellamy's going to make sure Oscar tells Daniel that I won't be taking up his offer. Right, Bellamy?"

Bellamy nodded. "Rightly so."

Riley was all but admitting he still cared for her. It shouldn't matter. She shouldn't encourage it, but she couldn't keep a breath of relief from blowing through her.

She sat up and drew the covers about her shoulders. Even though one of the blankets promptly slipped down, revealing Riley's shirt, her long hair fell like curtains and provided another layer of cover for her indecent attire.

Riley released an exasperated breath. "But I told Finola I wouldn't coerce her, and I haven't changed my mind about it."

"What if you don't need to coerce me?" The words came out before she had time to think about what she was saying.

All three men turned their attention upon her.

For long seconds, she didn't dare move, not even to squirm under the scrutiny as they waited for her to expound on what she meant. Maybe she'd been rash. Maybe she was making a terrible mistake. But she had to at least consider what she could do to help Riley.

"I'd like a moment alone with Finola," Riley said.

Father O'Kirwin still stood with his prayer book open. "Might as well not delay the inevitable."

"One moment." Riley's tone took on an edge that made it clear he was a leader and wouldn't be told what to do, no matter how much pressure the others put on him.

Bellamy was the first to step to the door, and Father O'Kirwin reluctantly followed. As soon as they exited into the hallway,

Riley started to close the door but then must have thought better of being alone with her again in his bedroom.

The gesture was noble of him, but their reputations were already in tatters.

He crossed toward the bed and stood at the edge. She could feel him waiting for her to look up and meet his gaze. But she couldn't, was too afraid of what she'd see in his eyes, that he'd be able to win her over all too easily.

"I meant what I said the other night," he whispered.

She knew he was referring to their parting of ways, when he'd informed her that if she didn't want to be with him, he wouldn't try to convince her otherwise.

"I'll stick to it, if that's what you really want."

Was that what she really wanted?

After the past few days of thinking she'd lost Riley, she had to finally be honest with herself and admit she wanted Riley Rafferty. But if she allowed herself to get married, she'd give up the peaceful and controlled future she'd planned for herself. How would she find peace when the nightmares and the sound of crying haunted her? How would she be able to be a good wife? And how could she ever be a good mother?

She didn't want any babies of her own, but from as passionate as Riley was with their kisses, she knew he'd never be satisfied with a chaste marriage. In fact, he'd already made it clear just how much he wanted her. She wouldn't be able to deny him—wouldn't want to deny him.

She clasped her hands to keep them from trembling. Was she really ready to abandon her vow to enter the convent? She didn't want to disappoint God or the Sisters. But what choice did she have?

She couldn't hurt her da or Riley. But she'd cause them both much grief if she didn't go through with the union. How could she stand in the way of their progress? Doing so would be utterly selfish on her part.

Aye, she'd questioned Riley about his stand against slavery, had confronted him about not adding it to his platform. But she still wanted him to run for mayor, still wanted him to make a difference in the city, still believed in him.

"Finola." He brushed the hair on her shoulder, his fingers skating along her collarbone. Even though his shirt was now in place and covering her, his touch turned her insides upside down and right-side up again. "Please talk to me. Tell me how you honestly feel."

Whenever she was with Riley, he seemed to demand that she speak openly, wouldn't let her get away with her usual subversive tactics.

"I want to marry you." His whisper was hoarse. "But I won't do it—absolutely won't—unless you're willing."

She tried to draw the blanket higher, wanting to hide within. But nothing could hide her emotions at this point, especially not from herself. Was she willing? Could she agree to it?

If she went ahead with the matchmaking plans, she'd do it for Riley and her da. But she would deny herself any pleasure or happiness in the union. Doing so would be a form of penance.

Steeling herself, she made herself say the words she knew she needed to. "Aye, Riley Rafferty, I'll marry you. Willingly. And I promise this time I won't try to find a way out."

He released a breath. Was it one of relief? Was he glad for her answer? A dozen questions seemed to radiate in his eyes. "You're sure this is what you want, Finola?"

She wasn't sure. In fact, she was suddenly queasy at the thought of what she'd just promised him. But she forced the worries down. "I'm sure."

He stuffed his hands into his trouser pockets. "Will you tell me how you really feel?"

She knew what he was asking, that she open herself up and share with him her truest feelings about him, about marriage, about their future. But a part of her didn't know what to feel or how to express herself. All she could do was express the wee bit she could. "You have nothing to worry about now, so you don't."

He held her gaze a moment longer, giving her the chance to say more.

She searched inside, trying to find an answer that would satisfy him. "I'll do my best to be a good wife. I promise."

After a moment, he opened his mouth, started to say something, then closed it. He gave her a nod, then crossed to the door and exited without another word or glance her way.

"As you just heard," he said to the people standing in the hallway, "Finola and I are still planning to get married."

"Today." Father O'Kirwin spoke above the others.

"No, we'll continue with the previous arrangements," Riley said, "and get married on Shrove Tuesday."

Father O'Kirwin protested, but Riley cut him off. "Shrove Tuesday and not a day sooner."

Finola flopped back onto the pillows, the bedsprings squeaking below her. Quickly she tabulated the days left until the start of Lent. Only three weeks. It was too much time. What if she changed her mind about marrying Riley between now and then? Maybe that's why he'd given her the extra time, to allow her to be certain.

But now that she'd agreed to the plans, she intended to go through with them, no matter how much she might doubt her decision.

25

"We have to do more to fight the spread." Riley's voice rose above those of the other men gathered outside the First Street tenements, the dirtiest and most crowded of the slums in the Kerry Patch.

The hazy late-afternoon sunlight was trying to peek through the low, dark clouds. For early February, the wind coming off the Mississippi still brought a chill to his cheeks and fingers, but the worst of the winter seemed to be over.

Unfortunately, the worst of the cholera only seemed to be starting.

"What more do you suggest?" One of the leaders of the gang that controlled the Clabber Alley tenements leaned against Riley's wagon, now empty of all the supplies he and Finola had already delivered.

In the past week and a half since his own battle with the deadly disease, the number of cases in the tenements had been increasing, especially those closest to the river where the poorest of the immigrants arriving in St. Louis crowded together. He didn't know the actual death count, but he'd heard over twenty-five people had died and dozens were now sick.

The few doctors willing to come into the Kerry Patch weren't able to do much but administer morphine to aid with the pain, but even that was often too little, too late for those suffering.

Riley only had to think back to the excruciating abdominal pain he'd experienced to know the suffering was terrible. After his recovery, he'd learned that he had a mild case, that the doctor had been confident he'd recover.

Bellamy had since confessed that he'd only retrieved Finola once he knew Riley was getting better, that he hadn't wanted to put Finola in danger. But, of course, the young matchmaker had led Finola to believe Riley was sick enough to die so that she'd rush over. Her efforts hadn't been for nothing. The sugar-salt water solution had helped him recover more quickly than normal.

Riley hadn't been sure whether to hug or throttle Bellamy for his scheming, not only getting Finola to his apartment but then also in finagling their getting in bed together and being caught in the indecent situation.

They'd been the talk of the town for a few days. But most folks he knew had brushed aside the indiscretion—or teased him mercilessly—because he'd ended up back together with Finola, and their wedding was still planned for Shrove Tuesday. Less than two weeks away on February 20.

Finola, on the other hand, had been dealt with more harshly among her peers, who were quick to judge and less forgiving. Her mam and da had returned to the city, having heard the rumors. They'd attempted to salvage the situation, spreading new rumors about how Finola had sacrificed greatly to serve her future husband at the time of his deepest need.

James Shanahan had approached Riley and suggested moving the wedding day up in another attempt to protect Finola's reputation. But in the end, Riley had convinced Shanahan and everyone else that waiting until Shrove Tuesday as they'd originally planned would prove that he and Finola had done nothing wrong and therefore had no reason to rush into marriage.

But the truth was, Riley had needed the extra time to assure himself that Finola really meant what she'd said about marrying him willingly and that she wouldn't scheme again. At the time she'd spoken the words, he'd been afraid that Bellamy—aided by Father O'Kirwin—had pushed her too hard.

Every day, he waited with the uneasy premonition that she'd only spoken the words as another ploy, that she would somehow devise a new way to get out of the match. But over the past days, she'd done nothing to undermine their relationship—at least that he was aware of.

Of course, she'd been on her best behavior, not wanting to give her parents any reason to make her go to the country home with them. They'd all but demanded she do so when they'd visited. But Riley had privately asked Shanahan if Finola could stay in the city, hinting that doing so would hopefully solidify Finola's feelings for him.

Riley glanced to the window of the tenement where Finola was helping, and he released a half sigh. If only her staying *had* solidified her feelings for him. He'd hoped she'd get to know him better and learn to care about him. He even hoped she would look forward to their marriage and starting a life together. But instead, she seemed to find excuses to hold him at arm's length.

Part of him had begun to wonder if that was her new strategy—agree to marry him but not allow herself to get too close to him.

If so, it was working.

The window with the dingy curtains hanging in a broken windowpane was open a crack. She'd been in the same apartment since arriving earlier . . . tending to several sick children. They didn't have cholera, but they'd been in a wretched condition.

Maybe he needed to go up and see how she was faring.

The group of men surrounding him outside the tenement

had swelled as more and more arrived home from work and worried over where the cholera would attack next, the unsuspecting new victims. The doctors had advised everyone to avoid exposure to the damp weather, to stop eating fish and vegetables, and to avoid large gatherings.

The instructions had been met with much scoffing since they couldn't do any of those things.

"There has to be more we can do to help the people," said the Clabber Alley leader. "Saint Riley, you got some ideas?"

Riley had been mulling over the options every time he came to provide assistance. Some of the ideas, like creating a better sewage system, would have to wait until he was elected as mayor. Even then, the task would be difficult since a large majority of the population was apathetic toward the poor and didn't want to pay more in taxes to create a sanitary method of disposing of sewage.

The same way the poor were apathetic toward the Black folks. . . .

Why couldn't everyone put aside their prejudices and embrace all people?

Ever since Big Jim had returned to the wagon shop somber and silent after having failed to help save his pastor and several of the pastor's children from cholera, Riley hadn't been able to stop thinking about the unfairness of everything. Here he was, helping poor immigrants find a way to survive cholera and have better lives, but he was doing nothing to advocate for the Black folks—free or enslaved. They deserved more too.

Finola's words from the campaign office had haunted him since the day she'd spoken them: *"One group cannot excuse the suffering of another because it makes life easier for them."*

Deep inside, he knew she was right. The problem was, what was he going to do about it?

All he knew was that with cholera becoming a bigger problem every day, he couldn't delay implementing programs to help. He had to start something now. And he planned to address the sewage problem first. The filth was everywhere—garbage in piles behind buildings, shallow pools of disposal in public areas, and muddy thoroughfares mixed with livestock waste.

The city council had allocated some money for the purpose of cleansing the city. But they'd taken little action. He would petition them to release the funds to aid his clean-up efforts.

"With spring on the way," he said, "the fumes will only get worse."

His predication was met with nods of agreement.

Riley pushed forward with part of his plan. "I suggest we cart away the waste and sewage to the city limits. If we can eliminate some of the noxious air people are breathing, maybe we can slow the spread."

"Aye," came a chorus of agreement.

"I'll get permission from the Board of Aldermen for safe places to dispose of the waste. In the meantime, we need to find carts for hauling it away and come up with a rotation of volunteers willing to lend a hand."

More nods and murmurs met his suggestion.

"We'll also instruct residents to clean their homes as often and as thoroughly as possible." Such efforts would be difficult. He knew from his own family's tenement how hard it was with so many people living together. Clean water wasn't easily accessible to combat the constant accumulation of mud dragged in from the street and coal dust produced from the cast-iron stoves.

At the sound of a woman's mournful wail from the cracked window above, Riley paused, the hairs rising on the back of his neck. Something had happened. And an urgency swelled within him, the same prodding he felt whenever he saw someone who needed rescuing.

Without concluding the plans with the men, he dashed into

the tenement and raced up the two flights of stairs to the apartment. The door was ajar and the wailing was louder, more heartbroken.

Riley pushed his way inside to the sight of the young mother, a recently arrived Irish immigrant, kneeling on the floor, clutching a baby in her arms, rocking back and forth and sobbing.

Finola was beside her, a hand on the woman's back. Her gaze was stricken, and her face was pale.

The baby had obviously died. And from the listlessness of the two other little children lying on blankets on the floor close by, Riley had the feeling death would call again soon. They were too weak from their hunger and the ship voyage to survive whatever illness they'd caught.

An ache lodged in Riley's chest. He hated to see the loss. The family had already suffered enough. But at this point, Finola had done what she could.

He approached quietly and touched her shoulder.

Tears streaked her cheeks, and she didn't move, didn't look at him.

"Finola?" He hesitated, then brushed the pad of his thumb down her cheek, wiping at one of the lines of tears.

She didn't shift her attention from the infant.

His pulse stuttered with the same sense of foreboding that had been growing all week. "We have to go."

Still, she didn't acknowledge his presence. It was almost as if she was somewhere else. Was she locked in the past, reliving what had happened with the baby sister she'd lost?

He had to get her away from the dead infant now. It was too much for her.

Without waiting for her permission, he bent down and scooped her up into his arms. As he straightened, he cradled her against his chest. She stiffened for only a moment before she buried her face in the crook of his neck.

As he carried her out of the apartment, the dampness of her

232

tears brushed against his skin, and he knew without a doubt that her sorrow went deeper than the dead baby back in the apartment.

Though the wails of the mother drifted after them, the dingy passageway was deserted, and he paused near the top of the stairway. "Talk to me, Finola."

She sucked in a shuddering breath and shook her head. "I'm sorry. I'll be alright in a minute."

Frustration reared up inside him. Why wouldn't she confide in him? The most open she'd been with him had been the night of their breakup. But the only reason she'd shared was because she'd known it would cause a wedge between them.

"Please. Tell me what's wrong." He held his breath and prayed she'd unburden herself. He longed to be the one she turned to and found comfort from. But, as before, he sensed that though she'd resigned herself to marriage, she was widening the distance between them instead of closing it.

"I'm just a wee bit sad. But I'll be right again soon."

He bit back a sigh. "You're thinking of Ava."

She didn't respond, which was answer enough.

"You're not to blame for that baby's death any more than you were for Ava's."

"I could have done more." Her whisper was harsh, but it was a start toward opening up.

"You're not God, and He's the only one capable of performing miracles."

She shook her head. "He doesn't help me anymore. Not after what I did to Ava."

"You have to let go of the past. It has nothing to do with what happened today."

"It has everything to do with it."

"And everything to do with why you won't allow yourself to love me?"

She grew so motionless he could almost hear her heart beating.

Had he finally hit on the truth? "Tell me, Finola, will you ever let yourself love me, or are you planning to punish yourself for the rest of your life?"

She held herself still for a moment longer, then began to wiggle to free herself from his hold.

He gently set her down on her feet in the hallway, and as he did, she took a step back and glared up at him with flashing eyes. "Who are you to speak of me letting go and punishing myself when you're the king of doing that very thing?"

"I don't punish myself—"

"Maybe you're not punishing yourself so much as having to prove yourself worthy of living when nearly everyone else in your family drowned."

The moment she whispered the words, her eyes widened and she cupped a hand over her mouth, almost as if she couldn't believe she'd spoken so bluntly and wanted to take everything back.

But it was too late. Her declaration hit its mark, stabbing his heart so that pain radiated out to the rest of his body. How could she bring up his past at a time like this and use it against him to protect herself?

She dropped her hand, her eyes growing contrite. "I'm sorry, Riley—"

"We need to go." He waved a hand toward the stairs, motioning for her to descend. He didn't want to hear her quick apology, didn't want to avoid important topics, didn't want to gloss over any more feelings. He wanted her to share deeply and be willing to give him all of herself. Could he live with any less than that?

The ride back to her house was silent. As he drew the wagon to a halt, she clasped her hands together on her lap and stared at them.

For a moment, he had the strange sense this was the end. Last time when they'd sat in front of her house, she'd been

the one to part ways with him—or at least tried her best to do
so. Now it was his turn. And this time, the breaking of their
match would be final. It had to be. He had to accept once and
for all that her desire for him wasn't strong enough to push
her into marriage.

Darkness was settling, but the Shanahan mansion was aglow
from within, a small staff of servants having returned to the
city to care for Finola. Regardless, he'd refrained from going
into the home over the past week, hadn't wanted to cause any
further gossip about their relationship.

But that didn't matter anymore. Nothing else mattered except what she wanted.

"Tell me one thing, Finola." He spoke softly, unable to keep
the sadness from his voice. "Would you have agreed to marry
me if you had no worry of the mayoral election or of your
father's steel contract?"

She fiddled with her mittens.

"Please. Just be honest with me."

After a moment, she sighed. "No, Riley. Probably not."

The words, like earlier, stabbed him. He sat back against his
seat, hardly able to breathe.

"But I promised I would marry you, and so I will." Her words
rushed out, as though she sensed his pain and wanted to make
him feel better.

The problem was, nothing could make him feel better . . .
except one thing—knowing that she wanted him. She didn't
have to love him, probably couldn't love him the same way he
loved her. He didn't expect that. But at the very least, he needed
her to give him—give them—a chance.

Maybe she'd agreed to marry him. But she was just as set
against letting him into her life now as the day Bellamy had
first brought them together. And as much as he wanted Finola,
for as beautiful and kind and amazing as she was, he had to
let her go, let her fulfill her vow to enter the convent, let her

ease her guilt, let her live in such a way that would make her happy and peaceful.

Because ultimately, that's what he wanted for her. Happiness and peace. If he couldn't provide it for her, then he wanted her to find it at the convent. Even though everything in him protested the prospect of losing her, he knew he had to set her free. This time was good-bye. And this time he intended to mean it.

With his heart crushed against his chest, he helped her down from the wagon and walked her to the front door. Winston met them as he usually did. But instead of moving into the house as she normally did, Finola paused, as though sensing he had more to say.

He was tempted to lean down and steal one last kiss from her. But he hadn't kissed her since getting caught in bed with her. And what would be the point of kissing her now, except to stir up more emotion between them that didn't need stirring?

He squeezed her hand, then released it and took a step back. "I want you to know I have loved you as I have no one else, and I've only wanted you and nothing else."

In the light of the hallway, her eyes glowed a bright blue, and her pretty lips parted with the escape of a short breath.

His muscles tensed in anticipation, and he willed her to say something in response. Anything he could take as a sign that she wanted him enough to fight for their match. But in the next instant, she bowed her head. "Good night, Riley."

The hurt rushed in again, this time more forcefully, like the tip of a bayonet plunging in for the kill. He bowed his head at her in return. Then he turned and walked away and didn't look back.

26

*T*he baby's wails echoed louder. But no matter where Finola looked, she couldn't find the infant—not in the cradle, not under the bed, not in the hallway, not on the long marble stairway.

Another cry echoed, this time the sobbing of a young woman, growing closer with each step Finola took. The woman was weeping uncontrollably at the bottom of the stairway. One of the immigrant women. She was rocking a lifeless bundle in her arms, the child wrapped in blankets that were frayed and thin and dirty.

Finola's legs trembled, and as she reached the mother, she peeked down to find that the baby in the bundle was Ava, her face pale, her eyes wide open, but her body too silent and still.

Horror welled up within Finola. "Ava?" She shook the baby. "Wake up, Ava! Wake up!"

Bile rose swiftly as she took the infant from the immigrant woman. Finola tried to scream, but nothing came out—except a gasp.

The gasp woke Finola to her bedroom bathed in morning light, and she covered her eyes with her hand, needing to avoid the brightness and ward off the remnants of the nightmare.

As wakefulness rushed in, the memories of yesterday in the tenement came back, the sick children, the frantic efforts to save the baby, the horror of failing—so similar to that helpless feeling she'd had when she discovered Ava's lifeless body.

The infant's mother hadn't blamed Finola for the loss. And deep inside Finola knew she wasn't at fault for the death. The baby had been too sick, and even though she'd worked with the mother, doing everything they could to save the child, not even their best efforts had been enough to keep the breath of life flowing through that baby's lungs.

Riley had been right when he'd told her, *"You're not God, and He's the only one capable of performing miracles."* She hadn't wanted to hear it yesterday. But all last night, his words had whispered within her over and over.

He'd also told her she wasn't to blame for the immigrant baby's death any more than she was to blame for Ava's. Was he right about that too?

A half sob escaped, the remorse of the past welling up once more. Would it never end?

From beside her on the bed, delicate, long fingers slid into hers and squeezed.

Finola released a yelp at the same time that she jerked upward. Who was in bed with her and holding her hand?

Her heart beating at triple the speed, she shifted and swept aside her long hair to find Enya lying on her side facing Finola. She was fully clothed, except for her cloak and shoes. Her stunning red hair was still fashionably coiled. But her face was splotchy, her eyes rimmed with red, and her cheeks damp with tears.

Finola squealed and threw herself against her sister, wrapping her arms around the young woman and drawing her into an embrace. Enya came to her willingly, hugging her in response, burying her face, and releasing deep, pain-filled sobs.

Finola didn't care that she was sobbing aloud too. Sobbing

for Ava, for the immigrant baby, for all the little ones whose lives had been cut short. And she was sobbing for Enya and whatever had broken her spirit.

When finally their weeping quieted to sniffles, Enya was the first to whisper, "You were dreaming about Ava again, weren't you?"

"Aye. How did you know?"

"I've known about your nightmares, heard your crying. And I know why you haven't worked on your doily creations again." Enya spoke as matter-of-factly as always but didn't pull away. Instead, she reached up and stroked Finola's hair. "I'm just sorry I was too selfish to comfort you before now, so I am."

Tears stung Finola's eyes. "I'm not sure I would have been ready for comfort." It was the truth. Before today, she probably would have pushed Enya away and denied that she had any problems. But since Riley had come into her life, he'd challenged her to be more honest about how she was really feeling.

"Tell me more, Finola." Enya continued to stroke her hair. "Tell me everything. I want to listen and be a better sister for you, the kind you've always been for me."

Finola's throat closed up at the offer. She swallowed and still struggled to speak. "First, tell me about you. I want to know where you've been and what's brought you back home."

Enya sniffled again, her voice layered with a new maturity and sadness. "I'll tell you everything. But first, we need to talk about Ava. It's a conversation that's long overdue."

Finola hesitated.

"Please?" Enya breathed out the single word. And as always, Finola couldn't deny her sister anything.

She stuttered and stopped as she shared her sorrow over Ava's death, blaming herself for it, then how the nightmares and crying had haunted her over the years.

"The crying became so troublesome, I finally vowed I would

go into the convent to do penance and there have peace," she finished.

Enya had pulled back and rested her head on her pillow, watching Finola during the entire retelling, her usually vibrant green eyes filled with something Finola couldn't name. "What if I tell you I'm at fault for Ava's death?"

"You're not. I was the one Mam assigned to watch Ava. I should have put aside my doilies and focused on Ava."

Enya reached for Finola's hand again. "Mam and I had an argument the morning Ava died. She told me I needed to help out more with the little ones instead of spending so much time on my music lessons."

Finola rested her head on her pillow, her face only inches from Enya's as they whispered just as they had when they'd been little girls. "You're not at fault, Enya. You weren't even present."

"But I should have been present." The words came out forcefully, passionately, in perfect Enya form. "I was selfish to focus on what I wanted and never allow you time to enjoy the things that give you pleasure."

Finola couldn't find words to respond. Maybe she'd taken on too much responsibility in caring for Ava on her own. And maybe she could have benefitted from having breaks from Ava once in a while. Whatever the case, was it time to stop carrying the heavy burden of Ava's death entirely on her shoulders?

What had Riley told her? Her mind went back again to their conversation in the wagon last evening when he'd brought her home. He'd asked her if she'd ever stop punishing herself by not allowing herself to love him. Could she stop doing penance? She wasn't sure. But maybe it was time to see if she could.

Enya lifted a hand and wiped Finola's cheek and the tears that had escaped. "I overheard Mam once tell Da that she blames herself for Ava's death."

"What? How could she blame herself?"

"She said that she was tired after Ava's birthing, never had

240

enough energy, and didn't want to take care of the baby. She said that she should have tried harder and done more instead of leaving so much up to you."

"She was busy with the other little ones."

Enya shrugged. "I guess we can all find fault if we look hard enough."

Finola wrapped her arms across her chest, suddenly chilled with the knowledge that both Enya and Mam harbored guilt the same way she had. How would her life have been different if she'd talked more about her grief and sorrows instead of keeping everything inside? Or using passive methods to express herself?

"I hope you'll finally give yourself permission to love a man, Finola." Enya's eyes brimmed with tears.

Enya's words echoed Riley's. For so long she'd denied herself the idea of marriage and family. Was it possible to change the way she viewed her life?

"And maybe— " Enya's voice cracked—"just maybe, he'll be someone who will love you enough in return to stay with you."

Finola's first thought was of Riley. But then as Enya's eyes squeezed shut and tears slipped out, Finola reached up and cupped Enya's cheek gently. "There, now. Tell me all about it."

Enya leaned into her hand but didn't open her eyes. "Bryan left me for the gold fields of California." Enya's whisper was laced with heartbreak and regret.

Even as anger reared up inside Finola at a man who would leave behind a new bride, she pushed it down. Enya didn't need her to belittle and berate Bryan. She'd likely done enough of that herself. Right now, Enya needed her to listen and offer comfort.

"I'm sorry, Enya," she whispered, taking her turn to stroke Enya's cheek and hair. "You'll miss him then, to be sure."

Her sister's eyes flew open and flashed with the sparks Finola was used to seeing there. "Oh no, I won't miss him. I told him if he left, I never wanted to see him again."

"And what did he say?"

"He said that was fine, that he didn't want to see me again either." Her expression hardened, and she pressed her lips together. "He ignored my love and walked away."

Finola squirmed at the realization she'd done the same thing to Riley just last night when he'd spoken of his love. *"I have loved you as I have no one else, and I've only wanted you and nothing else."*

She'd ignored it and walked away from him, had wanted to block it out and pretend he'd never spoken of love. In fact, she'd done her best not to think on his love all night long.

But now, the passion in his words returned to her with a force that took her breath away—with a wee bit of fear and wonder. Did she dare consider that he loved her enough to overlook her past mistakes?

She twisted the claddagh ring he'd given her on the day they'd eaten the gander. She traced the hands clasped together, the heart, the crown. Friendship, love, loyalty. He'd offered all three to her over and over again. But she hadn't done the same with him, even though he'd proven that he deserved it all, and more.

In some ways she'd been as callous as Bryan, maybe even more so.

"I don't think he really loved me to begin with." Enya's whisper ended on the note of a sob.

Finola pushed the thoughts of Riley from her mind. She couldn't dwell on him or their relationship at the moment. She had to focus on Enya, who was heartbroken that her husband had chosen to leave her for the lure of gold rather than to stay and love her.

Again, Finola gathered her sister in her arms. Enya's tears flowed once more, but this time with a bitter edge. She swiped at her cheeks as though to wipe away all feelings for her husband. Then she drew in a shuddering breath and spoke in an anguished voice. "I'm pregnant."

Finola froze. She mentally calculated the amount of time Enya had been married. Had it been three weeks? Maybe four at the most? Certainly, she could be pregnant in that short of time. But how would she know it already?

"It's rather soon to assume you're in the family way, isn't it?"

"No." Enya paused and drew in a breath, as though to fortify herself. "I'm late for my courses. And I'm never late, always early."

Finola scrambled to make sense of what Enya was telling her. Was it possible Enya had intimate relations with Bryan before they were wed?

Words of admonition swelled up within Finola. Mam and Da had taught them better than that. And Da, with all his rules regarding courtship, had worked so hard to keep them chaste and out of a situation like this.

"I can see what you're thinking," Enya whispered. "And no, I told Bryan I wouldn't—well, sleep with him before we were married even though he wanted me to."

Finola pursed her lips together to keep from saying something unholy about Bryan. Clearly, the man had cared about Enya only for what he could take from her. Once he'd had his fill, he decided to move on.

"Oh, Finola." Enya's voice wavered. "I was wrong about him. And now it's too late."

A knock sounded on the bedroom door, startling them both.

"Finola?" came the muffled voice of their da from the hallway.

Enya's grip tightened upon Finola. "Don't tell Da anything."

Finola hesitated. Enya wouldn't be able to hide her failed marriage and pregnancy for long. Wouldn't Da find out everything eventually?

"I need to figure out what to do first," Enya whispered, her eyes pleading with Finola.

The knocking thudded again, this time louder. "Finola?"

She pushed up from the mattress, but Enya clutched her arm. "Please?"

Finola nodded. It wasn't her place to interfere in Enya's life. "Okay."

Enya fell back into her pillow and pulled the covers up over her head, as if that could somehow keep her hidden from Da.

Inhaling a deep breath, Finola slipped out of bed. "Da? Come in."

The door opened, and he stepped inside. He was attired as usual in a finely tailored suit, his red hair neatly greased and combed, and his face cleanly shaven. Even though he looked as successful and put-together as always, something about him hinted at despair. Maybe it was the slump of his shoulders or the sadness in his eyes or the droop of his mouth.

"I'm sorry for waking you, Finola." He fidgeted with a piece of paper in his hands.

"I was awake already." She waited for him to look at the bed and to see Enya's outline under the covers.

Instead, he unfolded what appeared to be a letter.

She glanced at the draperies and the amount of light in an attempt to gauge the time. "You're in town early this morning."

"Aye." He ran his finger along the edge of the paper. "I came straight away so I could see if Riley Rafferty's message to me is true."

"Riley sent you a message?" Finola's pulse tapped an uneven pace.

"He had it delivered to me last night."

"Oh?" A strange foreboding came over Finola. She had the urge to stalk over to her da, rip the letter from his hand, and shred it into a hundred tiny pieces.

"You can imagine my frustration when I received the news."

"What news?" Did she really want to know?

"Don't tell me you aren't aware." His tone was suddenly edged with censure, and when he peered across the room at her, his normally kind and patient eyes were filled with disappointment.

"I saw him last night. He brought me home from visiting in the Kerry Patch. We said good-bye as usual."

But was it as usual? Or had there been a finality about the parting she'd overlooked?

"He called off the match."

Even as her da spoke the words, Finola guessed the truth—Riley's words of love had been his good-bye, that's what.

Protest swelled along with bile. What had she done now? "He can't call it off. He needs the match to win the election, and you need the steel contract."

Her da shook his head, frustration creasing his brow and crinkling his eyes. "He said that Rafferty Wagon Company would honor our contract anyway, that they would purchase the steel for their wagons exclusively from us."

"But the election?"

"He dropped out of the race. I stopped by his campaign office on the way home, and it's cleaned out. Everyone's gone."

His quitting wasn't possible. Not when she'd promised to marry him, had even begun to accept the fact that she would have a different life than the one she'd imagined.

Her muscles tensed. "The campaign must have moved locations."

"He's done, Finola. When I went to the wagon shop, I was told he left the city."

Riley was gone?

Her chest was achingly silent, her heart refusing to beat. "Why?" The word slipped out before she realized it.

Her da stared at the sheet in his hands. "He said he loves you but that he can't bargain for you or push you into marriage if you're resisting it. He'll have you freely or not at all."

Freely or not at all.

She pressed her fist against her mouth to hold back the cry that needed release. Riley had done this for her. Even though she'd stopped fighting against the match, he'd known that she hadn't wanted marriage, that she was just going along with the plans out of obligation to him and to her family.

He'd told her once that he wouldn't marry her unless she was willing. And even though she'd told him she was willing, apparently he decided her acquiescence wasn't enough. He wanted more from her than she'd offered.

Her da cleared his throat. "Riley said you have your heart set on joining the Sisters of Charity convent, and that we shouldn't deny you the opportunity."

Finola closed her mouth, opened it, but then closed it again. Riley hadn't just given her freedom, he was giving her what she'd always wanted—the chance to enter the convent. He must have written it in his letter to her da, had so easily communicated her wishes. If only she could learn from Riley to do the same.

Maybe people wouldn't always listen to her. But why should she let that stop her from expressing herself more clearly and directly?

"I'm sorry, Finola." Her da's shoulders slumped even lower. "Maybe we should have let you enter the convent all along instead of trying to find a husband for you."

"You were doing what you believed was best for me."

"And is the convent best?" Her da looked up and met her gaze levelly.

Was it? For so long, she'd thought she knew what she wanted, thought the convent with its orderliness was the only place she'd ever be truly happy. She'd even convinced herself that Riley's recklessness would be too hard to cope with.

But as her da held her gaze, the questions in his eyes sent doubt spiraling through her. One swirled faster and more turbulently than all the others. How much did she care about Riley? And could she give him up forever? How would she live with herself if she let Riley walk out of her life?

Because the truth was—the truth that she hadn't wanted to acknowledge—she cared about him much more than she should.

At her silence, her da began to fold the slip of paper. "Very well, Finola. I'll arrange a meeting with the Mother Superior for later today to begin the process."

"No." Enya pushed back the covers and sat straight up.

Da jerked back a step, obviously not having paid attention to the bed behind Finola closely enough to realize another person was there.

"No," Enya said again, this time more forcefully. "Finola cares about Riley Rafferty but is just too scared to admit it."

"Enya?" Da's voice cracked, and he pressed a hand over his heart.

She climbed out of bed and stood at the edge, beside Finola. "Hi, Da." Her hands trembled, and she clasped them together.

He raked his gaze over her, taking in her tear-streaked cheeks and wrinkled garments. "You're unharmed?"

"Aye."

Without another word, he started toward her, his stride long and hard. When he reached her, he grabbed both arms, searched her again, and then dragged her into an embrace. "Oh, sweet blessed mother, you're home."

The relief in his voice was so tangible, it brought swift tears to Finola's eyes. Enya couldn't hold back her tears either. Or her sobs. One escaped, followed by another, until she was weeping quietly in his arms. "I'm sorry, Da. I'm sorry." She said the words over and over while he clung to her and kissed the top of her head.

Finola's throat ached with the need to weep. Their family wasn't perfect. It wasn't even close to perfect. But they stuck together through all the difficulties of life. No matter their mistakes. No matter their faults. No matter the challenges.

They had each other and loved each other. It was something special. And maybe it was time for her to finally see that. And admit that Riley was special too.

He might have given up on her. But she wasn't sure she was ready to let him go.

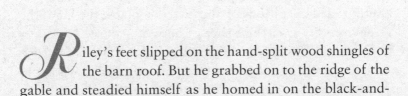

27

*R*iley's feet slipped on the hand-split wood shingles of the barn roof. But he grabbed on to the ridge of the gable and steadied himself as he homed in on the black-and-white cat crouched at the edge.

"Come here, cat."

In response, the cat flattened its ears and hissed. It only had a stub for a tail. One ear was chewed in half. And it was as fat as an overfed piglet. If the thing had ever been cute, it wasn't anymore, either in looks or in temperament.

Riley held out a hand, in what he hoped was a gesture of goodwill.

He was met with a swipe of claws and a low growl.

"Come now." Riley pulled back. "That's not the kind of appreciation I expect for risking my life and limb to save you."

He'd always told himself he wouldn't put himself in danger for animals. But here he was. On the roof of his uncle's barn. Rescuing a devil cat.

He paused and let himself take in the view. The land to the west of St. Louis was fertile for farming, and his uncle had cleared large swaths over the past ten years, earning himself a reputation as one of the largest corn and wheat producers.

He'd also taken to raising hogs and was making a decent profit at the endeavor.

Acres of the countryside spread out as far as Riley could see. Some of the fields were dark with newly turned soil in readiness for the spring planting. Others were fallow with the remains of yellowed plants and weeds that had sprung up and been left to wither and die. Pockets of lush, untouched woodland offered hunting grounds and provided protection against the unrelenting winds that blew in from the Kansas prairies.

Riley dragged in a deep breath and tried to find satisfaction in the beauty of the scenery. After the filth and mud and overcrowded conditions of the city, this place, the land, the wide-open sky, it was all a slice of heaven.

But as much as he wanted to relish the fresh air and the time with his family, his lungs squeezed painfully. In fact, his entire body felt as though it had been run over by a dozen teamster wagons.

Bother it. He'd been away from Finola for less than twenty-four hours and it felt more like twenty-four years.

"Call the kitty by her name, Riley," shouted one of the children watching him with wide eyes from below. "Her royal highness, Queen Victoria."

He'd lost count of how many cousins lived on the farm. The oldest was around the same age as Lorette, with the rest ranging down to a newborn babe. When he'd arrived earlier today, he was greeted by the whole crowd, including his sisters, who had never looked healthier with pink cheeks, bright eyes, and wind-tossed hair.

The country life agreed with them. And with his dad too. From what Riley could tell, his dad was back to normal, helping around the farm with chores as if he'd never had a heart attack a month ago.

"You have to do it properly." This came from his youngest sister, Colleen, who at eight was as bossy as a pecking hen.

Under normal circumstances, her ridiculous request would have made him grin. But not today. His grin was gone, along with his heart. He'd left both behind the moment he'd driven away from Finola's last night and gone straight to his campaign office.

There he'd done what he should have all along—he told his team he couldn't in good conscience run for mayor without taking a stand against slavery. The team argued with him, as they had previously. But he remained firm.

When Father O'Kirwin had told him to pull out of the election, Riley had done so willingly. In fact, even if Father O'Kirwin hadn't told him to, Riley had planned on it anyway. He'd realized he didn't want to join in political games where he had to compromise who he was in order to lead.

As soon as he'd left the campaign office and went back to the wagon shop, he'd written a letter to James Shanahan. He'd wanted to give Finola her freedom, needed her to know that she was no longer bound by the election or the steel contract. Then he'd paid one of the apprentices to drive it directly to Finola's father. He'd had to do so before he changed his mind.

And it was a good thing he had because when he'd woken up this morning, he was desperate to make her see reason. He'd almost driven past her house on his way out of town. He had to remind himself multiple times that he was leaving her because he loved her too much to keep her from the life she wanted, the one she believed would make her happy.

He knew he wouldn't be happy without her. But he'd made his choice. Now he had to resign himself to what he'd done.

He inched forward, trying to balance himself on the ridge. He'd been on plenty of roofs before. But the lusty wind and the light drizzle of the February afternoon were making this rescue more dangerous than he'd anticipated.

"You have to call her your royal highness." Colleen's call rose above the others.

Riley pretended to bow his head to the cat. "Will you please allow me to help you off this roof, your royal highness, Queen Victoria?" He raised his voice so the children could hear him and was glad the adults weren't around to witness his foolish antics.

"That's right, Riley." Colleen's voice contained happiness.

He shifted his attention to her, a forced smile at the ready. Before he could offer it, his fingers slipped again. In the next instant, he found himself sliding off the ridge and down the gable, unable to find a foothold to slow himself.

He clawed at the shingles, hoping to latch on to a loose one. The pitch of the roof wasn't overly steep, but the dampness and ice made everything too slick, and as he neared the edge of the barn, he had one thought—he was going to die and wouldn't get to see Finola again.

As his body plummeted over the side, he slapped a hand hard against the eave and managed to gain a grip.

He dangled precariously, the pressure tearing at his arm socket and stretching his fingers. He lurched upward and managed to grab on with his other hand. But even so, he wouldn't be able to hang on for long. His fingers were already losing their hold.

A glance down told him the drop was too far, but he wouldn't die today. Instead, he'd end up with a broken leg or arm at the very least. He couldn't do that in front of the children. They didn't need to see that sort of accident.

Rapidly, he assessed his other options. The window he'd crawled out of was at the other end. But the hayloft door was open below him. If he could get the right momentum, he might be able to swing into the upper-floor storage area. His landing would be hard. He'd probably still get hurt. But at least the children wouldn't see it.

Gritting his teeth, he swung his legs and let go of the roof, propelling himself toward the open door. A moment later, he

252

crashed onto the rough wooden planks that lined the rafters and were used for extra storage for livestock feed.

He attempted to roll and soften the landing. But his head slammed into something, and the world went black.

◆ ◆ ◆ ◆ ◆ ◆ ◆

Pain pounded in Riley's temples. He groaned and tried to lift a hand to ease the pressure, but someone else gently situated a warm heating pad against his head.

"Finola?" he whispered, sudden need swelling so that he pushed himself up. A mattress and bed creaked beneath him, and as he opened his eyes, he found that he was in the main bedroom on the first level of his uncle's farmhouse.

The room was dark with the shadows of the evening, but a lantern on the bedside table revealed the cluttered interior— pieces of cut material for clothing, colorful quilt squares, a half-finished braided rug, and a sewing basket.

He shifted his gaze toward the person at his side, only to find his dad seated upon a stool next to the bed. His dad's brows were creased and his blond-brown hair in disarray. "It's me," he said gravely. "Finola's not here."

Closing his eyes, Riley fell back against the bed and the pillow, the roaring in his head unbearable again. He pressed his lips together to keep from groaning.

"How are you feeling?" His dad shifted the warming bag.

"Like I got kicked in the head by a mule."

"After knocking your head against the rafter the way you did, the doctor said you're lucky you didn't crack your neck right in half." His dad's voice had lost all concern and was now filled with reproach, as were his eyes. "What in the name of all that's holy were you doing getting a cat off the barn roof?"

"The children asked me—"

"Balderdash, Riley." His dad stood and crammed his hand

through his hair. "Your excuses aren't worth a drop of water in a horse's trough."

Riley couldn't argue. He'd been stupid to go up. "I'm sorry—"

"I don't give a straw if you're sorry. *Sorry* won't keep you alive the next time."

His dad paced to the closed door and stood staring straight ahead.

The loud voices and the clink of dishes mingled with the scent of pork, which, thankfully, meant everyone was eating supper and not paying attention to their conversation.

"You're a good man, Riley. And people love you for your willingness to jump in and help when no one else can. But you take too many chances. And one of these times you won't survive."

"Maybe not. But at least no one can say I didn't try."

"Try at what?" His dad turned and stared at him. "What are you trying to prove?"

Finola's words came rushing back from the other night. *"Maybe you're trying to prove yourself worthy of living when nearly everyone else in your family drowned."*

What if she'd been right?

What if all these years, he'd been rescuing everyone else the way he hadn't been able to rescue his family?

What if all these years, he'd been attempting to show God He hadn't made a mistake in letting him live when everyone else had died?

He closed his eyes, wanting to avoid answering the question. But after he'd encouraged honesty from Finola, he'd be a hypocrite if he didn't acknowledge the truth hitting him square in the face.

"You're right." He forced himself to open his eyes and meet his dad's gaze. "Maybe I'm trying to prove that you made the right choice when you jumped into the river and helped me instead of Ma or one of the boys."

254

His dad leaned back against the door, almost as if the words had physically hit him. Pain etched lines into his face, and tears sprang to his eyes. "Saints above, Riley. I never knew you felt that way."

"I never thought about it either until just a day or so ago." A deep, dark chasm opened inside Riley's chest. "But it makes sense. Maybe if I do enough, someday I'll finally feel worthy of living when everyone else died."

His dad started toward the bed with heavy steps. When he dropped onto the stool, he reached for Riley's hand and bowed his head. His grip was tight, and he didn't speak. Instead, he pressed Riley's hand to his lips as tears bathed Riley's skin.

Riley never cried and had never seen his dad cry. But at this moment, he blinked back tears as the heartache that had been buried inside began to work its way up—the heartache that had tormented him by saying he wasn't enough.

His dad looked up, his cheeks wet, his eyes glassy. "Son, I want you to know that I love you, and you've never had to prove anything to me."

"But you saved me when you could have saved one of them."

He shook his head. "It all happened so fast. Everyone was in the river before I could jump off. The others were already too far away, and you happened to be the closest one. I didn't think I'd be able to reach *you* in time, didn't think I'd be able to grab ahold of you. But by the grace of God, I got to you."

It had been so many years, Riley's memories of the event had faded. Was it possible he'd remembered things all wrong?

"I came so close to losing you too, Riley. And I remember pulling you onto the shore and falling to my knees and thanking God that He'd allowed me to keep you." Dad's voice cracked with emotion. "Every day I look at you and thank God all over again that I at least have you."

The ache burned at Riley's throat, and he swallowed it. "I'm thankful God gave me you too, Dad."

"I hope you weren't running for mayor to prove something." He released Riley's hand, then wiped at his cheeks.

Riley started to shake his head, then paused. Had that been one more effort to show he'd been worthy of being rescued from the river? "I don't know. I don't think so. I genuinely want to do more to help the people of St. Louis, especially those in the Kerry Patch."

"And you think dropping out of the mayoral election will help them?" His dad's voice was gentle, but his eyes probed Riley for the truth.

The truth was, he didn't need to win the election to help the immigrants. The past month of serving with Finola and then his recent organizational efforts at trying to slow the spread of cholera had shown him that.

He didn't have to be in an official position to be a leader and make a difference for the immigrants. With his influence, maybe he'd even eventually teach them about the evils of slavery so that if he ran for elected office, he'd be able to do so with integrity.

"There are several reasons why I dropped out. And I admit, one of them is because of Finola. I didn't want her marrying me just so I could win the election."

"So you do want to marry her still?"

When Riley had arrived earlier, he told his dad about calling off his match as well as dropping out of the election. But they'd been surrounded by too many people for him to explain all the details of why. Maybe he hadn't been ready to talk about it. But now, after the conversation they'd just had, he needed to share, needed to know what to do next.

He pressed one hand to his throbbing head and one to his aching heart, not sure which hurt more. "It was agony living today without her. The thought of going tomorrow without her again makes me daft."

"Then don't go without her."

"It's not that simple. She wants to become a nun."

Brows lifting, his dad sat up a little straighter. "A worthwhile pursuit."

"And that's the trouble. Who can fault her for wanting to give her life over to God and the church?" Riley certainly couldn't, and he'd done the right thing in encouraging her father to allow it. Hadn't he?

"Sounds to me like you're faulting her."

Riley flattened his hand harder against his chest, but nothing could lessen the emptiness. "I've never loved a woman the way I love her."

His dad's shoulders relaxed, and a grin tugged at the corners of his mouth. "That's your answer, son."

"It is?"

"If you love her enough that you can't live without her, then you need to go and show her that love. Show her every day, even if it takes you the rest of your life."

Bellamy had once told him he was the one who could break through Finola's defenses and win her heart, that he had enough determination and daring to it.

Had he given up on Finola too easily?

"You're a scrapper," his dad said as if reading his thoughts. "Fight for her."

"But I don't want to push her into something she doesn't want."

"Then go slow. Be patient. Ask her to put off going into the convent to give you more time."

Riley nodded at the wise advice and relaxed against the pillow, the throbbing in his head turning more relentless. He wanted to close his eyes and go back to sleep.

"So, we're in agreement. No more idiotic stunts?"

Riley smiled. "Depends on the definition of *idiotic*."

"You want to know the definition of *idiotic*? Turning down the gift of a good woman. That's idiotic."

"Alright. I was an idiot. And I'll ride back to the city and tell her so tonight." Riley tried to fight against the sleep that was claiming him, but his eyes closed anyway.

"You're in no condition to go anywhere tonight." His dad's voice seemed to fade into the distance. "Tomorrow."

Yes, tomorrow the first thing he would do was ride to Finola's home, fall on his knees before her, and beg her to give him one more chance.

He would just have to pray he wasn't too late.

28

*F*inola slowed her steps as the Visitation Convent came into view. The simple brick building would soon become her home.

Her home.

The prospect didn't send a ripple of excitement through her as it normally did. Maybe because Da hadn't been himself since arriving home yesterday morning. Even this morn before he'd left to run errands, he'd seemed dismayed.

Aye, he was happy Enya had returned. His relief had been tangible. And perhaps because he'd gained back a daughter, he'd now have the strength he needed to finally let Finola go.

Whatever the case, he'd indicated that he intended to meet with the Mother Superior later today to begin discussing the terms for Finola's entrance into the order. Of course, he'd spoken with Finola again last night about the matter over supper and encouraged her to reconsider her desire for convent life. Enya had been adamant that Finola shouldn't go.

But in the end, Finola had done what she should have long ago—she gathered the courage to converse about it and asked them to respect her choice. Her voice wavered, her palms grew damp, and her heart raced the whole time she'd tried to explain that she loved the convent and the Sisters and their life of service and prayer.

Enya had shaken her head. "You might think you love the Sisters and their life. But the truth is, you're running into the convent so that you can run away from your problems."

Finola hadn't known how to respond.

When her da had cleared his throat, she'd expected him to agree with Enya. Instead, all he'd said was, "Bellamy McKenna is a very fine matchmaker if I ever did see one. I'll be using him again, that I will."

When Enya had brought up the issue of the convent in bed last night, Finola found her voice again, and she told Enya not to give advice about running away from her problems when she hadn't told Da about the pregnancy yet, not even after he'd made the announcement that he intended to get Enya's marriage to Bryan annulled.

Enya had started crying, and Finola had felt terrible for speaking her mind. Even so, she hadn't been able to get Enya's accusation out of her thoughts. Was she running away from her problems? She'd always believed that by going into the convent she'd be doing the right and brave thing. But what if it was the cowardly way out after all? What if she was simply seeking to escape rather than facing the fears and consequences of all that had happened with Ava?

Was it finally time to stop striving to control every aspect of her life? No matter how hard she worked to save the immigrants. No matter how much she'd done earlier in the week to save that sickly baby. No matter what steps she took to protect those she loved. She'd never be able to save everyone and control everything.

She'd never be perfect—not in an imperfect world where bad things happened even to the best of people.

Finola halted in front of the steps of the convent. She shifted her sack over her shoulder, the black habit inside. Today would be the first time in weeks that she went visiting with the Sisters and not with Riley.

And by next week on Shrove Tuesday, she'd make a pledge to become Christ's bride instead of Riley's bride.

Her heart gave a traitorous thump of protest, and keen longing for Riley rose so swiftly, it took her breath away. What was he doing? And how was he faring? No doubt he was enjoying spending time with his family in the country.

She slipped the bag off her shoulder and opened it. As she began to tug the black habit out, her heart gave another hard thud. She'd been wearing the habit the first time Riley had come to her rescue. What a rescue it had been with Riley on top of her, his face close to hers, his intense gaze captivating her.

She closed her eyes to block out the image, but her mind filled with the memory of when they'd been in his bed, his legs tangling with hers, his hands on her hips drawing her against him, his lips melding with hers in a blissful and endless kiss.

Heat spilled into her blood, pumping it hard and fast, and her muscles tightened with need . . . not only for his kisses, but for everything about him. There was so much about him that she loved—his easygoing ways, his mirth, his ability to relate to so many people, his genuine kindness, his willingness to do anything and go anywhere, his natural way of conversing.

Aye, he was impetuous and lived on the edge of danger, and it scared her. But he was everything she wanted and needed. And maybe she didn't just love his qualities. Maybe she loved *him*.

Holy mother, have mercy. She loved Riley Rafferty.

"Finola, dear," came a soft voice from the convent.

Finola's eyes popped open to the sight of Sister Anne standing on the top step. Attired in her plain cloak and the simple, wide-brimmed white bonnet, the older woman watched Finola with concerned eyes. "Is everything alright, dear?"

Was everything alright? Finola shook her head. How could anything be alright ever again when she'd fallen in love with

Riley? How had it happened? When? And why hadn't she noticed the feeling growing?

Maybe she had noticed it but had chosen to ignore it the way she did most of her feelings. But how could she disregard her feelings for Riley any longer? She couldn't, not when with every passing second, it was pulsing through her with growing strength and urgency.

Urgency for what?

Her gaze flitted up the length of the building, to the adjacent school, then to the interior of the convent through the open door. The other nuns were still donning their cloaks and bonnets. And the Mother Superior was standing in the hallway with them, admonishing them to spread the love of God everywhere they went.

As much as she loved the Sisters, she couldn't deny the truth. She loved Riley more, and she wanted to be with him. Aye, she wanted to be with him.

She released a long exhale as though she hadn't been breathing or really living until that moment.

"Finola, child, just the person I was hoping to see." The Mother Superior stepped outside onto the top of the stoop.

Finola bowed her head in respect to the revered leader. Had word already reached the Mother Superior of her da's intention to speak with her? Finola's chest burned again with a new resolution. She would need to return home and tell Da to wait to meet with the Mother Superior.

She needed to talk with Riley first. He might already have given up on her. After all, she'd relentlessly pushed him away. And their last parting had been so final.

She wouldn't blame Riley if he'd decided she wasn't worth the effort anymore. She'd been more than a little difficult. She could admit, she'd been impossible.

The Mother Superior offered her a rare smile. "I'm pleased to say that your father and I had an amicable meeting this morning and that he's given his blessing to you joining our family."

At the news, the other Sisters came outside, smiling and chattering excitedly. As they rushed down the stairs to hug her, she couldn't respond, the words lost inside a strangely dead and silent heart.

She was too late. After all these years of trying to convince her da to let her join the convent, he'd done it. He released her to live her life. She couldn't go back to him now and tell him she needed more time. How could she? That wouldn't be fair to him, and it wouldn't be fair to these dear Sisters.

Finola hugged the Sisters in return and tried to muster a respectable amount of enthusiasm, even though she felt none. Maybe she'd finally gotten what she thought she'd wanted. But in the process, she'd lost the one thing that mattered most—her match with Riley.

29

*R*iley stood outside the Shanahan mansion and fidgeted with his cravat and tall collar. He lifted his top hat and smoothed back a wayward strand of hair. Then he tugged at the lapel of his coat.

He'd taken extra care with his grooming, just as he had the first night he'd come with Bellamy to the Shanahans to discuss the possible match with Finola. That had been a momentous occasion, and he'd been anxious.

But this morning was even more important. And every nerve in his body was letting him know it. He wanted—no needed—to be at his very best before speaking with Finola. During the ride into the city earlier and while he'd gotten ready, he'd rehearsed a dozen different scenarios and exactly what he intended to say.

Though his head still ached from the fall from the barn roof yesterday, he hadn't let on with his family. If he'd shown the least bit of pain, Eleanor and Lorette and the other girls would have forced him back to bed and made him rest the entire day. After the women had clung to him and doted on him over breakfast, his dad had finally been the one to encourage the womenfolk to let him go.

With midmorning already upon him, he'd wasted enough time. He'd heard James Shanahan was in the city for a few days, had likely come when he'd gotten the letter canceling the match. And now when he saw Riley, he would probably greet him with a fist to his nose.

Shanahan had been counting on him to win over Finola, had believed he'd succeed where every other man had failed. And Riley had let him down.

Riley lifted a fist to the door and hesitated again. Today he intended to rectify that. He'd let Shanahan and Finola both know he would wait as long as it took for Finola to care about him in return.

She might not punch him in the nose, but she'd think nothing of slapping him in the face. In fact, he missed her so much that a slap from her was preferrable to nothing at all.

After clearing his throat, he rapped against the door, then took a step back, clasped his hands together, and waited.

Brisk footsteps echoed on the tile of the entryway inside, and as the door rattled and began to open, Riley arched his neck, then forced himself not to fidget and to present himself as a gentleman and not a rogue. He could do so once in a while.

The butler answered the door. Attired as usual in an immaculate black suit, not a strand of his silver hair was out of place. Rather than the welcoming nod, Winston remained overly stiff and formal. And silent. Without a word of greeting.

Riley supposed the aloofness was the butler's signal of displeasure for Riley calling off the match. He stifled his frustration and forced out his request. "May I please speak with Finola?"

Winston started to close the door. "Miss Shanahan isn't home this morning."

Riley shot out a hand to keep the servant from slamming the door in his face. "When do you expect her to return?" Was she already out visiting among the immigrants? If so, she'd likely gone with the Sisters of Charity. He glanced down the street, not daring to hope that he'd get a glimpse of her riding away in the wagon, but hoping nonetheless.

The residential area was quiet, almost deserted for the February morning. He supposed more families were leaving the city if they could find a safer place to temporarily live. Not everyone had a country home like the Shanahans or relatives like he did. Many people would have no choice but to stay in the city and suffer as the cholera spread.

In fact, just a short while ago as he'd been changing, Big Jim had informed him of a dozen more cases of cholera that had sprung up over the past two days. Riley had sent word to several of the Irish leaders and asked them to gather tonight at their usual Front Street meeting place to rally more men, even women. It was time to step up their efforts to combat the spread of the cholera. And he needed all the help he could get.

Winston pressed against the door again. "I really cannot say when Miss Shanahan will return."

"Is Finola visiting the immigrants with the Sisters of Charity?"

"Riley?" A woman's voice came from the winding staircase.

Riley's pulse skipped ahead. Was Finola home after all? He tried to peer into the entrance room, but Winston blocked him.

A moment later, however, Winston stepped aside, and Enya sidled beside him, wearing a fashionable day dress with her red hair tied up into a neat chignon. Though she was a pretty girl, she couldn't begin to compare to Finola's mesmerizing beauty.

When had Enya returned? And where was her husband? Riley glanced beyond her, expecting to see the fellow. But from the quiet of the interior, he guessed no one else was home.

He shifted his attention back to the prodigal daughter who'd caused the entire Shanahan family heartache over the past month. He was glad, especially for Finola's sake, that Enya was back and appeared to be safe. "It's pleasant to see you, Enya. I hope you're well."

"Thank you, Riley." Her eyes welled with sudden tears, and

he had the sinking feeling that not all was well and that Enya's story wasn't ending but just beginning.

He didn't know what to say, didn't want to probe, but he also didn't want to ignore her obvious distress. Rather than say the wrong thing, he stood silently and waited.

"I'm glad you're here," she said after a moment. "Maybe you can put a stop to the nonsense."

"What kind of nonsense?"

"Da went over and met with the Mother Superior this morn and made arrangements for Finola to enter the convent, with plans to give them her dowry."

That sounded official, and each word drove a nail of dread deeper. Was he too late? "Has she already gone then?"

"I'm not sure when she's moving, but I suspect it will be soon, so it will."

Bother it. He should have come earlier this morning, maybe even left the farm last night. Regardless, he needed to go now and find her. In fact, he had no time to waste. "Do you know where she is?"

Enya pressed a hand to her stomach, and her face blanched, almost as though she might be sick to her stomach. She wavered, and Winston gently steadied her. "Careful now, miss. Maybe you should be resting."

Enya nodded and then drew in a deep breath, allowing Winston to guide her away.

Riley waited just outside the door, hoping Enya wouldn't forget about him and would give him more information about Finola's whereabouts.

But as Winston led her up the stairs, he called over his shoulder, "Do be kind, Mr. Rafferty, and close the door as you take your leave."

That was Winston's way of telling him that he'd gotten more information than he deserved, and he'd get no more.

Within minutes, Riley was racing his gig as fast as the muddy streets would allow. First, he went to the tenements that the Sisters normally visited. A few Sisters were there, but Finola wasn't among them, and the Sisters claimed they didn't know where Finola had gone.

He drove to the tenements closer to the waterfront. After asking around and not finding her anywhere, he decided he needed assistance. And there was only one person who would be able to help him get Finola back. If anyone could do it, Bellamy McKenna could.

Riley rushed to Oscar's Pub, hopped out of the gig, and barged inside.

As usual during daylight hours, the interior was quiet with only a handful of regulars, mostly older men. And Bellamy was at the bar counter, this time with what appeared to be a financial ledger spread out in front of him.

"Bellamy!" Riley shouted, the flood of memories returning from the last time he'd been at the pub right before he'd gotten sick with cholera. He'd been in a similar situation that night, Finola having rejected him. He hadn't fought for her that time. But starting today, he would always fight for her.

Bellamy was writing with a stubby pencil in the book and didn't glance up.

"Bellamy!" Riley called again as he strode around the tables through the familiar waft of cigar smoke and beer. His pulse was still charging forward, hadn't seemed to have gotten the message that the horse and gig had come to a halt.

"Bellamy." As he reached the bar counter, he slapped both hands down, startling Georgie McGuire, sipping from his Guinness, so that he jerked his mug and spilled liquid on the bar.

The older man set his mug down and turned to the matchmaker. "Bellamy, Saint Riley is here to see you."

"Is that a fact?" Bellamy tallied another number.

"Oh aye, so 'tis." Georgie nodded at Riley as though giving him permission to proceed with his business.

Riley took off his hat and fiddled with the brim. "I lost Finola again."

Georgie shook his head sadly and made a humming noise at the back of his throat.

Bellamy wrote down another mark. "So I heard."

It was downright uncanny how much Bellamy knew. Riley wouldn't be surprised if Bellamy McKenna had gotten wind of the breakup even before the angels in heaven had. "I need your help to win her back."

"Naturally you do."

"Naturally," Georgie echoed.

Bellamy didn't look up, but his lips quirked with humor.

"This is life or death, Bellamy."

"Is it now?"

"Yes, I need her. I can't live without her." It was the truth. He couldn't fathom his future without Finola Shanahan in it. "Tell me what I can do to convince her not to go into the convent, to give me more time to win her."

Bellamy finally stuck his pencil behind his ear and looked up from his ledger.

"You orchestrated getting us back together last time and did a right good job of it. Surely you can think of something again."

The matchmaker's eyes sparkled with merriment. "If I remember correctly, the last time you accused me of scheming."

"I need you to scheme again."

"How much scheming do you want?"

"Enough that Finola will fall in love with me."

Bellamy crossed his arms and leaned against the bar. "Maybe the love's already there, Saint Riley. And maybe like a jammed spigot, it needs a wee nudge to get it flowing."

Riley prayed Bellamy was right. Not that Finola loved him. Bellamy couldn't be right about that. But maybe she cared about him and just needed him to show her that more clearly.

Riley put his hat back on and then rubbed his hands together, eager to get started. "Do you have any ideas?"

Bellamy's grin was slow and crooked. "Do I have ideas? Now, Riley Rafferty, I wouldn't be the world's greatest matchmaker if I didn't have ideas, would I?"

Riley quirked a brow. "World's greatest matchmaker?"

Georgie was sporting a toothless grin wide enough to span the Mississippi River. "Oh, aye, Oscar is good. But let me tell you, I've never seen a matchmaker better than Bellamy."

Bellamy grabbed a bottle and began to fill the man's glass. "You don't have me fooled, Georgie McGuire. I know you're lavishing on the praise to get a free drink."

"No one is better," the old man insisted with wide, innocent eyes. "Who better than me to know it?"

Bellamy chuckled as he topped off the glass. Then he motioned toward his brother-in-law at one of the tables with customers before he wiped both hands on a towel and leveled a look at Riley. "Oh, aye. It's time to finish making the perfect match. And I know exactly how we're going to do it."

30

*F*inola's knees were numb on the prayer cushion. She hadn't moved from the spot at the front prayer rail of St. Vincent de Paul's for the past two hours. Not only were her knees sore, but her back ached and her stomach was starting to growl.

She'd thought the time of prayer would comfort her and clarify what she needed to do. But her thoughts were as jumbled as when she'd left the Visitation Convent and the Sisters. She probably should have gone with them to the Kerry Patch, but her heart had been too heavy.

With a sigh, she sat back on her heels and released her rosary, letting it fall idle into her lap.

"Miss Shanahan?" The kindly priest who'd let her in spoke from behind her. The hour for mass wasn't yet upon them, but perhaps he wanted her to leave anyway.

Finola pushed herself up, gathered her bag, and stuffed the rosary inside, her fingers gliding against the habit. She hadn't taken the time to change into the garment, was still attired in her day gown. Absent of the usual multiple layers of petticoats and crinoline, the light blue skirt hung limply. She'd always left the extra off on her visitation days with the Sisters for the ease of changing. She wouldn't have to worry about that soon enough.

Gathering her cloak, Finola turned. "Thank you for allowing me the time, Father."

The priest stood in the aisle, his hands folded beneath the wide sleeves of his cassock. "You're welcome here any time, Miss Shanahan."

She wouldn't need to come again, would soon join the Sisters for prayer time in the chapel in the convent during the multiple holy hours they spent on their knees each day. In fact, the gong of the bell in the church's tower was now signaling Sext, the call to noon-hour prayer.

"I hope your prayers brought you the answers you were seeking," the priest said quietly.

She'd hoped today she would feel peace, especially after Enya's revelations about her guilt over Ava's death. But she was feeling anything but peace. "Why is forgiveness always so hard to find, Father?"

"Forgiveness is never difficult to find, my child." The priest offered a kind smile. "It can't be, not when it's right in front of us in an abundant measure just waiting to cover any and all of our sins and mistakes."

A soft but bitter laugh slipped out. "It's not in front of me."

"God never hides or withholds it. Perhaps you just need to open your eyes to see it."

Could she do that?

"Sometimes we mistake our own inability to forgive ourselves as God's inability. But Holy Scripture says that God forgives us so deeply that He puts our mistakes out of His mind as far as the east is from the west."

Was the priest right, that she'd simply been unable to forgive herself for what had happened with Ava? If God was so willing to forgive her, was it time to forgive herself?

She nodded. It was past time. She had to let go of Ava, let go of all that had happened, and let go of the guilt. And maybe the first step in letting go was to acknowledge that she no longer wanted to punish herself for the mistakes, not in light of God's deep forgiveness.

"His forgiveness sets us free," the priest continued. "Free to truly live and love."

Free to live and love. Free to be with Riley. Free to live her life with him. Free to love him.

Her heart resounded with the truth. Aye, she wanted nothing more than to spend her every waking moment living with and loving Riley.

Did she dare ride out to his family's farm today and tell him how she was feeling? How would he react? Fear rushed in and rooted her feet to the floor. He'd already tried so hard to convince her to give him—give them—a chance.

She straightened her shoulders and lifted her chin. It didn't matter. Today, right now, she would go to him and tell him everything she felt. She had to, no matter how hard it would be and no matter the consequences.

Before she lost the courage and before she could convince herself not to go, she started down the aisle toward the door. "Thank you again, Father. Your words have helped me more than you'll know."

"You're welcome, Miss Shanahan." The priest stepped aside to let her pass. "Also, I wanted to let you know I just received some news you might find of interest."

Something in the priest's tone halted her steps. And she braced herself.

"I know you were recently matched with Riley Rafferty." The priest glanced toward the door.

She followed his gaze, praying Riley would be standing there willing to offer her another chance. But the door was firmly closed, and Riley was nowhere in sight.

"I thought you might want to know that Saint Riley is getting married today."

"What?" Her heart jumped up into her throat, and she could only squeak. "Today?"

"Yes. Today. Now, at the noon hour."

A tremble started in her hands and spread quickly into her limbs. "How—where—are you certain? 'Tis rather fast." But, of course, after their last breakup, Riley had all but made arrangements with Daniel Allen the same night. So it wasn't impossible he'd done the same this time, maybe had renewed the plans with Daniel Allen to marry Bets.

The priest nodded as though confirming her worst fears. "Bellamy McKenna was the one who told me."

"Bellamy?" The matchmaker surely wouldn't allow Riley to marry Bets, not when he'd been working so hard to match her and Riley.

"Bellamy came by a short while ago asking if I'd perform the marriage ceremony."

Finola glanced to the door again and swallowed hard. Were they all waiting outside even now?

"I told him I couldn't do so. Not with you here." The priest seemed to be trying to reassure her, but a panic was rising and threatening to drown her.

"Then it's true." Riley was getting married. She cupped a hand over her mouth to hold back a cry of distress. What if he was already married?

"That Riley Rafferty is such a good young man. We've all been hoping he'd find a good wife."

"Aye, to be sure." She wanted to be that good wife for Riley. She *could* be that good wife with God's help, couldn't she?

She twisted the ring on her finger. The ring he'd given to her. His mother's ring. Surely he wouldn't get married without it. Did she have time to go to him? Did she dare interrupt the ceremony?

Her insides quavered at the prospect, but how could she stand back silently and watch the man she loved pledge himself to another woman?

She shook her head. She couldn't remain silent, had to speak up, even if doing so would take more courage than she had. "Did Bellamy say where he might go next?"

"I suggested the Cathedral."

Finola flew down the aisle and burst through the door, with only one thought at the forefront of her mind—she had to get to the Cathedral of St. Louis before Riley wedded Bets.

Her limbs were still trembling, but she didn't let that slow her down. With her pulse pounding a fearsome rhythm, she picked up her skirt and ran down the street, not caring that she was splattering mud, that she was drawing attention from the many people out at midday, or even that she was about to make a fool of herself.

She had to stop the wedding. That's all that mattered.

By the time she neared the waterfront and glimpsed the Cathedral's octagonal steeple with gilded ball and cross on top, she was breathless and her side ached. More than that, she was frantic with the need to make sure Riley heard everything she had to say. She didn't know what that would be, except that she had to tell him how she felt.

As she finally reached the church with its towering Greek Rival columns, she didn't pause to admire the limestone front with the marble slabs engraved with various Scripture verses like she usually did. Instead, she raced up the steps directly for the middle of the three doors.

When she was only feet away, the door opened, and Bellamy stepped out.

"Bellamy." She wheezed, halting and pressing a hand against the sharp ache in her side. "Stop the wedding."

He closed the door behind him, then leaned back against it and crossed his arms. "No, Finola. I can't do that."

She straightened, only to find that in her vigorous efforts to reach the church, her hair had come loose from its knot. She'd run at least a mile—if not more—and she was breathless, disheveled, and now her hair hung in disarray. She was in no mood to be told no.

"Let me in." She took a step forward and pushed against his chest.

He didn't budge. In fact, his expression was much too smug. "Give me one good reason why I should let you."

She sucked in a breath and tried to still her body. What reason could she offer? She glanced to her hand and the claddagh ring. She tugged at it but couldn't make herself take it off. "Riley needs his ring back."

Bellamy cocked his head. "Really? That's all you can come up with? I expected more creativity from you than that, so I did."

"Creativity? Whatever do you mean?"

He shrugged. "You've given me a good challenge so far. If you're planning to keep playing your games, then at least make your excuses believable."

She wanted to deny that she'd played any games during this whole matchmaking process. But what purpose would that serve now? Especially since he already knew, maybe had known from the start. "Fine, Bellamy. I'm done playing games. I really just want to see Riley."

"Why?" His dark eyes held hers and demanded she tell the truth.

Could she? After years of keeping everything locked inside, she had to keep moving forward down this new path of being more vulnerable and sharing more honestly.

She clasped her hands together to stop the trembling, then she closed her eyes and said the words that Bellamy was waiting for. "I love Riley."

Bellamy didn't respond.

She opened her eyes to find him grinning.

"Will you let me see him now? Before I'm too late?"

Bellamy was already moving aside. "Oh, aye, go on with you." He swung open the door to reveal the darkened interior, lit only by a few sconces.

She stepped past him into the narthex. He didn't follow and instead started to close the door behind her. "You're not helping me, Bellamy?"

"I already did." He winked, then finished shutting the door.

Silence surrounded her. In addition to the sconces, soft light filtered past the rows of windows on both sides of the nave. The pews were empty, and the chancel and marble altar at the front were deserted.

She paused. Where was Riley? Daniel Allen? Bets? Their families?

Maybe there was no wedding after all. She started to release a tight breath, but then Riley stepped out of the east side chapel.

Attired in a suit, with his cravat neatly tied, he held himself rigidly, formally. His hair was slicked back with pomade, although one strand had escaped the comb and fell across his forehead rebelliously, as if to remind the world that though Riley Rafferty could look and play the part of a gentleman, he was a rogue at heart.

A rogue whom she loved.

As Riley walked toward the prayer rail, her mind tried to make sense of what he was doing. Maybe he was getting into position for the wedding. Perhaps Bets, her family, and all the guests had yet to arrive.

Did that mean she still had time to convince Riley not to marry another woman? And how would she do that? Should she persuade him to marry her instead?

Her heart answered with a loud and excited pounding. Aye, she not only loved Riley, but she wanted to marry him.

When in position at the prayer rail, Riley finally glanced

down the aisle in her direction. She expected his eyes to widen in surprise. But he didn't move.

He made a handsome picture standing there waiting for his bride to arrive. He filled out his suit well, so strong and yet so humble.

She wanted him, couldn't let any other woman have him. Maybe that was selfish of her, but in this case, she wasn't sorry for her selfishness. In fact, she was greedy for Riley—greedy for all of him, for his heated gazes, his searing touches, his delectable kisses. She wanted his eyes, his smile, his love to be upon her alone and never on another woman.

"Hi, Finola," he said, and something in his voice wavered.

Was he sad he wasn't marrying her? Did that mean she still had the chance to get him to change his mind about his union with Bets?

She opened her mouth to greet him in return. But the words she needed to say got lost somewhere inside. Instead, she stood frozen in place.

Riley seemed to stiffen. Was he afraid she'd come nearer?

She couldn't keep from taking a rapid step back. Maybe she'd made a mistake in coming here. Maybe he didn't love her enough to overcome the obstacles and issues she still carried with her from her past. Maybe he was glad to be through with her.

Should she leave?

31

*R*iley's heart constricted. Finola was going to run
away again. He could see the growing panic in her
expression.

Bellamy's plan to get her to the Cathedral had worked ini-
tially, but now it was falling apart. . . .

Riley had hardly dared to breathe when Bellamy had called
down to him from the tower that she was on her way. With how
well the matchmaker knew everyone and everything, he'd easily learned of her whereabouts at St. Vincent de Paul's. When
she'd left the church, he'd tracked her progress nearly the entire
distance from St. Vincent de Paul's. When she'd gotten close,
he ordered Riley to go into one of the side chapels and wait
with the priest and not to come out until he heard Finola enter
the church.

Even though Riley had wanted to be the one to greet her
when she arrived on the doorstep, Bellamy had gone out. Riley
didn't know exactly what Bellamy had said to Finola, but he
was trying to trust the matchmaker to work his magic.

When she'd walked in, Riley's heart nearly stopped working. And he grinned like a madman at the realization that she'd
come, just the way Bellamy had predicted she would. But Riley

had wiped away his smile, walked calmly out of the chapel, and took his place in front of the prayer rail the way Bellamy had instructed.

Bellamy had said to wait and let Finola come to him, that he wasn't to encourage her in any way, that she had to be the one to pursue him this time. Bellamy's advice made sense. Finola had to recognize her need for him on her own.

From where she stood at the back of the church, she was more beautiful than he'd remembered, with her hair flowing in long waves around her, highlighting the paleness of her skin and framing all the freckles. Her blue eyes were bright and intense, and the dimple in her chin was adorable.

Even so, her fear was escalating, becoming more palpable with every passing second.

As she took another tiny step back, Riley couldn't restrain himself any longer. He wouldn't risk losing her again. He loved her too much.

He held out his hand toward her, hoping she knew he was offering her another chance together, that he still cared, that he would wait for her as long as she needed.

Her attention dropped to his hand. She studied it for a moment before she lifted her gaze to his. *Please be mine, Finola*, his heart whispered.

Her eyes suddenly turned glassy, almost as if she'd read his thoughts. She glanced at his hand again, still outstretched toward her. Then she started down the aisle toward him, tears spilling over onto her cheeks. She picked up her pace, and in the next instant she was running toward him, as if she couldn't get to him fast enough.

His heart kept time with her so that it was racing too. She didn't slow down when she neared him. Instead, she launched herself against him, wrapping her arms around his torso.

He eagerly gathered her close, but before he could completely draw her in, she lifted on her toes and touched her lips to his.

Not in a chaste, quick kiss. No, she opened up fully and passionately, hungrily tasting him as if she'd been denied what she wanted for too long.

Since he wasn't in the habit of denying her anything, he gave her what she was asking for. He let her feast, while at the same time giving himself permission to do the very same.

He savored the softness and the heat of her lips, dipping in, sampling, nibbling. Her fingers glided up his chest, to his neck, and into his hair. And she dug in, as if she couldn't get enough, wouldn't ever be satisfied until she had all of him.

Each stroke of her mouth and of her hands lit him so that he was burning. His blood, his muscles, his body—every inch of him was on fire. A fire that only she could fuel, and a fire that would only burn for her.

With each passing moment, he knew she was telling him what she couldn't express with words—that she needed him, needed him more than she needed anything else in life. He was her sustenance. Without him, she had nothing.

As he tore his lips from hers, she released a murmur of protest. The sound only added to the desire building inside, the desire to make her his, once and for all.

But as much as he wanted to sweep her up in his arms, take her away, and kiss her for the rest of the day, he had to be patient with her. Just because she'd thrown herself at him and kissed him as if she never intended to stop, didn't give him permission to lose self-control.

He had to be careful, couldn't scare her away again. He gentled his touch, kissing her jaw, then her neck, then her ear.

Her fingers tunneled deeper into his hair. "Oh, holy mother, Riley." Her nose and mouth hovered against his ear too. And the desire in her whisper, the warmth of her breath, the brush of her skin—he had to close his eyes to fight against the raging need to claim her lips again.

She pressed in harder, as though feeling the same urge. "I

love you." Her whisper was breathless. "I'm just sorry I didn't say it sooner."

"You're saying it now." He nuzzled his nose into her hair. "That's all that matters."

"Will you marry me, Riley?"

He closed his eyes against a sudden swell of emotions. When he'd ridden away from her house this morning, he never dreamed he'd be standing here with her. Not only had she just declared her love. But she was agreeing to marry him, *and* she was asking him.

"Will you?" She kissed his ear, giving him no choice but to slide his hands into her hair and let the thick, silk waves float through his fingers.

"Yes."

At a loud clearing of a throat, Finola hopped and broke away, glancing in the direction of the sound.

There standing a dozen paces away in the center aisle were James Shanahan, Enya, and Bellamy, having been witness to not only their passionate moment of kissing but to Finola's proposal of marriage. Their eyes were rounded with surprise. Likely at seeing the way he'd been kissing Finola.

What would James Shanahan say to him now?

"Da?" Finola's question contained mortification. "Enya?" She pushed against Riley's chest, trying to back up.

But Riley held her fast. "Stay here with me, Finola. Please?"

Thankfully, she ceased her attempt to extricate herself, because now that he had her in his arms, he wasn't sure he'd ever be able to let her go.

"What is everyone doing here?" Finola's cheeks were rosy, and she didn't meet their gazes.

"They're here for the wedding." Bellamy spoke with a confidence that made Riley want to grin. How had Bellamy been able to make this all work?

"The wedding?" Finola's delicate brows rose. For a second, Riley could see her mind at work piecing together Bellamy's shenanigans. An instant later, she leveled a glare in the match-maker's direction. "You told the priest at St. Vincent de Paul that Riley was getting married."

"Oh, aye, that I did." Bellamy nodded. "And Riley Rafferty is getting married, so he is. To you, Finola Shanahan."

"So all the while you were planning my wedding today, you were letting me believe Riley was marrying someone else?"

Bellamy held up his hands as though he had nothing to hide. "All I said was that there was a wedding. I never did say who would or wouldn't be in it. Can't help it if you mistook my intentions for another woman and decided you wouldn't let anyone else have the man you love."

Finola locked eyes with Bellamy for several more heartbeats before a smile turned up the corners of her lips. "Bellamy Mc-Kenna, you once told me that you were cleverer than me. I didn't believe you then. But you were right."

Bellamy's grin worked free. "Naturally."

Her smiled widened, so that it took Riley's breath away. He couldn't hold himself back. He bent in and touched his lips to her smile. And when she responded with a delicious kiss, he smiled too.

"Ready, Father?" Bellamy peered beyond them toward the altar, where a priest now stood with a prayer book in hand. "It's not Shrove Tuesday, but we all knew Riley and Finola wouldn't be able to wait until then."

"We all knew?" James Shanahan chuckled, his shoulders relaxing and his expression filling with relief.

"The barmbrack ring predicted it." Bellamy winked at Finola. But the nod he gave Riley said it all—Bellamy didn't want to give Finola another chance to change her mind any more than Riley did.

Enya tried for a smile, but it didn't reach her eyes. Instead, the young woman seemed weary and worn, just as she had when Riley had called earlier.

"I never once lost faith that Riley and Finola would find their way to each other." Bellamy beamed at them. "Some journeys take longer than others. Some need a little more help to get to the right destination. But in the end, a good matchmaker knows how to make it all happen just so."

Riley guessed Bellamy had received help from heaven too.

Bellamy waved the priest forward. "Let the ceremony begin."

The priest seemed to have been instructed by someone—probably Bellamy—to keep the service short and to the point. Within minutes Riley had spoken his vows, and the priest turned to Finola and asked her to state her intentions.

Standing facing each other, Riley hadn't let go of her hands, and she hadn't seemed to mind. Now, with her beautiful blue eyes peering up at him, wide and filled with promise, she spoke softly: "I, Finola, take thee, Riley, to be my wedded husband, to have and to hold, from this day forward, for better, for worse, for richer, for poorer, in sickness, and in health, to love, cherish, and to obey, till death us do part, according to God's holy ordinance, and thereto I give thee my troth."

As she finished, she offered him another smile, and before the priest could speak the final words of the service, Riley leaned down and kissed his wife. *His wife.*

He kissed her without reservation, not caring that they still had an audience, that the service wasn't over, or that everyone would now know—if they didn't already—that he couldn't keep his hands off her. The priest cleared his throat and waited, but after a moment he continued the service, raising his voice, as though to make sure they heard him through the kissing.

Finola broke away first, biting her lip, casting her eyes down, but not before he saw the eagerness there and knew their kisses affected her just as much as they did him.

After the service ended, Riley shook hands with Bellamy, squeezing hard. "I don't know how to thank you, Bellamy."

Bellamy clamped him back. "Seeing you happily married is all the thanks I need, so it is."

"I'm more than happily married." Riley hugged Finola to his side. "I'm the happiest man alive."

"So you are, Riley Rafferty, so you are."

Shanahan and Enya had already left for the mansion to organize a small dinner to celebrate the union. Before leaving, Shanahan had informed Riley that he wanted the two of them to live in the mansion. By summer, if the cholera was gone from the city, then Shanahan would build them a house of their own as a wedding present.

It was a generous offer, and Riley had tried to turn it down. But Shanahan had been adamant that he wouldn't have it any other way.

Now with Bellamy strolling casually down the street on his way back to the pub, Riley stood with Finola just outside the church door. He pulled her close again.

"Tell me how you're feeling, Finola. I want to know. Was this all too much, too soon? I didn't want to rush you, and I'm sorry if I—"

Her mouth cut him off with an almost-desperate kiss. It was hard and full of need, but she pulled back before it had time to truly begin. "I knew from the moment I walked to the convent this morning that there was only one place that would ever be home for me. And that's with you."

He was partially afraid he was dreaming. If he was, he never wanted to wake up.

Her eyes filled with adoration. "I can't promise I'll always be able to share my feelings well. And I can't promise that we won't have hard times ahead. But I can promise to love you through it all with every day that I have breath."

"That's all I need." He drew a line on her cheek, tracing the pattern of freckles. "That, along with permission to kiss every freckle on your body, which is what I've been dreaming about doing since the moment I met you."

She gasped at his bold statement, then shoved his arm. "Riley Rafferty, you'll be getting no such permission."

He chuckled, then leaned into her ear. "It might take me a lifetime to kiss each and every one, but I intend to do it, Finola. You are forewarned."

She shivered, but the light blue flames flickering in her eyes told him all he needed to know, that her reaction was one of pure pleasure, and that she would relish a lifetime of his kisses.

"So you're happy?" He brushed a kiss against her forehead.

"Aye." She released a contented sigh. "As long as I can make you the happiest man alive, then I'll be the happiest woman."

Riley smiled. Spending their marriage making each other happy? That would indeed make the perfect match.

32

*B*ellamy McKenna tossed the towel over his shoulder before he grabbed the handles of three empty mugs in one hand and three in the other.

For a Tuesday evening, the pub was deserted—the tables and chairs barren with only the dirty dishes to signal that anyone had been there at all over the supper hour. Most men were out celebrating, as right they should on Shrove Tuesday, the last day before Lent. And a day filled with weddings. Thankfully, the cases of cholera in the city seemed to be subsiding with a recent cold spell, and it wasn't overrunning the city the way everyone had predicted it would.

Bellamy knew of at least a dozen weddings, mostly from the matches Oscar had made. They'd gotten invitations to all of them, and Oscar was making the rounds to each home, never one to waste the opportunity for craic. In fact, Oscar anticipated Shrove Tuesday all year, eager for the feasting and dancing and the chance to mingle and talk to his heart's content.

Bellamy had never enjoyed the celebrations as much as his father, so it hadn't been much of a sacrifice to offer to stay behind and mind the pub. Besides, even though he'd been successful in matching Finola Shanahan and Riley Rafferty, Oscar hadn't provided any other opportunities to help with matchmaking, which meant he didn't have a vested interest in attending any of the wedding celebrations.

Not that he was sore about it. Okay, maybe he was a little. Oscar could have given him another match or two to work on his own instead of relegating him to his normal role as assistant, following the master around like a pup.

But Oscar had made it clear that he hadn't liked Bellamy's unconventional methods with Finola and Riley, had felt as though Bellamy had taken too many risks in trying to get the couple together.

"You got lucky, Bellamy," Oscar had boomed into a pub full of customers. "You managed to make a match this time, but you won't be able to do that again, not like that."

Bellamy had wanted to retort that he didn't intend to do it again the same way, that each couple was different and needed a unique approach tailored specifically to them. But he'd held in his views, knowing his dad would think those were unconventional too.

Bellamy pushed in a chair with his hip before starting on his way to the bar counter. Captain Sullivan O'Brien was still sitting on one of the stools, the only man left in the pub—even old Georgie McGuire was gone for the night.

The captain never drank any of the hard spirits, only ever asked for a bowl of stew and sipped the watery ale that Riley's sister Jenny brewed.

Sullivan had finished his supper but was lingering. The question was—why?

The steamboat captain was a brawny man, made of more muscle than three other fellows combined. With his dark hair and eyes and perpetual layer of dark facial scruff, he had an almost menacing appearance. At the very least, he put off an intimidating aura. Not only that, but he was quiet, introverted, and gruff.

Bellamy suspected Sullivan used those aloof qualities to hold others at bay because he was insecure. And if Bellamy had to take a guess at what was causing the insecurity, he'd say it was the burn scars.

The captain did his best to hide the scars behind his high collar and cravat. But a slight line of puckered red skin showed anyway, and no doubt it covered a good portion of his shoulder and maybe even his back.

After rounding the bar counter, Bellamy placed the empty mugs into a basin with all the others that needed washing, a task Jenny would take care of in the morning.

Sullivan shot a dark glance his way, and something in the man's expression told Bellamy now that everyone else had gone, he wanted to talk but didn't quite know how to get the conversation started.

Bellamy arched his brows at the fellow's mug. "Looks like you need a refill, so you do."

"No." Sullivan issued the curt word while he rose from his stool. "I'm leaving."

Bellamy quickly sifted through all the information he'd learned about Sullivan O'Brien over the past couple of years the man had frequented the pub. He was from New Orleans, was in command of a host of steamboats, was the oldest son of a wealthy steamboat magnate, fought for a year in the war with Mexico, and was close to thirty years old.

And he was single. On Shrove Tuesday.

Oh, aye. Bellamy knew exactly what the captain wanted. He leaned against the counter and nodded at the fellow. "Go ahead and ask me."

Situating his flat-brimmed captain's hat on his head, Sullivan tossed Bellamy a glare. "Ask you what?"

Bellamy loved when people made things more challenging. "Ask me the question you've been wanting to since the moment you sat down."

Sullivan didn't react, and his eyes remained unreadable.

Even without the usual clues, Bellamy guessed the captain had lingered longer tonight for only one reason. Because the pub was empty, it was the perfect opportunity to ask for help in finding a wife.

Bellamy considered crossing his arms and taking his sweet time. But he sensed that Sullivan wasn't normal and wouldn't be as easy to guide as Riley and Finola had been. Sullivan was stronger willed and would need different tactics. Bellamy had to figure out the approach to take or he'd lose the chance to help the fellow.

Was directness with Captain Sullivan O'Brien the way to go?

Sullivan started toward the door.

"Tell me what kind of wife you want."

The fellow halted abruptly but didn't turn back around. His thick shoulders were tense, and his big hands tightened into fists.

Bellamy once again scrambled to put together all the clues. On the surface it would be easy to conclude that Sullivan didn't want a wife. The fellow had obviously tried to force himself to bring up the issue tonight but failed. And he obviously still wasn't comfortable talking about it, even though Bellamy had given him the opening to do so.

But Bellamy had to dig deeper to find out the truth of the matter. And the truth was that Sullivan needed a woman in his life, even if he didn't think so.

Sullivan uncurled his hands, as if trying to ease the tension radiating through him. Then with stiff movements, he turned and made himself do what he'd come to do. "I want a woman who's soft spoken, gentle in manner, and doesn't take stock in appearances."

The fellow rattled off his list so rapidly and succinctly that Bellamy knew it had been rehearsed. The other thing Bellamy knew was that Sullivan's list was all wrong for a man like him. He didn't know how he knew, only that he did.

He supposed it was one of those instinctual aspects of having matchmaker blood in him. He could read people well, often better than they could themselves.

The deckhands and stevedores who came into the pub hailed Captain O'Brien as the best captain anywhere on the Mississippi for his fairness, loyalty, and generosity.

The captain might be tough and crusty on the outside, but underneath he was a man with a good and kind heart.

A good and kind heart that was clearly being pushed to get a wife. By his father? That was likely the case. But why?

From the way Sullivan clenched his jaw, Bellamy guessed the list wasn't quite finished.

"Anything else?" Bellamy kept his tone nonchalant.

Sullivan paused, took a deep breath, then continued. "I need a woman who is willing to be married before midnight."

"Tonight?"

"Yes."

Bellamy reached for his towel and began to wipe at the counter, mostly to hide his surprise. The captain had thrown him a twist he hadn't seen coming. He supposed he should have expected it. After all, the church frowned upon weddings during the holy weeks of Lent, which was why it had become the custom for most people to get married on or before Shrove Tuesday.

Sullivan scowled. "I'm too late, aren't I?"

Bellamy made a show of looking at the clock above the mantel even though he already knew what time it was. "It's only seven. We still have five hours."

Sullivan didn't move, was likely trying to decide if Bellamy was being serious or sarcastic. Bellamy preferred sarcasm. But with the captain, he decided seriousness was the best route.

Mustering as much genuineness as he could manage, he met the man's gaze levelly. "I'll do my best, Captain O'Brien, so I will."

Sullivan's expression remained doubtful, even gruff, but

Bellamy thought he saw a glimmer of vulnerability in the captain's eyes.

Bellamy's mind went to work, racing through all the possibilities, but the options were slim. "You should know that most of the eligible women are already matched and married."

"I understand."

"And you should know that I may not be able to find someone meeting all the qualities you're looking for."

"It's not a long list."

Bellamy shrugged. "'Tis short enough, so it is." In this case, he wasn't making any promises, not when he planned to find a different sort of woman for the captain.

Sullivan paused, clearly debating whether to push forward with a match even if the woman didn't meet his standards. Finally, he expelled a tight breath. "If you do your best, that's all I can ask for."

Bellamy nodded solemnly. "I vow I won't match you with the wrong woman."

"Fair enough."

"Meet me at the Cathedral in four hours attired in your Sunday best and ready for a wedding."

Sullivan held his gaze for several long moments. As though realizing he had no option but to trust Bellamy, he nodded, spun, and stalked out the door.

When he was gone, Bellamy blew out a long breath. What in the wee devil had he just done? Not only were there very few eligible women left in the marriageable pool, but tonight he'd have a devil of a time trying to track people down since many roved from party to party.

His gaze shot to Oscar's leather-bound ledger sitting open on the back table. He hated to snoop, but he had no choice. He'd have to take a look at all the names of people who'd come in over the recent weeks and sort through those who hadn't been matched.

The odds were highly stacked against him in finding a match for Sullivan, but that's why he hadn't turned down the opportunity to take over for Oscar. Because he loved the challenges that came with matchmaking. And tonight, he'd face an even bigger challenge than he had with Finola and Riley.

He wouldn't rest until he'd done his best to find a woman the captain would learn to love, no matter how unlikely the match.

Jody Hedlund is the bestselling author of over fifty novels and is the winner of numerous awards. Jody lives in Michigan with her husband, busy family, and five spoiled cats. She writes sweet historical romances with plenty of sizzle. Visit her at jodyhedlund.com.

Sign Up for Jody's Newsletter

Keep up to date with Jody's latest news on book releases and events by signing up for her email list at the link below.

JodyHedlund.com

FOLLOW JODY ON SOCIAL MEDIA

Author Jody Hedlund   @jodyhedlund   @JodyHedlund

More from Jody Hedlund

On a trip west to save her ailing sister, Greta Nilsson is robbed, leaving her homeless and penniless. Wyatt McQuaid is struggling to get his new ranch running, so the mayor offers him a bargain: he will invest in a herd of cattle if Wyatt agrees to help the town become more respectable by marrying . . . and the mayor has the perfect woman in mind.

A Cowboy for Keeps
COLORADO COWBOYS #1

Traveling the Santa Fe Trail on a botanical exploration, Linnea Newberry longs to be taken seriously by the other members of the expedition. When she is rescued from an accident by Flynn McQuaid, her grandfather hires him to act as Linnea's bodyguard, and Flynn soon finds himself in the greatest danger of all—falling for a woman he's determined not to love.

The Heart of a Cowboy
COLORADO COWBOYS #2

While Brody McQuaid's body survived the war, his soul did not. He finds his purpose saving wild horses from ranchers intent on killing them. Veterinarian Savannah Marshall joins Brody in rescuing the wild creatures, but when her family and the ranchers catch up with them both, they will have to tame their fears if they have any hope of letting love run free.

To Tame a Cowboy
COLORADO COWBOYS #3

❖ BETHANYHOUSE